About the Author

J T Craft is an urbanist by profession with a passion for writing about the social and economic systems that define modern life. He divides his time between Dallas and Toronto where he leads multiple urban design practices. He is a graduate of the University of Guelph, with a degree in Landscape Architecture and the London School of Economics and Political Science, with a Masters in Cities. This is his first novel.

The Jesus Chronicle

J T Craft

The Jesus Chronicle

Olympia Publishers
London

www.olympiapublishers.com
OLYMPIA PAPERBACK EDITION

A CIP catalogue record for this title is
available from the British Library.

ISBN: 978-1-80439-388-8

This is a work of fiction.
Names, characters, places and incidents originate from the writer's
imagination. Any resemblance to actual persons, living or dead, is
purely coincidental.

First Published in 2023

Olympia Publishers
Tallis House
2 Tallis Street
London
EC4Y 0AB

Printed in Great Britain

Dedication

The people to whom this book is dedicated know who they are, and why.

Why are there trees I never walk under but large and melodious thoughts descend upon me?

From Song of the Open Road

Istoia (EL): the past of mankind

Prologue

The leather-bound book in the wooden box was in nearly perfect condition. Exactly as I was told it would be. The panels on the front and back were deeply cracked but supple enough to open along its bound edge without breaking. The loose vellum sheets were clear and white and had not yellowed, which was proof that the book hadn't seen any light. I found it in the unmarked limestone ossuary, which in turn had been placed in a niche in the stone wall in a spot marked simply with an incised PAX, or peace, symbol. The book, or manuscript such as it is, had aged very little from the day it had been hidden. It contained no illuminations and was written in the common language of the time without the calligraphic skill of a scribe. The vellum was clearly of high quality and cut neatly by a well sharpened knife, but the pages were not uniform in size, and they were without incised guidelines as if the author had no apprentice to prepare his pages. The script was in a tight and determined hand and in a high, and what I assumed from my non-academic experience, to be courtly prose. It began with an introduction as *The st'rye of an embasy of a land from across the ocean. A true account by Robert FitzEdward, Duke of Cornwall, in the year 1481.* There was no mention of Edward IV whose reign in which it claims to be written, and curiously, its title reads in a very simple and elementary Latin:

inde Iesus venit in posserum

13

What follows here is reading of a story hastily written by a man whom I was assured was of the greatest credibility. I am presenting it here, to the best of my ability, in *our* common language and the proof of its veracity is meant to be the very existence of the manuscript itself. Although I can't yet vouch for this truth, all I can add at this time is what I have read and been told, and that this is the story of a Jesus who comes from the future.

Chapter One

Austin

I easily identified David as an advanced form of a Hollow. Even if the technology that projected him was vastly superior to our present capabilities the unusually warm temperature and the lack of give in his skin, as evidenced in his handshake, was the tell. Billions of people walk the planet and at any given time and amongst those billions there are always a few hundred Hollows on walkabout, projected by us. Even though I was one of only a handful of people that even know what a Hollow is, I have never seen a random one, or one that we had not projected ourselves. I hoped my alarm didn't show, but I could tell by the look in his eyes that he knew that I knew right away what he was.

My first thought was that the Chinese had made some technological leap that we were unaware of, or perhaps some science-tech-private sector group (STPSD)—most likely Russian—had somehow hijacked our technology and progressed on their own. The Chinese scenario seemed implausible since they rarely had an original thought and had never taken anything we had done and made it plausibly better. The Russian thought had some legs, since we too had started small before we were sucked into the *supposedly* non-existent Office of Strategic Services (OSS). From the very beginning we feared that some other private sector group working out of a basement somewhere was doing the same thing as us. We may have been allies with

Russia for the past couple of hundred years, but there are still outliers in every state that can't be trusted.

Since birthing our first Hollow in our own basement (actually, a warehouse in San Francisco's China Basin) we knew that we couldn't be alone in developing projected technology. Our research began in a graduate lab at Stanford and there were eyes all over us back then. The move to San Francisco was our way of hiding in plain sight while begging from every major venture capitalist in the city to raise enough dollars just to keep the lights on. And even now as part of the OSS, with unlimited funds at our disposal, and after our migration to Austin like everyone else in tech, we were not naïve to believe that we necessarily had the creative edge. Tech doesn't work that way. Hunger and hustle count too. And anything and anyone could be hacked, so what you believed to be proprietary could be floating out there and you wouldn't even know it.

Our problem is that we have a master now. Every group that is poached by the CIA, even those that fall under the top-top-top secret and not-really defunct-OSS (even though the world thinks so) had to answer to a bureaucrat at some point, and nothing makes you go limp quicker than someone from Langley standing over your shoulder. In the brief seconds of his introduction, I wondered whether I was really talking to some kid in a basement in Novosibirsk, or one of my own checking up on me.

I was very surprised by the detailed quality of his transmission and the character of the actual projection, which we had begun to describe as a projection's caste. As I said, I had never seen a Hollow in person that we hadn't birthed, and when we purposefully projected one into the population it was done so under carefully controlled conditions, and we never deliberately allowed close contact with the civilian population. Even so, they were often noticed by people. And more than a few have even appeared on social media as presumed ghost encounters. If you search the web, you will find quite a few examples, from Russia mostly, of what appears to be *whole*, meaning solid appearing, people disappearing into walls, passing through moving cars or simply evaporating into the ether.

We track the Russians closely to follow their progress and worrisomely there have been recent Chinese sightings as well, but none can match the quality of the joint Great Britain-US versions that we have been projecting. We certainly cannot currently match the quality of this guy.

I knew he was a projection, but only from touch and not his caste. Visually he was whole and moved without distortion or any telltale aliasing, his voice had no perceptible oscillation and there was no aberration in his chromaticity that I could detect or had reason to suspect—at first that is. But, like our own lab work had shown to date, the heat that prevented annealing, or hardening like in glass making, could not be reduced sufficiently to normal body temperature without considerable breakage. All of our testing had produced severe fractures in the skin when we cooled the projection down to below 40 degrees Celsius. And even if we could get the temperature down to approximate normal body temperature the transmission alone was still so unpredictable. The further we got from the router the cooler the skin got, often leading to complete breakage. A normal man's hands at David's temperature would have meant he should have been in the hospital with a raging fever akin to one of those long-conquered Corona viruses.

I had no reason to suspect that he was anything but a random encounter when he approached me at the farmer's market. He started the conversation as anyone might when discussing produce with a stranger. It was a normal, if not a distracted, conversation between two people waiting for the guy manning the booth to finish bagging up a sale so we could each select some vegetables of our own.

What I did find immediately suspicious was his friendliness. We are trained to be attuned to behavioral cues in others that are uncustomary in nature, be it man or beast. And Austin may be a friendly place, but it is not overly familiar. As Texans our politeness does not preclude a discussion on religion, politics or guns. It does, however, have its limits at how close you talk, and how you position your body when meeting a stranger for the first time.

The stalls were not crowded that morning and so I immediately felt his approach was way too purposeful. I tried not to show any alarm, but I felt my training kick in as he began some small talk. I had to ask myself whether he was genuinely a friendly guy, which was possible, whether he was into me and his small talk was an awkward attempt at a pickup, or whether he was the enemy? All options were plausible, and so I introduced myself with an outstretched arm, inviting him to shake hands in an attempt to take some control of the awkward situation.

"Paul," I said. Nothing more.

"David," he responded.

We shook hands quickly, and I noted a slight hesitancy in his initial outreach. His hand was hot but dry. His skin texture had the unmistakable feel of sharkskin, and there was no perceptible give in the flesh. While most men shake hands with an assertive grip, his seemed affected and a little detached from the intent which didn't seem to match his stature and his approach. I also took note, as I am trained to do, that he was a little taller than me and toned in an athletic way, more like a runner rather than someone who concentrates on weights at the gym.

When our eyes met, he simply nodded. I nodded back. He knew then that I knew, and disappointingly, my training had failed at that moment. I may be a Commander by title, but I am a science nerd first and an agent second, maybe even third. As I attempted to find the right words, and before I could say anything, he suggested we go for a walk. I should have run the other way because that is what I am trained to do. But I didn't.

The market was in the parking lot of a failed strip mall just north of the University. It was beginning to get crowded with Saturday morning shoppers jostling at the stalls that lined the parking lot, so we walked down the less crowded center aisle towards some random benches beneath an old oak at its edge.

"Where are you?" I asked as we sat down. Not certain that he would answer willingly.

He laughed a little, and said, "Wrong question."

"What do you mean?" I responded, genuinely perplexed by what he was saying.

"I mean, I thought you might have asked a more clever question. It would be far more interesting if you asked *when* am I?"

"When?" I responded.

To manage the lag time between operator and projection was a skill that took many hours to master. The gap in transmission time could be worked like a pause in a sentence, but it took real talent to affect a natural flow in conversation and ensuring that the lips sync'd with the sound of the voice. We had perfected the lag to less than a second, and so there was no way with the quality of his caste that he was less than that behind me. I had no reason to question *when* he was and assumed him to be current.

"OK, let me guess. 900 milliseconds."

He looked at me quite quizzically and said, "Come on. You need to be more creative than that. You've never seen anything like me before, what makes you think I am behind you?"

I had not considered otherwise. We had been working on the lag time for several years while simultaneously correcting all character issues. We had gotten the temperature almost correct, but we couldn't get closer than 900 milliseconds. Could he be ahead of me, I wondered? I naturally assumed we were sync'd in real time and that he appeared with the lag per normal. I felt like he was playing with me with, and I didn't like it.

"This game is not very entertaining," I responded. "You've obviously sought me out, so quit toying with me. If you've got something to share then do so, otherwise I am going to walk away."

He knew I was bluffing. There was no way I was going to walk away from a Hollow this good. I needed to know more, but I needed to play it cool. If he was Chinese, he would give it away soon enough since their Hollow's lifespans were directly tied to remote batteries that never lasted long. If Russian, his vocabulary would give it way, as they never had enough money to hire real Americans. I needed to keep David talking.

"I am with London," he responded, sensing my frustration.

"So, you are one of us?"

"Yes, in a manner of speaking."

"Then where is the router? Because if you were one of us, I would know about it."

My first thought at hearing this was that London had gone rogue and that I was looking at a colossal failure of intelligence, which would mean my own failure and that of my team. We had been working directly with the covert British Secret Service Branch MI-8 since the start and had never had a breach of protocol, or even the slightest mishap in communication. We operated with complete openness. But of course, we treated all partner interactions with healthy skepticism and always ran our missions with the caveat that trust had to be verified. And vice versa.

He pointed to a car across the street, a newer looking Lexus. Silver, with very darkly tinted windows. "It's the silver car, notice the tires, they are a little too round. We're still working on the embrace. We have the edges down pat, it's the way light bends around inorganic matter that we still haven't perfected."

I would never have noticed the detail, no one would have. But once he mentioned it, I could see that the tires looked over inflated. We considered such imperfections as non-perceptible.

"But you haven't asked me: *When* am I?" he continued.

I had not forgotten the question, but I considered it somewhat unimportant. A few milliseconds meant nothing to me at this point, since I was more concerned with why London had projected without my knowledge. I was genuinely concerned that I was out of the loop. But he wanted me to ask, so I did.

"OK, when are you? And does it matter?" I added.

David looked at me and our eyes locked, he smiled a bit mischievously and said, "Twenty-Two Twenty-Eight."

I was stunned and I am certain it showed in my face. He wasn't behind me in the past. He was ahead in the future by nearly two hundred years. I wanted to say it was impossible, but I knew it wasn't. It was very possible. We had projected inanimate objects several seconds into the past, and we had sought permission to try to project mice backwards as well. We had not been authorized to do so yet, but our calculations had shown it was possible.

We knew that first we needed to build a battery to support a router before we could project a living creature. Sort of a chicken before the egg thing, but with another egg thrown in. David, and whomever he was working with, had managed to birth a projection from 2228. That is, if he was telling the truth.

"Why should I believe you?" I asked.

"You have no reason not to, you know the technology, you know it's possible, you just don't know how to do it quite yet," he answered assuredly.

I had so many questions, but I had to remind myself to remain skeptical. He could be telling the truth, or he might not be. He could be projecting from London as it was technically possible, but that doesn't mean he was necessarily MI-8. He could be rogue, or worse, he could be Canadian—our true nemesis.

"Why are you here, why now?"

"We've got a problem and we need to solve it, here and now, and we need your help."

"You need my help in the year 2228? Seems like a long way off for me to be of any use to you," I answered earnestly, totally ignorant of the depth of the problem he was speaking of—but also very interested in learning more. "Are you MI-8?" I continued, wondering if he would answer truthfully.

"There is no MI-8, no OSS, no CIA. We don't have agencies anymore. We don't have governments anymore, not in the way that you understand. We don't need them," he said with a wry smile. "There is only one organization now, and it has a singular mission to correct the fucked-up messes we make before we make them. That's what I do, and I need your help."

It was difficult to process what he was saying, and I had more questions than I could possibly ask at once. If it was true then I was looking into the future, and if it was a ruse to hack or hijack our tech then it was a ballsy move to do so in public, in broad daylight, at a farmer's market.

"What the fuck, man. Are you Chinese, Russian, Israeli maybe? Cause this really sounds like a load of crap."

As interested as I was, I was also growing a bit angry. Frustrated might be a better word for how I was feeling. Try as I may, I did not fully comprehend what he was saying. I had basically invented this technology and here I was lost in the conversation. It was like handing Alexander Graham Bell an iPhone.

"Where is your battery?" I asked. I could see the Lexus router parked on the street, but he was at least thirty minutes into his caste, and he had not even twitched once.

"We don't use batteries. We are nuclear. It's self-contained and travels with the projection."

The conversation was making me uncomfortable. I was being schooled in my own science, yet I couldn't really grasp how it worked. We too had considered projecting an energy source, but we could not figure out how to do it without frying the Hollow. The generated heat could not be mitigated, and we had never even considered the possibility of dimensional time, let alone using nuclear in any form.

"We can't bend the energy, so I am here now,' he answered, "and I can't go back further from here otherwise I'd then be in a different future. So, from this point forward you are part of the correction, whether you understand it or not," he continued, assuming correctly that I didn't.

"So, you didn't need the battery first, you could build the router after the birth?"

I was beginning to understand the energy component of what he was talking about, but not the *correction* he had mentioned.

And I didn't get the bent energy part either.

"Yes, we can, it just takes time—and we've been here a while", he chuckled again, perhaps enjoying my ignorance. Like he was talking to a child.

"A car is a perfect router, it's mobile, no one looks at it twice. Fits in perfectly with the surroundings. And we can build them when we arrive, quickly and easily. It basically comes with all the parts we can use, except the rubber and plastic bits, we don't need those. Hence the tires. We usually just project those. We can only use the metals and the silica, and we don't need the chips anymore, but I am guessing you are figuring this out."

It seemed so plausible, and even technologically possible, but there were many other reasons that I was so uncomfortable with the conversation.

"Why are you talking to me? I've got bosses, why didn't you go to OSS? And what is this correction you mentioned," I asked, reluctantly.

"They don't know what your team is capable of, yet. And when they do figure it out, they will want you to make a ghost army, won't they?" He asked, but before I could answer he went on, "But I am not a ghost, and I am not a Hollow. I am a Solid."

It was true, he was not a simple projection like a hologram, he had true mass and his caste was human-like, enough to fool almost anyone. He appeared to be made of solid material.

"I have read everything you have ever written and seen every note in your files," he continued, "even the files you've never seen, the ones your so-called bosses keep on you. They suspect what you are really doing, but they don't know yet what you have achieved. But I do, and I need you to do something for the future that does not involve them."

It was true. The people at Langley had tasked us to create a facsimile of an intelligence army, but what they didn't know yet was that in a true sense our product could be an actual army—that is if the technology was ever perfected. They wanted us to create spooks, and we had pretty much done that. With David sitting across from me, I now knew that it was possible to perfect the technology.

But the bosses don't know that our 'ghosts' can be made solid, and in a sense made real. If they knew that we could create one Hollow that had caste—a Solid, then we could be made to create an army of the same; an army that felt no pain and thus could not be destroyed, an army that could move spatially and theoretically could kill without being killed.

This was potentially another hidden Oppenheimer moment. He knew what his atomic bomb was capable of and hid it from the world for decades. We have been hiding our tech for less than a year knowing it was only a matter of time before they found out.

The projected Solid was not our original intent, but it was the logical extension of our initial experimentation. We knew from the moment OSS first contacted us at our lab in San Franciso that whatever we produced for them would be bastardized over time—for good or for bad. But we also maintained amongst ourselves a thoroughly altruistic attitude towards all we produced, even when we knew that from the moment we began working for OSS that we had lost control of the evolution of the technology.

It wasn't like we had a choice in selling to them, since they would have just taken it from us anyway. The price we demanded was high, and we certainly made us a lot of money, but not nearly what we could have in the private sector. We maintain some of the patents and each of us had more money now than we could ever spend in a lifetime but that said, we had each given up a piece of our souls when we entered the service.

None of us ever considered ourselves special agent material and so the training was a real eye opener. We were aware that in the private sector the risk of espionage was very real, but in the corporate world there is little training; just lots of protocol to follow in the hopes of protecting intellectual capital. As spooks we had to go through genuine training, both physical and mental. None of us are James Bond now, but we can all shoot, we know how to surveil, we can read a room, and we certainly know when we are being marked. I was being marked big time.

Our initial experiments in the warehouse in China Basin began with the idea that there was a need for remote medical assistance to humanize robotic surgeries, and to provide humanitarian relief during disasters. The original idea came to me after the last big earthquake in Haiti. I thought if we could get huge amounts of manpower on the ground in dangerous places without needing to provide additional support such as food and shelter for relief workers, it would be a game changer.

It was very altruistic and very naïve, but I was a different person then and I would be lying if I didn't think that we'd make a shit load of money from the idea too. But to my mind, the result justifies the reward.

We began by projecting simple holograms which were terribly unreliable. Frightening really—imagine you've just been pulled from a collapsed building, and you are undergoing emergency robotic surgery to repair a shattered leg when a ghostly apparition starts talking with you. So, we thought we could create teams of medical aid workers that would appear in real-time, provide diagnosis, guide surgery, comfort the needy etc., but they would actually be housed like gamers in a facility safe and sound and far away from the disaster.

We imagined so many other possible applications and we were under no illusion that this technology wouldn't, or couldn't, be used for nefarious purposes if in the wrong hands. It was almost a given. When our first Solid was projected, even for a brief and unstable moment, we knew the game was changed forever and that it was only a matter of time before we had to share it with the bosses.

"What needs correcting?" I asked.

Looking out over the parking lot and the people milling about the stalls he began to speak without looking at me.

"We need to make a very small adjustment to your future. A nudge in a certain direction to modify some pretty bad stuff that is going to happen."

"You mean *prevent* something bad from happening?"

"No, bad shit still happens, but we can correct the path so other things happen too, less bad, hopefully."

"I don't understand," I said. "Can you be more specific? How do you nudge the future?"

"I can't explain it now, and it wouldn't make much sense to you anyway, but I know you get the basics of what I am saying otherwise I wouldn't be here, and you wouldn't still be talking to me. So, please just roll with it."

"If you aren't able to explain it fully, then at least tell what you want from me?" I asked, not able to hide my frustration.

"You are going to London tomorrow, right? He answered. "I need you to find something—a book of sorts. It will explain things, or at least make it all a bit clearer. I will meet you there."

My going to London was not a secret. The lab knew, my sister knew. So if he thought he could convince me that he was legit by sharing with me this bit of intel he was wrong.

"Why don't you just get the book yourself and bring it to me, wouldn't that be easier for both of us?" I asked in response.

He paused and looked out at the crowd again, as if collecting his thoughts, before returning to look at me. "To answer your question in the simplest terms, I can only project to this future that we are creating right now, to the specific future that we are constructing together. If I went anywhere tomorrow ahead of you, say to get the book, it would put me in another future, and I need to project to your future. It's just a fact that I can't go back beyond the point in time that I am in right now, nor can I go ahead of yours without you."

He could tell I was confused by the look on my face, but he continued anyway.

"Think of time like a measuring stick, or ruler of sorts—metric, or imperial—you choose. And suppose today we are now on day number one, on the number 1. When you go to London tomorrow, which would be day number two, I could meet you *there*, or rather on the number 2, or on 3, 4. for that matter, but I cannot go back to day 1 since I have already been *there*. If I were to go to London tomorrow and you weren't *there*, I would be on another measuring stick altogether than the one you are on, make sense?"

As a scientist I needed proof of what he was saying for me to believe him, and he knew this. In the abstract it made some sense, but time travel was not my specialty, or anyone's for that matter. At least not until this very moment.

"How do I know if any of this is true?" You could be setting me up in some way. You could be OSS or MI-8 testing my loyalty."

I had listened to him and provided him with nothing except my first name. I had asked questions, but they were innocuous enough to not be incriminating. He had talked about my work and my future and I had given him nothing except my time.

"Tell me something from my future that only I know? Prove to me that this whole thing isn't a load of shit."

"You intend to break up with Sarah while you are in London. The long-distance thing is too much for you," he responded.

It was true. I had intended to call things off with Sarah. We had been dating for almost two years, and although I cared for her, the distance is too great between Austin and London. And I was not willing to commit, nor is she, to living in each other's city. That said, this may have been a private thought, but not a secret. I had discussed this with my sister Jane, and whoever David really is he could have had access to that conversation. I always assume my phone is hacked, any conversation, text or email is open source as far as I am concerned.

"That's not the only reason," he continued, "you've been questioning your sexuality for a very long time—you always have, and you haven't had the courage, up to now that is, to discuss this with Sarah. Or anyone for that matter. It's your intention to do so this trip, correct?"

"How could you know that?" I was incredulous. It was plausible that he knew I was planning on breaking up with Sarah. But he couldn't know my deepest private thoughts. There was no way.

"I know most things about you from the measuring stick you were on before today. The truth is that you are not an insignificant player in a major bit of technological history and it's possible that your life becomes more public later in life than you can imagine at this very moment. I told you before that I have read everything you have ever written, including the diary entry you will make tonight about our meeting today. So, I know a lot about you. But what I don't know for certain, at this precise moment, is whether you will actually go to London and participate in the correction we have planned."

This was a lot to process, and it required some intense internal deliberation. I needed to weigh the pros and cons before buying this explanation, but I also knew that I didn't have a lot of time do so. I had to make a choice whetherto participate or not, but first I had some questions.

"Is time linear?" I asked.

"Yes," he explained. "Directional, but not exactly straight. It's like a tree branch growing from the main trunk on a tree. A tree that's bigger than the universe.

"Is time constant?" I continued, "yes, and it can't be stopped, but it can be interrupted with insertions, and that's what we are doing right now."

I pondered his response for a moment because he didn't answer my question, not really. But I chose a different tack for my next question.

"Can I have more than one future?" I continued, "I mean, you say you've read my diaries, and all my working notes I presume. So, does that mean that even if I don't go along with what you are saying that the future I had before we met will continue ad finitum?

"We like to say that there are an infinite number of branches on the big tree, and if you meet me in London we will be on a new branch, while the other branches on the tree trunk continue to grow. It's true, I know all about your original branch, but it's this new one that has the best possibility of helping mankind avoid an uncertain peril."

"Peril? That's a heavy responsibility you're putting on me."

"Meet me in London and we will see how it unfolds. Either

way, time continues whatever branch you are on until the branch dies," he smiled wryly and continued, "and if it's any consolation, you still have the branch you were on before you met me and yes, in answer to your question, it too will continue to grow even though you can never go back to it. It's the same for me, I can't go back either."

"So, what you are saying is that you've already removed me from one possible future?"

"No, we like to say that we have seeded another future for you, but I have no idea what you will choose for yourself from this moment forward. If you choose to never see me again, chances are the variables in your current future will be little to no different than the one you had yesterday. If you choose to meet me in London, then the chances are that your new future will be considerably different."

I remained silent for a moment before responding. "I always stay at The Hoxton on High Holborn."

"I know," he said. "I will see you there."

London

I had seriously overthought my conversation with David and was left with a throbbing headache for my efforts. I had spent the four hours of the British Airways Concord flight from Austin to London playing our conversation over and over again, and I still had so many additional questions for him, and so many doubts about the truth of what he had said. Try as I may, I could not fully reconcile the fantastical nature of his own projection with the fact that he knew some deeply personal thoughts of mine. Did both things need to be true for me to believe one or the other, or could he be simply trying to trick me into believing that the if one thing is true than the other must be as well?

This was one of the most basic manipulations used to build confidence in any mark, and we had been trained to spot it—the trick of making two things true by association. Admittedly, this was also a basic tool of child psychology and even toddlers could figure when it was being used against them—and he would know this, so why would he attempt something so transparent with me?

During the car ride from London Heathrow to Whitehall my thoughts turned more predictably to my work and the seemingly impossible reality of projected time travel and not just the milliseconds we had already achieved. Not to mention the perfected birthing of Hollows—now Solids, using some form of nuclear energy. I kept coming back to when he said that sometime in the future I had written all these thoughts down, and that they had seemingly entered the public record. It was no wonder my head hurt.

What was more overwhelming than the thought of the perfected technology, or even the fact that he knew something so personal about me, was the possibility that there was more than one future for me. Which meant that there was now more than one possible past as well. David had said that even if I chose not to go to London that the future that had been cast the very moment before I met him would go on regardless. So that meant that I had at least two futures progressing simultaneously, and yet I was only conscious of the one.

If this was true, then for every correction he, or others like him had made or were planning to make, there would be a new past, present and future for those involved. And if he had imposed himself on my future, then to whom else and how many other times had he done this? How many branches are on this metaphorical tree he had described, and where are all these branches located? Is the Cloud even big enough for all these futures?

I was reluctant to consider the idea of multiple planes of consciousness since it seemed like something from a bad sci-fi movie, but for the moment I had no other explanation for how this was all working.

I had so many questions, but the answers would have to wait until our next meeting. I had made some very specific plans for this trip. Even though it was supposed to be business as usual, meaning *usual* in the sense that I met monthly in person with our British counterparts to ensure that our conversations were not corrupted, and that there was no perceived ambiguity in our correspondences. In the meantime, I had important business to attend to with Sarah, as well.

Meeting in person allowed for stronger bonds between the two labs and kept us accountable to each other. The *unusual* part of the trip was that I had planned on breaking up with Sarah. I was mostly convinced it was the right thing to do, including trying to share some of my deeper thoughts and insecurities, even if I was not exactly certain what I was capable of saying.

I had never had this conversation with anyone before, so I was filled with great angst about the whole idea, but I also knew it was the right thing to do after the couple of years we had spent together. My thought that she deserves to know about what I was struggling with was challenged by the fact that I am not sure anyone deserves anything in life. I feel like she should know the truth, but if I chose to simply stop seeing her would the truth behind my decision ever really matter? Our futures would go on regardless of whatever I said, admittedly with different realities born from the reason for my actions. The similarities between what David was asking of me, and what I was asking of Sarah, was not lost on me.

My regular schedule dictated that I went right to the office from the airport, which the redeye allowed me to do, and although I often lamented privately about not going to my hotel first to freshen up after my flight this time, I was grateful to not have to go the hotel where I was worried that David would be waiting for me.

I called Sarah when I landed and arranged to see her later that evening and so I was looking forward to a few busy hours at the lab as a diversion from my racing mind. I hoped I might even get a few minutes to myself in the walk from Whitehall to the hotel to clear my head before seeing either David or Sarah—whomever came first—since both meetings posed very specific and very different challenges. Both required a deep personal commitment on my part, and in this particular moment in my day, in the car from Heathrow to Whitehall, I had mostly made up my mind: I was going to break up with Sarah *and* tell David that I wasn't interested in helping him with whatever the correction entailed. I was going to take control of my own destiny.

Stepping out of the car on Admiralty Place changed that decision in an instant. From the corner of my eye, I caught sight of David standing conspicuously on the sidewalk, just a few short paces from the building entrance. He looked like any of the other civil servants milling about, his navy pinstriped suit nicely tailored and crisply pressed, polished shoes, umbrella in hand and with a newspaper under his arm.

Our eyes met briefly, and he nodded slightly. I made no other attempt to acknowledge him and quickly made my way into the lobby and through security. I turned back just before passing through the metal detector and tried to catch a glimpse of him through the glass panes in the narrow steel door. I lost sight of him just before I was met on the other side of security by one of my colleagues and was whisked downstairs to the lab. I tried to appear as normal as possible, but I was deeply unnerved by David's sudden appearance.

He said that he would meet me at The Hoxton but for some reason he had felt compelled to make his presence known to me in advance. I didn't know if this was his way of reassuring me of his legitimacy, or whether he was checking to see if I would follow through on my plans to go to London. Either way, when I saw him, I immediately second guessed my decision not to help him. What if it was all true? And what if my participation might play some part in the advancement of the projection technology beyond anything that I had imagined to date? And had I just committed to an unplanned future?

Compounding this uncertainty was the fact that I hadn't pressed him adequately on what he meant by helping him with this correction, which seemed overly dramatic on his part, and in hindsight—a point that really had been lost in the totality of the conversation. He had used the word peril in describing his need for my help, but he had been a little too nonchalant about the *peril* part for my liking, so I had not pressed him further. But now I wanted to know exactly what he was implying, which meant that I had to meet him again.

My description of our offices at Whitehall as a lab is not quite accurate. The term lab is more of all catchall term to describe where our teams spend most of their days when not in the field. Austin, however, is a lab in the true sense of the word— a series of clean rooms and light boxes, suspension tanks, and dozens of people working on computers, white coats, etc., all in support of the experiments we are conducting around the world. In London, the lab is more like a traditional office, albeit set in the basement of the old War Offices Annex where protocols are mapped and traced, and non-conforming performance methods are tested and graded.

The two locations work in sync, but Austin is blind to London's testing mechanisms and only receives criticisms of the operating procedures that we jointly establish before each projection. London cannot send spike samples, or even blanks, since they have no ability to make a projection, but their arms-length verification of our work is integral to our success. They aren't our bosses, but we rely upon their oversight, and their endless and constant criticisms (always well documented) to guide our experiments. They observe in-field, and with CCTV from all over London their network of public surveillance cameras is greater than anywhere else in the world, and so we use the city as the base for most of our test projections. The distance from Austin pushes the limits of our abilities which provides the challenge we needed to drive our work.

The decades of shared intelligence between the two agencies, prior to the establishment of our actual collaboration, means that there are few political barriers between the two locations, and this makes the teamwork that much easier. Our cultural differences are minimal since the US's return to the Commonwealth after Reagan's presidency. The short stint on our own in the 1980s seemed to have done us no harm, even if he and Thatcher had been arch enemies. Our shared colonial past and smooth transition to independence soon after the ratification of the Slavery Abolition Act by Westminster in 1833 had laid the foundation for a special relationship, even after the violent uprisings that ended the constitutional monarchy and laid the ground for the modern American Republic. We are no longer one people under a single flag, the Brits and us, but we think in sync and our special relationship has kept the peace in North America for the past couple of centuries—with the unspoken, yet common goal of keeping Canada's insatiable expansionist policies in check.

In the beginning, admittedly, I had been reluctant to share any of our work with London. My work, really. Our team was very small then and we were quite protective, just three of us working in the dingy warehouse space in San Francisco's China Basin. Yet we had achieved so much so quickly, and our vibe was so dynamic, and we were just so enthusiastic about our work that we hardly noticed how shitty the place was. The move to Austin, like all the other tech companies, after being acquired (sucked in) by OSS put us on a more disciplined track and gave us access to the all the other tech headquartered there.

My initial reluctance to share our product was soon replaced with a more collegial approach, and we even learned over time to trust our MI-8 colleagues. We had been able to handpick our own team with the move to Austin, and all team members went through the same spook training so there was a genuine sense of loyalty and camaraderie amongst all of us, which extended to the present day for both teams. We had grown much more professional with the marriage between Austin and London, and yet I had broken all the rules of my training—and maybe the law—yesterday by not reporting my meeting with David. Worse still, I had seen him outside Whitehall, and I failed to report him. I had willfully broken the most basic and elementary rules of tradecraft, and yet I had no regrets.

Sarah

The walk from Whitehall to The Hoxton after a day of meetings, and a night flight, was tiring but I didn't mind. The low autumn light and the crowds on the Strand, coupled with the sounds of the traffic was a perfect distraction for my raging mind. The autumn sky glowed an amber hue that enlivened the usually dull limestone buildings so that even the centuries of wear had a welcoming warmth. Over the past several years this walk had become somewhat ritualistic for me. It gave me time to decompress from the flight and the hours of meetings that usually followed, and the change of seasons seemed to bring new delights with each walk.

In the summer the sun set so late that the streets teemed with people long past the normal commuting hours—tourists mostly it seemed—but I preferred the fall and winter when the light was low, and the air was damp and cold and the smell of chestnuts roasting in braziers hung about the street corners. The city seemed more alive when the weather changed, and my delight in the chill and wet was probably due to the repetitive heat of my regular life in Austin, and the constant sun of my younger years spent in California.

London has an ancient history that is still very much alive— that is, if you looked for it. Especially if you got off the Strand and dove deeper into the city proper, where the remnants of the medieval city could still be found in the pavestones of the alleyways, in carvings on the Temple, and in the leaden glass of the facades of Lincoln's Inn.

I take comfort in this history, and not just as a diversion from my own thoughts, but because I genuinely appreciate the sense of permanence that comes from a stone cornice that sits atop brick and mortar laid by hand five hundred years or more prior. It is reassuring to me to know that there is a genuineness in the built form of the city, and that some things in life can still actually be tangible and permanent, and that they can endure for so long when so much about modern life is virtual.

I find it disappointing that we don't hold photos in our hands anymore, and that books are rarely printed now. They exist on a screen, and even art is now available in a non-fungible form which renders it inaccessible to most people. Life has been reduced to a unit of data, a non-thing on a blockchain and even my own work has so much about it that is ephemeral that I find I need to walk the city just to reassure myself that life is real; to smell the city, and to wipe its grit from eyes. There are certainly quicker ways to get to my hotel, but on foot I feel connected to a reality that has a permanence that I fear escapes me in my everyday life.

The Hoxton is a respite of sorts too. The large lobby lounge is usually full after the work hours with young academics from the neighborhood, and of course professionals from the city. Admittedly, the space is contrived to encourage socializing with sofas and club chairs littered about the place, and the occasional tables and bookshelves give it a residential feel, and since I know few people in London it is a perfect place for me to feel comfortably anonymous in a crowd.

I can enjoy a bourbon in quiet while the room buzzes around me with 20 and 30-somethings engaging in conversations that I get to hear, but not have to contribute to. It was here that I first met Sarah, and so it has become, over the past two years, our meeting place for my visits. If my work takes me over a weekend I typically move to her flat in Kensington after a few days at the hotel, but for short visits and as a creature of habit, I take great comfort in the familiarity of the hotel and in its unpretentious vibe.

Sarah is convinced her flat is bugged, and I continuously lie to her in response and assure her that it is not true. In my profession I work from the premise that everything and everyone

I speak to is known to someone in the agency. Even my meeting with David in Austin was most assuredly noted by someone, but I felt it was innocuous enough to not raise any alarms—for the time being anyway.

She also thinks her office at the university is bugged, and rightly so. Her research in the field of Behavioral Economics has minimal theoretical relationship to my work, but it does have a lot of practical similarities. Whereas my research creates facsimiles of people mimicking real-world behavior through social transactions, her research attempts to reproduce genuine transactional behaviors using real-live people. This is where our work is similar: I experiment in crafting artificially socialized motor skills to improve interactions between live and holographic subjects, and she theorizes how to socialize behaviors in complex monetary transactions between subjects that are all very much live, and in real-life.

For obvious reasons I have not been able to completely share my work with her, and she knows that it is classified having gone through the necessary clearances herself once things got more serious in our relationship. Her position at University College London as an inconsequential PhD candidate raised very few flags at Whitehall, and this means she is able to share far more about her work than I am able to share about mine.

She knows this implicitly, but she is quite unaware of how much of our regular conversation I allow to influence my own thinking. Her theory, that how people relate to the construct of money, and how it is pre-programmed or hardwired in us is very interesting to me. And her belief that this preprogramming is not entirely a product of current, or real-time socialization, has made me question almost all aspects of the transactional quality of how our projections function in the proto-real world. So, I've applied

40

some of the more practical aspects of her theory in our work without sharing any of it with her.

In the beginning we would work our projections like old fashioned drone operators, and we relied upon deeply subconscious, and one might argue inherent, behaviors to govern how we functioned; pilots were required to use instinctive reactions to circumstances that they were not always preconditioned to process or predict. For example, a couple of years ago we projected to a barely socialized indigenous group in the Amazon. We sent our pilot in blind and she had no idea when the projection birthed where she was and whom she would meet. All she was tasked with, wherever she appeared, was that she had to build trust via a transaction of some sort. The form and manner of the transaction was hers to decide.

The indigenous group we had chosen for our experiment had previous, but very brief and intermittent contact with missionaries and government officials, and therefore they had very few associative transactional experiences, and certainly none with a sudden appearance of a westernized white woman. The pilot herself had no fear of physical harm, for obvious reasons since she was a Hollow, and so with no prior knowledge of the place or the people she was projected to the edge of a village and had to use her acquired instincts, which is a form of social conditioning itself, to enter the village without causing alarm. Interestingly, the experiment relied upon the pilot's ability to communicate without a shared language, to gain entry—for a short time anyway—without a prior relational history, and for the experiment to be deemed successful she was required to make at least one mutually beneficial transaction.

We had chosen the projection to be naked, which meant that the pilot had nothing but her wits to rely upon, and the results of her first interactions surprised us all when she entered the village and encountered a group of children first. Their curiosity was tempered by a conditioned wariness born from lives spent in concert with a physical environment that could be hostile, yet the pilot was able to convey that she was no threat, and her nudity was certainly not an odd occurrence. Through a cautious and unassuming approach over a few short minutes, she convinced, or maybe permitted, the children to bring her to the center of the village and into one of the communal grass roofed structures.

She had a limited time to act, and with that in mind she humbly approached a group of indigenous folk, and with some graciousness managed to be invited into a group of women who offered her a drink from a gourd-like vessel. Of course, projections can't drink or hold solid objects, but feigned acceptance of what was offered and went through the motions of pretending to do so, and then reciprocated—her part in the transaction—by smiling and impassively singing a song: A very soft and quite melodic acapella version of Mary J. Blige's Family Affair.

This completed the transaction, but, why this song? She could offer no good reason during the debrief, apparently that was all that came to her mind at the time. Maybe it was the last song she heard on the radio before starting the projection, or maybe it had some deeper meaning to her. She then got up from the hut, walked back to the edge of the jungle, and the projection was ended leaving no trace of her on the footpath.

None of the actions of those involved was preplanned and none of the reactions of the parties, from the accepting children to the offering of the drink by the women of the village, to the pilot's singing, were conditioned by any form of pre-contextualized behavior. Certainly, there were *preconditioned* behaviors exhibited, and not just limited to the general welcoming of a stranger, but ultimately, we concluded that the small series of transactional events that made up the projection were all prefaced on the initial trust of the children and their acceptance of a naked stranger—and tellingly a woman—into their midst. This trust came from a programmed place somewhere inherent within the psyche of the children that bred additional trust and acceptance by the other villagers.

Sarah has told me that her research had indicated that the most successful transactions were those that were made quickly and instinctively, and that the more people thought about the cost, or the disaggregation of their actions, the less willing they were to complete a monetary transaction. It was this principle, that she called the Child's Purchase (after Nathaniel Child not the small humans) that we used to improve the interactions of our projections.

We tell our operators to use instinct, and to not think too hard if you need to make a decision and do so from the premise that all people at their core share one common behavioral attribute, and that is the inherent need to bargain for their life. For example, a mother feeds a newborn and in return it smiles and gives love: The basic premise of the Child's Purchase theory.

We learned very early on that in most cases that survival of a projection required the pilot to navigate a transaction of some sort—and that women, inherently, made better pilots overall. We think it is their ability to project trust and that maybe there is some residual memory of all of us in our physical passage from womb to the world.

Sarah's research was frequently published, which meant there was no conflict for her when she shared her work with me, since it was readily available online. I, on the other hand, could only offer a cursory insight into what I did at Whitehall, and I rarely talked about my regular daily work in Austin. As far as she knew my work was based in surveillance technologies, and that I simply and boringly, worked for one of the Commonwealth agencies, and hence the requirements for security clearances and secrecy.

This meant that our relationship was built on an element of deception from our first meeting, and it was probably why I was able to justify to myself my lack of complete honesty and really my lack of commitment to her from the very beginning of the relationship. I couldn't tell the truth, so I didn't. It was easy to be noncommittal when you get to leave at the end of a weekend, and you didn't need to be entirely truthful about yourself and your feelings for someone when you are safe in a lie that had been institutionalized from the very beginning of relationship.

I know that not telling the truth about what I did for a living was not the same thing as not sharing my uncertainty about my sexuality, but I had convinced myself that if one deception was acceptable than the other deception was acceptable too.

I assure you, it was not lost on me that I had been playing the same psychological trick on Sarah that I suspected David to be playing on me as well.

The Hoxton

I spotted Sarah through the window, sitting on one of the orange velvet sofas near the bar. Her long brown hair loose on her shoulders, a slight kink still visible from the elastic that she usually wore to tie up her hair while she worked, now free as she enjoyed a cocktail while waiting for me to arrive. She looks the very same as when we first met, classically beautiful but not pretty, not in the English sense. Her features are angled and sharp, not round and soft like the Anabelle's or Chloé's found in the shops in Mayfair, and she would sooner argue a fine political point than gallery hop. True, she can ride and shoot like all the other girls from her school days, but she is more at home at a football game rooting for her beloved Chelsea than at a country home for a weekend party. I love these things about her, but I do not love her. This is tough to admit to myself, but it is going to be tougher to admit to her.

Three years younger than me, she turned twenty-eight a few weeks prior and I had not been in London for her birthday. We had planned for her to come to Austin to celebrate shortly thereafter, but I had cancelled her trip at the last moment feigning a work commitment. She had been disappointed, to say the least. I think she had been expecting a marriage proposal in Austin, and if not then, soon. Which is why I cancelled her trip.

Our subsequent conversations had been strained by an undercurrent of an unmet expectation that I sensed was more disappointment on her part than a lack of belief in my commitment to our relationship. In other words, I don't think she has a clue what's coming. This meeting today was going to be my first since her cancelled trip to Austin, so I knew that at this very moment, seeing her face to face, was going to be difficult for both of us.

She too was trained to observe and therefore could read me easily. So, I entered the lobby lounge prepared to appear happy to see her, which I believed I could do if I tried hard enough, but I struggled to mask my anxiousness and the anxiety I was feeling prevented me from showing any real joy—no matter how hard I tried.

Turning right towards the bar I steeled myself for the greeting and noted with some alarm that she was not alone. I had caught sight of her from the window as I walked by outside, but I hadn't noticed that she was sitting with a stranger, and that they appeared to be heavily engaged in conversation. She spotted me as I walked towards her and she jumped up to greet me with a kiss, but I was not able to maintain eye contact with her because my gaze was fixed upon David, who also stood up from his place beside her on the sofa. I could not hide my alarm, which was much greater than any sense of surprise since nothing could truly amaze me now after the revelations of the last few days. His presence frightened me.

I had been worrying about who I would see first, David or Sarah, but I had not anticipated seeing them together at the same time! These two people were not meant to meet, and all my mental preparation for this evening had not steeled me for this possibility.

Kissing Sarah first, I then turned to greet David with an outstretched hand. Again, I noted the artificial feel of his projected skin. He took my hand readily as if it was the most natural thing in the world for the three of us to be meeting in the lobby bar of The Hoxton.

"Paul, you didn't tell me your friend David would be joining us this evening," Sarah said before I could say anything. This allowed me to buy some time to process the situation. "But we've been getting to know each other a little while waiting for you," she continued.

I could hear the uncertainty in her voice.

"I am not sure I knew myself," I said with a mixture of sarcasm and wryness, trying not to sound too confused or bothered.

"I hadn't confirmed with him, Sarah," David interjected quickly. "I was uncertain of my own arrival time in London. But he mentioned the other day that he was meeting you here and I thought I might surprise you both."

Having to think on my feet here was proving to be a bit of a challenge. I always considered that the early successes of my projections was due to my ability to improvise in an unfamiliar situation, but here I was engaged in a charade in real time and it was a genuine challenge to my skills as an operator. I needed to tap into my instincts here to get through whatever was about to unfold.

"How did you happen to both end up on the same sofa, and how long have you been here?" I asked, directing the question to David.

"I recognized Sarah immediately from your Myspace page," he responded with a wink directed towards her. "I introduced myself and have been imposing myself upon her for the last few minutes or so."

His familiarity was unwarranted, and it made me uncomfortable.

"David was telling me that you two had met through work not long ago, and that it was quite coincidental that you would both be in London at the same time," Sarah interjected, bringing herself into the conversation. I could see her in eyes that she too was uncomfortable by David's presence.

"Is that so?" I responded, not masking my irritation very well, and not really posing a question. "I don't remember that part of the conversation."

"It was just a couple of days ago, at the farmer's market in Austin," he replied without a trace of deceit in his voice. "You remember," posing a statement in the form of a question, as well.

"Ah, yes," I said. And before I could respond further the waiter came by and I was able to order a double bourbon, which couldn't come quick enough for me.

I could tell that the interaction between the three of us was growing noticeably awkward for Sarah. David's presence was not only presumptuous, but it was also unnecessary to his cause, and I could not even begin to surmise why he had chosen to interject himself into what was supposed to be a very private moment for Sarah and me. The circumstance of his arrival was unusual, to say the least, and I know this was not lost on Sarah. Here is a stranger that introduces himself to her, claiming he knows her boyfriend, and begins a conversation while waiting for said boyfriend to arrive.

She had every right to question the situation. This sort of interaction with a friend, or supposed friend, was not normal for us. We did not have a shared friend group due to the long-distance nature of our relationship, given what she knew of my need for a level of security in my work, I could only assume that she was suspicious of his approach and the story about how he recognized her from my Myspace page would not seem credible to her. She knew that I was old school and used the barely functioning Facebook app, and not the ubiquitous Myspace, like the rest of the world.

"Tell me again, David, what brings you to London?" I asked, trying to take some control of the conversation.

"You, Paul. For you," he responded in earnest.

Sarah showed no outward sign of surprise to David's response, but I could see in her eyes that this comment was as much as a revelation for her as it was for me. So, before she could question anything further, I attempted to intervene with a request to clarify what he meant, but before I could ask, he cut me off again.

"Sarah, I am sorry," he said, directing the conversation and his gaze towards her. "Paul hasn't had much of an opportunity since his arrival to explain to you why I am here. And I am guessing that in any conversations you two might have had either yesterday or today, on the phone or via text, that he didn't mention me."

Sarah nodded in agreement. I tried to jump in again but was abruptly cut off by David.

"I told Paul two days ago, in Austin, that I would meet him in London, but I didn't tell him when exactly. Earlier today I waited for him to arrive at Whitehall and watched as he entered the building, making sure that he saw me on the pavement."

This was an odd admission and explained nothing to Sarah but confirmed his intent towards me.

"Paul," Sarah begged. "Will you tell me what is happening?"

"What the fuck, David. You should leave," I exclaimed angrily, my voice raised loud enough that other people in the bar were now watching us intently.

There was a long uncomfortable pause between the three of us while the other patrons returned to their own conversations.

"Sarah, I need Paul to tell you that he doesn't love you, and that it would be best for all concerned if you just moved on from one another."

Sarah looked at me wide-eyed, and David continued, "Because he isn't sure he's totally straight, but he's too afraid to tell you. And unfortunately for all of us, I can't risk that he might not have the courage to tell you this, so I am compelled to do it for him. He has important work to do and getting on with it requires him to be without you in his life. This may sound harsh to you now, but it's for the best—for both of you and many other people."

"Why is he saying this, Paul?" Sarah asked, looking at me

pleadingly.

My first instinct was to physically lash out at David, but I knew it would be fruitless since he couldn't feel pain. But I certainly would if my fist encountered his annealed skin which is like tempered glass. Punching him would give me some satisfaction, but it was more important in the moment that I attempted to soothe a visibly distressed Sarah. I got up from my chair and began to move towards her, but she got up too, grabbed her coat and bag as if to go towards the door. She paused to look at David who was still sitting on the sofa.

"Who the fuck *are* you?" She asked him, coldly.

"Please, sit back down. Paul can explain," he answered calmly without lowering his voice, while gesturing her back towards her place on the sofa.

She reluctantly sat back down but kept hold of her coat and bag resting awkwardly on her lap. She looked at me pleadingly, her eyes searching for an explanation without saying anything.

I felt as if my head might explode, and I caught myself rubbing my right temple and wincing as I struggled to come up with a plausible explanation for Sarah as to what was happening. Nothing came to mind. Was I to tell her that I met David a couple of days ago when he appeared from several hundred years in the future using the very technology that I was working on at this very moment? How plausible would that sound? Could I tell her that he wasn't actually sitting beside her, but rather that he was a projected image made of silica that had been formed using some sort of radioactive material and that at any moment he could turn to dust if he wanted? Where could I say he actually was, or who he was, when I wasn't certain myself?

I was struggling to rationalize the moment. I felt so foolish for having listened to him in the first place. I had not committed to anything he had asked of me. I owed him nothing. I had simply listened to him. I had not agreed to join his correction. I came to London as I usually did; he chose to insert himself into my life, and now he was making decisions for me without my permission.

I had no explanation for Sarah, and I was doubting what I knew myself to be true, yet I chose to continue despite this fact.

"I don't know what to say, Sarah. I guess some of its true, I do love you...but I guess not enough. Please believe me that this isn't how I was planning on telling you. He had no fucking right to say these things to you." I was now looking at David.

"You have no fucking right to speak for me."

There was another long pause, while the three of us sat looking at each other. David bemused, with a slight smile, and Sarah and I visibly angry with him and at the situation in general.

"Why? Why have you done this?" I asked him earnestly.

"Once again, I apologise Sarah. But not to you, Paul," he said, turning towards me now. "I told you before that I don't have much time and I can't wait for you to find the courage to have this conversation with her. It's painful for you both, I know this, and I understand how this could be awkward for everyone," he gestured to the small circle of three of us, "but its for the best, trust me."

"Best for who?" Sarah asked. "How do you know what is best for me? And I've asked you once already, who are you? I think I deserve to know after this stunt you've pulled."

He didn't answer. She then looked directly at me. "Are you two sleeping together?" she asked.

I answered "NO," and looked to David for support, but he remained irritatingly silent. However, it did seem like a logical question given what David had told her about me.

Sarah got up to leave again, and I knew I couldn't stop her

this time. I followed her out through the lobby doors and onto the busy sidewalk of High Holborn. She knew I had followed her, but she chose to ignore me as she searched the busy traffic for a cab.

"Sarah, please," I begged. "Give me a moment, I need to talk to you." But she was ignoring me as she struggled to put on her coat while juggling her handbag. I tried to help her, but she shrugged me off.

"You don't have to believe me," I pleaded, "but I have to say again that I don't know David. I just met him the other day and he asked for some help with some work thing. I told him I was going to London, and he said he would see me here, but I didn't know if he was telling the truth. I had no idea he would show up here, of all places."

Sarah turned to speak to me without making eye contact, her attempt at hailing a cab fruitless during rush hour. I could tell she was contemplating the tube and whether to walk to Covent Garden or head back towards the Kingsway.

"If you just met him, then how did he know so much about us? You must have told him that you wanted to break up with me, how else would he know? And why would you tell that to a perfect stranger, and why couldn't you not have talked with me about the other thing? I mean, for Christ's sake Paul, we've been together for more than two years. Could you not have had the decency to tell me yourself? Why subject me to this public humiliation?"

"I didn't know he was going to show up here," I stammered nervously. "I had planned to speak with you this evening, I promise you…to have an honest conversation about a lot of things."

"I think David, or whatever his name is, is right. I don't think

52

you have the courage to be honest with me. I think our entire relationship has been an illusion. I don't think I even know who you are!" Sarah paused for a moment before continuing: "I think you are a coward."

With that, she turned away from me and began to walk towards Covent Garden rather than try to hail a cab or walk back against the tide of people moving from the Kingsway towards the lights of the West End. I called out to her, but she chose to ignore me, and I couldn't blame her. We had argued before over little irritations and had had general differences of opinion on minor topics, but I had never hurt her before like I had this evening. I knew that what just had happened was irreparable, and worse yet, I wanted it to be irreparable. It was painful for me to admit, but there was something inside me that was grateful to David for forcing the conversation, which unfortunately did make me the coward that they both said I was.

Chapter Two

The Hollow Truth

I returned to the bar with every intention of forcing David to answer the many questions I had, but I also knew that I had been unable to master any control over my dealings with him. He possessed an internalized immunity that came from the detachment of his projection. He wasn't actually here, and therefore he didn't face any repercussions in real-time for anything he said and did. So, he held all the power in this situation. This was one of the negative attributes we noted in our pilots when they first began to master their projections. Their initial trepidations, like a baby's first steps, were hesitant and cautious, but as they grew accustomed to their own body movements and the mirroring of the projection, they grew bolder and more daring, sometimes quite reckless with their actions.

This was mostly true of male pilots rather than the female ones, but it is a common trait in most people irrespective of gender to accept more risk when there are no personal emotional, or physical repercussions for their actions. We have had Hollows walk off cliffs, step in front of trains, pick fights in bars, insult strangers, you name it, they've done it with impunity in the name of experimental science. Sometimes there are witnesses to this recklessness, which is what you see on the internet and on the conspiracy theory and ghost encounter channels that proliferate on the web. This is why our work with the Brits has been invaluable. They helped established the rigorous protocols that limit a Hollow's interactions with live subjects. Not that we weren't capable of academic rigor at the time, but within the intelligence community they had a much longer tradition of applied science.

The experiments we now jointly devise have highly specific and well practiced controls which prohibit protracted discussions with live bodies. There are never engagements in personal matters of any kind. All our encounters are purely transactional and limited to in-and-out scenarios. Apparently, things have evolved in David's time where there is now highly intrapersonal contact and deep engagement in personal matters. Fuck!

Where we continue to struggle is when our projections lack sufficient bandwidth and the Hollows come in and out of focus, we call this twitching. This is where the screen captures and surveillance footage of 'ghosts' come from on the web. We find it amusing, of course, but there are millions of believers hooked on this stuff. People really think they are seeing ghosts, when in fact it is just our failures visible to the world. Ghosts don't exist, and even the least rational among us knows deep down that there are no spirits even in our deeply spiritual society. The whole notion of entities from beyond death fails in the face of the basic tenets of the Judeo-Christian-Islamic (JCI) faiths that govern modern society, even if the belief still has a home among agnostics and their kin: the Qanon quacks.

Even with our Hindu and Buddhist brethren, the idea of spirits is anathema, and the universal acceptance of the JCI prophets has sustained a tentative world peace for a very long time, even with Canada's continuous sabre rattling. I wondered if, perhaps, David might share with me now when and why these protocols ended and why he has chosen to impose himself upon me?

David hadn't moved from his place in the bar. The token drink he had ordered remained untouched on the table before him. I rejoined him with every intent on giving him a piece of my mind, but I found that I had little to say at first and instead downed his drink as well as my own while collecting my thoughts. Our eyes locked on one another.

"You are an asshole, David."

"I am not sorry, Paul," he said, his voice giving little in the way of emotion. His eyes as glassy and lifeless as always.

"I can see that," I replied. "She is gone, you got what you wanted. So, are you going to tell me why, now?" I asked.

There was a long pause before he asked me what I wanted to know.

"I have a lot of questions."

"Ask away," he responded. "I will answer them all."

"Truthfully?" I enquired, knowing that it was a hollow question.

"I have not lied to you yet, not really. When you asked me where I was, when we first met, I avoided the answer by saying I was with London. If I had told you the whole truth, then you would have walked away from me. But you must admit, I have been more truthful than you could have ever expected...or perhaps wanted of me, correct?"

I nodded in acknowledgement. His abrupt and forthright exchange with Sarah had left me shocked, and the bourbon had yet to fully help in my recovery. I waved the waiter over and motioned for another while we sat in protracted silence. I was going to ask questions now and I wanted to make sure that I had them well ordered in my head. The silence between us gave me pause to collect my thoughts.

"Where are you, then?" I began.

"On the moon," he answered plausibly. "You were thinking the ISS, weren't you?"

"I was wondering. The International Space Station (ISS) is on the cards for us in 2036. A permanent base? You live there, on the moon?" I asked with wonder at the future possibility.

"Yes, a permanent base since 2092. We've been here for over one hundred and thirty years. I return to Earth every few weeks, but things have been hectic the past few months and I find myself up here more than usual."

"That explains your ease of movement," I interjected. "Even our best pilots still look like marionettes sometimes, no matter how much practice they get."

"Your cabling is pretty good," he continued, "but your pilots are still limited by their lateral movements, and their subtleties of motion are still not credible, the ones that aren't really noticed till they're not there. Like blinking, and smirking. With Zero-G we move effortlessly and can project as we are. Totally normal."

I nodded in agreement. Our biggest challenge is relating body movements in real-time to the movements in projection. For a Hollow to walk up stairs, sit, climb, or even navigate the minor changes on a ground plane in the place of their projection the pilot needs to feel the matching resistance to their limbs, or at least be suspended in a way that allows them to parrot motions in their projected space. In our early experiments we used simple rigging with pulleys and counterweights, but that was extremely clumsy and resembled a circus act more than a serious experiment. We then tried water-based suspension but risked electrocution and drowning our pilots, and now we use a very sophisticated gimbal system and a 360 LED screen to connect via live feed from local CCTV or even drone cameras—satellites too sometimes if the projected space is remote. We still can't effectively parrot the minor movements that make us more relatable, such as the arched eyebrow or David's wide-eyed sarcasm, and he is correct, our lateral movements still need work.

"We have hoped for Zero-G from the beginning. It's the perfect medium, but how do you remain static and not float around, do you still use cabling for stability?"

"You will still use some cabling when you finally get to the ISS, but now we moderate gravity."

"With magnetism," I asked earnestly. It was what we were working on here in Austin right now.

"Yes, we use the Zero-G for suspension and manipulate the natural magnetism in the body using low energy magnetic domains. We align the domains to get bigger forces where needed and misalign them in gradients to allow for smaller movements. Like the subtle hand movements, we use when talking," he lightly strummed his fingers on the arm of his chair to illustrate, "pretty basic stuff, really."

I was impressed and eager to learn more, but I think I understood the basics…in abstract, anyway. David was in an oxygenated room on the moon; gravity was non-existent, so he was suspended in space, magnets were being used to provide resistance to his movements and to give them credibility, and his Hollow was being projected two hundred years back in time, with mass and as a perceived Solid…and with the ability to see and speak with me in real-time. This was fascinating. I knew the human body was mildly magnetic, everything is, but to my knowledge no one had ever mechanized it before. As much as I wanted to push him further on this, and I had other questions that went beyond the mechanics of his projection, I needed to press him on other aspects of his projection.

"So, you are naked in space?" I asked, attempting to interject some humour in the conversation.

"Yes," he laughed in response. "A bare ass is funny in the future too."

"How do you legitimize the projection?" I continued, "I mean, how do you clothe yourselves? Buy the shoes you are wearing now? Hire a car, pay for the food, and drinks you can't eat? How do you pull off and maintain the charade in the present time?"

The questions were elementary, but the simple logistics of legitimizing a project are always a challenge for us. We can create Hollows in the lab and outfit them with everything they need to walk out into the world as credible entities since they are just reflections really, but not when we are remote. How do they project into the past, and with mass, and expect to pull it off, I asked earnestly.

"It's surprisingly easy to project to your time. We hack the web and there are routers everywhere, we blockchain servers all day long, and simply buy what we need. For example, we book a hotel room online, we pay online, we have a wardrobe delivered to the room that we buy online—all the best hotels have a concierge that takes care of everything. We deliver wallets, IDs, cash, credit cards...everything we need. We project to the hotel room, dress, and walk out the door."

It is genius really, and very simple.

"You taught us this," he continued, "everything we do is transactional."

"Sarah. My diaries?" I asked knowingly. And he nodded in agreement.

"What about farther back, before the internet? How did you pull it off, because I have my suspicions that you've been doing this for a while now?"

"The challenge has never been acquiring what we need logistically. We project and steal where necessary, and since we don't need to anneal fully in dim light or darkness, we can be nearly invisible. Your YouTube has thousands of video clips of smoky entities and shadows that people want to believe are ghosts. They're not," he laughed. "And yes, we've been doing this a while."

I laughed a little as well, because we too found the whole notion of our projections being mistaken for ghosts highly amusing. But I was also laughing out of nervousness because we started this phenomenon, and it is still happening hundreds of years later. I was growing concerned that we, and me in particular, might be caught in some time loop, where my work in the present is being influenced in the future, but now it was too complicated a thought to fully process.

With further prodding on my part, he then explained that the further back they project they tend to use Hollows which consume less energy and form easily even with the weak routers that can be fabricated from rudimentary materials. Interestingly, he said that they're able to create mass illusions, theatricals he called them, Hollow projections with multiple participants, lights, and even music. I could not imagine the need for this, but I listened attentively anyway.

"The challenge for us, the further we go back," he continued, "is the need for a functioning router. We have infinite possibilities in your era, since the 1950s really, and the ability to build them is simply done by hiring the right people and paying them well. Venmo for you, tele-banking in the 1990s, phone-banking back through to the 1930s, then telegrams, then mail…the further back we go the more creative we need to be to acquire the basic raw materials, and the appropriate currency for transactions. Silica is basically everywhere, so is copper in some form, but steel as we know it has an origin point in time not so long ago, as does usable aluminum. The further we go back in time the more we rely on gold, which is not plentiful by any means and hard to access since it is usually locked away. Further back than the invention of steel and we are challenged."

I nodded, understanding the basic limitations, but the chicken and egg scenario kept nagging me. What comes first, the router or the projection?

"I know what you are thinking. But when we finally accepted that the universe is flat and that spacetime can be bent by mass and energy, think nuclear, we were able to bend it just enough to get a projection in place to enlist craftsmen to fabricate what we needed without having to appear in solid form. We can talk to anyone in any time, kind of like Alexander Graham Bell asking: Watson, come here."

I think I understood what he was saying. They didn't need routers to project at all, they only need them to amplify for movement. It really was like the chicken and the egg. And so they could convince people via voice technology to build the tech they needed to take the next steps in the projection. This must be painstakingly slow the further you go back in time, and the less technologically advanced the era. But the premise was really the same as a telephone.

"Da Vinci, Gutenberg, Franklin, Marconi, Tesla, Musk, and a few more. They were super helpful and since time is basically a straight line whatever they built for us remains on whatever branch of time we are on."

He was using the tree branch metaphor again. I wanted to press him further on this, but it needed to wait for the time being.

"Next question," I continued, "how can you see from where you are? I mean, we use cameras, our Hollows exist in real time...or nearly real time, and so we can see where we are precisely in the moment. But how can you see into the past? And how can you hear and see me from the future?"

"Same principal that you use—matter is matter. We use a camera to see as well, but with rectilinear light motion. It's not video, so we aren't refracting light. Very old school, we went back to basics since digital imagery cannot travel very far, no matter how much light you use to focus the image."

I nodded, but I could tell he sensed my lack of complete understanding.

"Our camera is no different than a pinhole camera that a child makes in elementary school, except we use remnant nuclear light from fusion, not just daylight."

I nodded again, still uncertain.

"It's like the light from a distant star that we see at night. Its source is not in current time, it travels through space having originated millions of light years away. If someone near that star could see the light when it hits the earth, he or she would be seeing back in time."

"You mean ahead in time," I asked, confused by the notion of light traveling backwards.

"No, but that is the most basic misunderstanding of time. You'll need to work on this thought a bit more. In the meantime, all you need to know is that nuclear light is the same as light from a star," he continued, "we just focus this light intently and use it quite easily to see since it only has to travel a very short distance, meaning not so far back in time. We really don't need much light energy at all."

I pondered what he was saying and took his cue that he could not answer all my questions at once, and that I had some responsibility to figure out the mechanisms sometime later. I was now fully invested in the correction he was planning.

"How do you instigate the fusion, and capture the energy to create the Solid?" I asked, genuinely flummoxed by the complexity of all the processes it would take to create the fusion, capture the energy, focus the energy, and create a Hollow that has mass...all while projecting back in time.

"I don't think we have the time to unpack all those questions, and even if we did have the time, I don't think I have all your answers. I am a pilot, not a physicist," he answered wryly. "You drive an automobile, don't you?" He asked, offering an analogy that I could relate to, "do you know how all the parts of an engine work? I don't think you do, but you know how to drive it, right?"

I had to agree. But his analogy did little to quell my desire to know how it all worked. But there were more pressing questions in the moment.

"Same principle with sound?" I asked, but already guessing the answer.

"It piggybacks on the light energy."

"So, how does the energy bounce back? How can my image and voice make it back to you?"

This seemed to me to be the weakest point in his explanation. He said that he can't go forward in time, but if he can see and hear me then I am doing just that...time traveling to his future.

"It's an echo, like when you stand at the top of mountain and yell. Your voice bounces back, that's what I see and hear. It's a facsimile of you and everything around you, nothing more, you are not here with me on the moon."

I think I understood what he was saying, I was not time traveling like him. I was a static echo, nothing more.

"Why are you here, then?" I continued.

"We need you for a correction," he answered.

"You've said that before," I interrupted. "But I don't know what you mean. What *exactly* is a correction?

I had been slowly piecing the puzzle together with every small bit of information he had been feeding me. I now knew that he was he was purposefully affecting things in my time to change things in his. I was genuinely worried that he was making irreparable manipulations to the present reality that would have lasting impacts on future events, and that I was already a part of whatever he was doing, and I had little control over my participation."

"Paul, I have read all your diaries. I know that you already know what I am doing."

There was a long pause before either one of us spoke again. I looked around for the waiter, I needed another bourbon, but he was no where to be found.

"Do you believe in God and the JCI prophets, Paul?" He asked intently.

"You've read my diaries, you tell me?" I answered.

My patience for this line of conversation was very thin, but regardless, I pulled my pocket New Testament out of my jacket and held it up to him as evidence.

"I have not read your conscience. Up to this point in your diaries you've written very little about your beliefs. I want to know how firmly you adhere to the basic tenets of the Judeo-Christian-Islam belief system, right now, right at this moment?"

My mind was racing with this question. Where was he going with this? I had shown him my New Testament, most people carried one, or a pocket Quran or Torah. My fear was that if all that he said was true, and that if he had projected here to 2028, that there was a possibility that he, or someone else, had projected further back and maybe had interfered with the JCI Prophets. If he could manifest convincingly as a Solid to me, and I was one of the creators of the entire technology, what would people several thousand years ago have thought of someone like him?

"I believe as most people believe. One God, many prophets," I answered truthfully. "I don't go to church or anything, I mean you know already that I was raised as a Christian, but I keep my faith to myself generally, as do most people. Proselytizing hasn't really worked out for mankind, has it?" I asked, hoping he might share some insight from the future.

We suffered through another long pause, our eyes locked on one another. I was using the time to think, but he already had this conversation planned, so I got the distinct feeling that he was just toying with me.

"So, were they real, or did you project them?" I asked, breaking the silence.

"Oh, they were real people, completely legitimate. Maybe not exactly as the books say, I mean Moses was not one hundred and twenty years old when he died. It was 1271 BCE. Not the most sanitary time in our history, life expectancy was quite short back then. He might have been sixty at best. And Krishna, well, the whole Hindu thing is a tough one, so many gods, so not sure about him. And Buddha, totally real. A prince, a wanderer, an eternal sitter."

"Christ? Mohammed?"

"Yes, all real people, genuine prophets as far as we know. But we don't really care for that matter. The point is, they existed, in what context I am not an expert in theology, so I can't really say. We know some things, but we don't know most of what is true in the past, just what we read. But I can say that we are not in the habit of correcting things unless there are catastrophic consequences to not doing so."

"So, you interfere in things for the good of mankind? Is that what you are saying?" I asked skeptically.

"I like to think so, "he continued, "I mean, that is the basic tenet of our mission."

"Who decides what is good for mankind? You?" I asked.

"I know you want a simple answer here, but there isn't one. We humans are not capable of making that decision, it's morally impossible for us to do so. So, we rely on an algorithm. It provides us with a carefully scripted scenario that we apply to existing situations." There was a thoughtful pause before he continued, "remember, I am just a pilot, same as you."

I couldn't help but picture some august body of moral purists sitting in judgement, plotting corrections to manmade catastrophes, wars, and political malfeasances. Like the Gods atop Olympus.

"Surely there is still some need for human choice, some form of deliberation before you project into some situation. I mean, the implications of making a mistake could be catastrophic. We know this ourselves from firsthand experience. That woman we projected into the Amazon had direct and lasting impacts on those children. The tribe is no longer isolated, they rapidly began interacting with outsiders right after our experiment, and we know for a fact that they very quickly succumbed to disease and alcoholism. We attempted to clean up our mess, but we failed badly at that too. We knew there would be impacts, we weren't completely naïve, but we didn't adequately play out all the scenarios, because we genuinely underestimated how impactful we would be on the tribe. We can't undo what we had done, and the tribe has suffered for it. I think about it all the time and its pretty painful for me."

David didn't respond immediately. He just looked at me knowingly, and I was reminded that he knew all this, already.

"The algorithm is not qualified by humans. We don't meet to debate its validity because we don't need to deliberate its rationale. History is riddled with so many examples of our own moral failings for us to qualify anymore about what what's right and wrong."

I pondered this for a moment and noticed that the bar was thinning out. The afterwork crowd was leaving. I looked at my watch for no apparent reason, absentmindedly really since I had no other place to be, as David continued talking.

"In my training, on day one, an instructor shared an alarming story about the early days of the Algorithm, about an Austrian baby that a pilot had to murder in its crib. I remember clearly that he said it was in 1889, and the baby was a boy. He said the projection was required to materialize as a Solid, and the only assigned task was to smother the baby with a pillow. The pilot was not allowed to ask why she had to kill a baby, and that it broke her...emotionally and spiritually. She was devastated by the act and couldn't return to service again. Up to that point we were not told the *why* of our missions, and of course we weren't given the possibility of reasoning, ourselves, any decisions that were scripted for us. We were just told how the scenario was to unfold and whatever acts were necessary for the success of the correction."

I was shocked by what he said. I couldn't imagine what that baby could ever have done to deserve to be killed like that, but I guessed it had to do with something that the baby might have been responsible for in its future, had it lived.

"What would have happened if the baby had lived?" I asked.

"The algorithm is not fallible. There is no moral question that can be applied to a mathematical solution, but there are ethical questions that pilots have about their own actions and the role they play in corrections. We humans are unable to separate our conscience from our actions, that is unless we are psychopathic or narcissistic, and pilots can never be either for obvious reasons. But to mitigate the mental health fallout the pilots are now told the reasons behind the correction."

He didn't answer my question.

"The reason, but not the outcome for not doing so?" I pondered.

"That's the thing. The outcome, or outcomes more precisely, are not entirely known since there are so many variables at play. However, there is a predictable and probable outcome that is benignly weighed against a particular act or set of actions. Pilots are not told the probable results, so we have no burden to carry, just the *why*, which helps us mitigate our own possible ethical dilemmas."

"Did you ever find out what why the Austrian baby was murdered?"

"Not really, I mean we were simply told that the kid would be responsible for genocide, mass killings, war, and most likely more terrible stuff. The *more* of which was never shared with us."

He answered with a cold detachment, as if all that terribleness was stopped from happening and the potential ethical impacts of killing a child carried little weight to David.

"So, what do you want me to do, and for what reason?"

David didn't answer right away. He asked instead if I wanted to order some food from the waiter, or perhaps another drink, but I had had enough bourbon and felt the need to sharpen up a bit for the rest of our conversation. He seemed distracted, or perhaps bored with the room, and wondered whether we might go for a walk and continue our discussion outside.

I signed the tab to my room, and we left The Hoxton and began walking west for no apparent reason. The crowds were thinner now than when I had followed Sarah out to the street. The night was clear and slightly crisp, and the walk felt good after sitting for so long. We didn't began talking again until we reached Drury Lane.

"We need you to retrieve a book that's been hidden for a very long time," he finally answered me. "As for the *why* of it, well, *you* need the book, which means it has some importance to your future."

"That's not much of an explanation, there must be more to the correction than simply retrieving a book, and why can't you just get it yourself?" I asked, wondering in earnest why he needed me for such a presumably simple task.

"It's not the act of retrieval that is important here, it is the message contained in the book that matters. Granted, getting the book will not be that easy, but not that difficult either. You can do so, and you need to know what is says inside its pages. You are at the core of this correction, at this point, anyway."

"Why can't you get it yourself?" I asked again. "You seem to have the ability to manifest almost anywhere."

"It's in Whitehall and the security is too sophisticated for us to project inside without being noticed. Even if we don't anneal, our motion is detectable, and we have a heat signature that is very distinct. We'd be immediately picked up by censors. It's just not possible, believe me," he replied. "The book is located almost directly one floor above your own laboratory," he continued, "you have the necessary clearances and can access the floor at will."

"That seems a little too coincidental, don't you think?" I responded sarcastically. "You need a book, and it just so happens to be in the office just above my lab."

"Paul," he stopped walking and halted me with his arm, turning to me he continued sternly, "you know by now that there are no coincidences. The book is there waiting for you, and you need it. I am just the messenger here. The correction needs to be performed by you and it starts with the retrieval of the book. The script couldn't be simpler: I will give you the specific location of the book, and all you have to do is get and read it. The rest plays itself out from there."

We continued walking south before crossing over towards Covent Garden and in the general direction of Whitehall, but paused beneath one of the streetlamps, away from the pedestrian traffic on the corner.

"But there's more," he continued, "it may not be that simple to access. It's been walled up for centuries and from what we know there is a veneer of limestone between you and the book. You'll need some tools to scrape out the mortar from the joints, but it's old and dry and should come out easily. After that you'll need to use some leverage to dislodge the limestone block. There you will find a small ossuary, a casket of sorts, also cut from limestone. The book is inside it, untouched since it was placed there in 1481."

"I will need masonry tools of some sort, and won't it be noisy" I responded, "I mean talk about arousing suspicion. I am not particularly known there for carrying tools or performing manual labor. I can't just walk around popping open limestone block walls without security noticing."

"It won't be too difficult for you. The location of the book is in a small anteroom, a closet really, adjacent to the men's room on the second floor, right above the reception area of your own laboratory."

I could picture it. I had used the toilet there before.

"You are aware that your particular wing is older than Whitehall itself, it's part of the original York Place, the former residence of the Archbishops of York, which is why the layout of the rooms is so choppy. The anteroom has a heavy oak door and the block you need to remove is just a veneer, not a solid piece of stone, so, there will be little noise, and it is easily identified by a pax symbol that has been carved into its face. Its just a few feet from the door on the left-hand side after you enter. All you will need is a flathead screwdriver and a metal edged ruler to scrape out the thin-set mortar. Both of those are readily available to you in your lab."

I nodded in agreement, listening carefully, but not certain that he could see my head move in the dim light of the streetlamp.

"In the ossuary is a yew-wood box of about 16 inches square and 4 inches thick, and in the box is the book itself. It is bound with leather boards and contains no outward markings. You'll need to remove the book, put the box back in the ossuary, place the ossuary back in the wall and replace the limestone block as you found it."

"And what do I do with the book?" I asked.

"You need to take it someplace private and read it. We'll connect again after you've had a chance to digest what it says."

"I am only here for another two days, and I have meetings stacked up for most of that time. I am not sure I can sneak away," I said skeptically. Angling for an excuse, and a weak one at that.

"You know that since I am still here, and we are still talking about this after all these hours, that you do participate," he responded sternly and without having to mention my diaries again. He continued with more than a hint of anger in his voice, "Paul, this isn't a game. There are real and tragic consequences if you do not perform the correction per the script."

"That's what you've said," I responded with equal indignation. "But you still haven't given me the reason why I must do this. You said, not but a moment ago, that you always give the pilots in your projections the reason for their actions, and you are telling me that my reason is simply because I need the book. I have to say that *just because* is a wholly unsatisfactory reason in this case. I mean, you people killed that Austrian baby to prevent genocide, which admittedly seems like a plausible enough reason, but I need a bit more from you here."

I could tell he was carefully thinking about what to say in return, or perhaps he was just cautiously choosing just the right words, because there was a long thoughtful pause before he finally responded. "Same reason."

Chapter Three

PAX
(Kiss of Peace)

There was little in the way of conversation between us after David told me that I had to be a baby-killer of sorts. We parted ways and I headed back towards The Hoxton without turning around to see which direction he was headed. I didn't care. As interested as I was in the conversation we had been having, I was quite eager to check into the hotel and call Sarah from the quiet of my room. The callousness in which David dismissed our relationship and the anger and hurt that I knew Sarah was feeling was eating at me. She did not deserve the abrupt treatment she received from David, and I had been cowardly in not being more assertive in the conversation. Ashamedly, I was relieved that David had instigated the breakup, and even though I found his callousness rude and hurtful to Sarah, I was secretly grateful for not having to instigate the conversation myself. But this did not absolve me of the hurt I had caused her, and I owed her both an apology and a further explanation of my feelings. That is if she would even take my call.

The hotel lobby and bar had pretty much cleared out by the time I arrived back, and I quickly picked up my key and headed to my room. The car service had taken my luggage directly to The Hoxton and it was waiting for me in my room as usual. Sitting down on the bed I pulled out my phone to call Sarah and

I noticed that she had already sent me a text sometime earlier in the evening, probably while I was walking with David. It simply said that I wasn't to call her and that when she was ready, she would reach out to me. Nothing more. My first instinct was to call her anyway, and as I searched for her contact under recent calls, I noticed, ashamedly, that it was way down the list, too far down for a girlfriend's number to be.

As I stared at her name I lay back on the bed and thought about how badly I had treated her, not just this evening, but over the past several months. It was as if I had been slowly ghosting her—how ironic—and whether this was a conscious act on my part it must have been very painful for her and this evening's performance by David must have seemed to her as the inevitable end to our relationship. She was right. There was no good reason for me to call her.

I must have fallen asleep shortly afterwards because I awoke fully dressed in the early morning hours, just after sunrise. The bourbon and the jet lag had knocked me out, and unfortunately the light of a new day did not cleanse me of my shame I felt for my behavior towards Sarah the night before. I had been a coward and if any good was to come from my shame it was to be in the resolve that I would follow through with David's plan. I would search for the book as per the script and live with the consequences. If he was correct, so would many other people. I would go to work as I normally would, but with determination to find the book.

Finding the opportunity to use the toilet on the first floor was not a simple as David made it seem. The lab was not a single room, but a series of cleanrooms, offices, and storage facilities that were all connected via a central monitoring system complete with CCTV. I do not have free reign of the building, and my movements, like everyone else, was chip tracked and my access to certain floors and doors is blocked. The anteroom David had mentioned was on a half flight up from the ground floor entry and was located on a mezzanine to which I did have access. It served as a central corridor running the full length of the building, connecting to other parts of Whitehall via a maze of smaller corridors and fire doors. To get to the anteroom I would have to pass by the primary security at the building entry, doors and do so without raising suspicion. The guards were not particularly attentive, but they had been trained to notice the unusual. They knew me and knew my regular movements and I rarely, if ever, crossed the mezzanine.

I knew if I wanted to pass the security station without being seen I would have to do it while other people were also entering the building. The return from lunch at one p.m. sharp offered the perfect opportunity. The British were nothing if not punctual, and the lunch rush was reliably busy with people returning from Pret a Manger and the like to allow me to get lost in the sea of returning staff. I knew the subterfuge was possible, but timing was going to have to be the key to my going unnoticed.

Arriving to work at my usual time, and with the usual greeting from the security staff, I went about my normal morning routine. I waited patiently through my morning meetings and surreptitiously—in preparation for the deed—took a small flat head screwdriver from one of the work carts and a metal ruler from one of the secretary's desks and placed them in my briefcase. I normally didn't leave the lab for lunch, as it was typical to have my lunch brought in, but today I headed out on my own, briefcase in tow, and spent a short hour walking along The Mall and through Trafalgar Square, too nervous to get get any food to eat. I kept a close eye on my watch and made certain to time my return to coincide with a group of my colleagues without hovering on the pavement beforehand. I managed to re-enter the building clearing security without the slightest indication of nervousness. Passing the desk with the bank of monitors was the make-or-break moment for me. I typically turned left and headed down the half flight of stairs, but this time I turned right and headed up the other half flight. For some reason I turned back towards the guards, which was unusual for me, but something clicked inside my head that told me to look back. The guard who oversees the monitors glanced up at me and I could tell from the look in his eyes that he was wondering why I was headed in a direction different than my usual route. Instinctively I ran my hand over my stomach and made an exaggerated wincing motion with my face and nodded towards to the men's toilet along the corridor to the right. He smiled and nodded knowingly in return.

Taking advantage of my fake gastro-intestinal emergency I hustled along the corridor and quickly found the anteroom that was adjacent to the toilet. The door was as David described it—heavily panelled oak, and with a very old latch set and handle. I let myself in and noted with interest that the lock only worked from the inside, which was illogical for such a secure building, but I recognized that it must have been a remnant from when the room was part of a larger suite, sometime in its ancient past. I turned the latch to secure the door and searched for the light switch, but quickly noted that with the amber light streaming in from a narrow-slit window on the outside wall that there was no need for additional illumination. The room was practically empty save for a few boxes labelled as cleaning supplies and an assorted collection of mops and brooms.

Two of the walls were panelled in an aged, darkened oak like the door, but the wall immediately to my left upon entering was made of neatly trimmed limestone—as was the exterior wall with the window.

Worrying about time, I quickly began to search for the pax symbol etched into one of the stones, and at first glance it seemed like an impossible task. The wall had been scratched, scraped, and generally defaced over the centuries with graffiti of all sorts. There were scribbles of initials and dates harking back as far as the fifteenth century, with some quite obscene examples of very poorly etched male and female genitalia. I imagined that this anteroom, or closet as it is now, might have housed servants at some point in time—and most likely juvenile male servants judging from the quality of the etchings.

The X with the overlaid P, usually so easily recognized, was nowhere to be seen and so I began to use my hands to see if I might be able to feel the etching in case it had worn so thin over time that it wasn't visible. After a few minutes of running my hands over the cool stone I grew quite frustrated and worried that perhaps I was missing something important, but having scanned the walls and run my hands across them multiple times I knew there had to be something more to the missing symbol.

Was I in the wrong room? Possibly, but David had been quite precise about the location of this room and the description, so far, fit perfectly. Perhaps I had the wrong symbol in mind, but I was pretty sure I knew what the pax symbol looked like. I might not attend services regularly, but I had been in enough churches to recognize it. But had I been in enough medieval churches? Perhaps there was a different version of the symbol than I was aware of.

Pulling out my phone I quickly AOL'd 'medieval pax symbols' knowing that the ubiquitous search engine wouldn't fail me, and I was dismayed to see that the familiar X with the P overlay was the reference example for endless entries. But something told me to dig a bit deeper. I scrolled past the images and decided to read the actual definition of pax and was surprised to learn that medieval meaning was different than I had imagined.

In earlier times it was known as the 'kiss of peace' and in early forms of the Christian mass an actual kiss was given between congregants. Armed with this information I began to visually rescan the walls with a different perspective and quickly noticed something I had missed before. The etchings on the wall were mostly puerile and rather haphazardly placed, and some even migrated across mortar joints, but there was one graphic that seemed to be more determined in its execution. Perfectly centered in one of the rectangular stones, just above knee height, there was an incised image in what I guessed was a medieval styling, crude but credible, of two men kissing. One was wearing a crown and the other a chainmail head armor that I recognized as a likeness of a knight of some sort. Both characters had swords hung about the waists of their tunics. It was a kiss of peace.

Time was not my friend, and although I was certain that the guard had forgotten about me, I knew I had to get back to the laboratory before someone came looking for me. So, I pulled the screwdriver out of my bag and began to remove the mortar from the joint and quickly realized that it was too narrow and the mortar too deep. This was the reason for the thin metal ruler. It was a perfect tool to saw through the sandy cement, and I was able to easily excise the mortar on all four sides. Using the screwdriver, I then began to slowly pry the stone loose, working it slowly away from the wall without chipping the edges of the stone. It came free easily, which surprised me, since it turned out to be a thin veneer of a stone not more than an inch thick and not nearly as heavy as I had imagined it would be.

Placing it carefully on the floor beside me I used the flashlight on my phone to illuminate the cavity left behind. The wall itself was made from rubble stone and mortared very crudely, but solidly, with a niche carved out where some rubble had been removed. In the niche was a stone box. The ossuary David had mentioned. Typically used as a resting place for the bones of the dead, this small ossuary could only have been meant for a baby. But its small size made it manageable and allowed me to easily remove it from the niche. There were no markings carved into the ossuary surface, and its lid lifted off effortlessly to reveal a wooden box of highly polished amber colored wood.

The box was beautifully made and had two strap-hinges made of iron that had been neatly inset into the wood. The box was also free of markings of any kind. The lid did not have a latch or keyhole, so I was able to open it immediately revealing a book bound in leather with just a few noticeable cracks, but generally looking like it had been bound just yesterday. Having not seen any light since it had been placed in the box, it looked new and even retained a slight hint of the smell of tanning. I knew that time was running against me, but I had to open the book out of curiosity to see what it contained and noted that the writing was calligraphic and on quite bright white vellum.

I was eager to dig deeper and although I wanted to begin reading it right away, I knew it was more important to follow the script and get the book out of Whitehall and read it in the quiet of my hotel room. So, I placed the book in my briefcase and using my hands I carefully scooped up the dry powdery mortar from the floor and threw it in the hole in the wall. I put the wooden box back in the ossuary and placed the ossuary back in the niche before lifting the limestone block in its place. It was not a perfect job and if anyone looked carefully, they would notice that the mortar lines of the block looked different than those around it, but judging from the condition of the room I was certain it would go unnoticed. Undoing the latch, I peeked out of the door and with the empty hall in sight I slipped out and made my way back down the mezzanine, nodded at the guard who gave me another knowing smile and returned to my office in the lab.

The whole exercise took no more than thirty or forty minutes, but in my anxious state it seemed like it had taken much longer, but my worry that I might have been missed by my colleagues was unfounded. However, I found it difficult to concentrate on the remaining tasks of the day, and although I had committed to a series of meetings, I was highly distracted by the presence of the book in my briefcase, which I had placed in its usual place on a corner chair. I had to correct myself repeatedly from gazing over at it too frequently. My lack of concentration was in anticipation of the continuing adventure that reading the book promised to offer, and of course, this meant that time seemed to creep and whereas most days in the lab flew by for me, this afternoon was by far the slowest I could ever recall.

I had no work commitments for the evening and meeting up with Sarah was not in the cards, so when I was finally able to excuse myself from my final meeting. I quickly packed up my things and left the building. Too eager to walk I arranged for a car to take me the hotel, and without stopping for my usual drink in the bar I headed right up to my room pausing only briefly to scan the lobby for any sign of David. I hadn't seen him on the street, but that didn't mean he wasn't observing me from somewhere unseen.

I had not considered that he might project into my room and therefore was surprised upon entering to find him sitting in an armchair in the sitting room of my suite wearing one of the hotel's complimentary terry cloth robes from the closet. I hadn't eaten all day and I had hoped to settle in for the evening with the book and a room service hamburger, but I was now faced with another interaction with David.

"That's my robe," I said only half jokingly. Wanting to ask him how he got in my room, but I already knew how.

I was genuinely surprised to see him, but it was not unexpected.

"I could have chosen some of your clothes, but I wasn't sure they'd fit. You are quite a bit shorter than me, so I thought the hotel robe was a safer choice," he said dryly. "Shall I take it off?"

Part of me was genuinely interested in seeing him naked, but not in a sexual way. David's entire demeanor was distastefully haughty and not the least bit attractive. His all-knowing self assuredness and fixation on his script made him unlikeable to say the least. My curiosity was purely scientific.

Our Hollows had little to no body hair, even on their heads. Hair is comprised of dead cells and therefore has poor projection capability. Just as we remove all metals and plastics from the body before projection, we do the same for hair. It's not that it doesn't project per se, it manifests as a mass without texture and on a Solid, it would look more like a helmet than hair. Similarly, pubic hair would appear as a block, hair in the armpits appears to the observer as a dark hole, and arm and leg hair, if dark in color, would look like stain on the skin. So, we rely on wigs or hats to complete the reality of our projections, but I noticed early on that David had hair on his arm visible from above his shirt cuff, and with his short-cropped hair his scalp was visible—meaning no wig or toupee for him.

"Keep the robe on but open it. I want to see your body hair."

"Is that all you want to see?" he asked with a chuckle while opening his robe. There was little humor in his laugh, and I was not amused.

Remarkably, he had visible body hair. A small amount hair between his pecs, a light dusting on his stomach and legs, and a small patch of pubic hair, all very dark or nearly black. I was going to ask him how it was possible to project his hair, but he beat me to it.

"You already know that infrared light allows us to see what visible light cannot," he said, while closing the robe. "What *you* see is what we capture in our camera, and simply made visible with shorter, more controlled projected wavelengths. This is my hair," he ran his fingers across his scalp. "This is me as I am right now…on the moon."

"Remarkable!" I said and I meant it.

We couldn't even dream that this quality of Solid could be possible. Our Solids are problematic because of the annealing and heat generation and in the briefness of their birthing they appear plastic when static and like marionettes while moving. David's projection was as perfect as I could ever hope to achieve. His skin appeared flexible, and his hair moved with him when he moved. I wondered if the key to this technology is contained in the old book safely tucked away in my briefcase.

"You have the book?" he asked, his eyes narrowing in seriousness now that he was fully robed again. He sat back down in the chair.

I raised my arm holding the briefcase, indicating its presence within.

"Surely you know I have it. You've known everything so far. That's why you are here, isn't it?"

"No, I don't, or I should say, I didn't know for certain," he answered and continued for clarity, "I think you misunderstand the purpose of the script. The most plausible variables are all accounted for, but *none* and *all* are assured. An algorithm can run forever and nearly instantaneously but my mind cannot, and so I am unable to process quickly enough all the variables you might pose for me. I may not actually be here in this place and time with you, but I must rely on my own thoughts and intuition in these, *your* moments. When you walked in, I had to decide the probability of whether you have the book, or not. Not the likelihood. I assumed you did, the script says you do, but there is the possibility that you don't for whatever reason, which means the algorithm will adjust and so will the script. It's just a matter of time. Literally."

I had come to expect over the past few days that all my thoughts and actions were preordained, or at least known by David in advance of my own realization, but I now knew that they were not, and that David was not certain of anything I might do or say, which might explain his anxiousness. I thought that I was a game piece of sorts on a very big board, but with this bit of knowledge I realized that I had some control over the situation I found myself in.

"So, what would have happened if I didn't have the book," I asked, while eyeing the minibar.

"Whatever. That's the point. Things happen," he answered, his frustration obvious in his tone followed by a long pause. "I need to clarify something," he continued, "I am not here for the book. I am here for you, and to make sure that you read it."

I nodded, not in acknowledgement, but in agreement of what he said.

"Can you show it to me?" He asked.

I crossed over to the desk and placed my briefcase on it,

slipped off my jacket, and undid the latch strap and pulled out the book. His eyes grew wide, and he smiled in a way that I had not yet seen. I had seen him laugh earlier with some mirth, or maybe ironically, but now he appeared generally happy as he walked towards the desk and touched the book and ran his hand across the leather cover before quickly opening it to the first page.

"Cornwall. 1481," he said aloud. "Yes, this is it. I've never actually seen it, but this is the book."

As he carefully flipped through the pages, its binding stiff with age, I helped myself to a little bottle of Jack Daniels from the mini bar, unscrewed the cap and drank it down in one shot.

"What's next?" I asked.

He looked up from the book while closing it slowly. We were only a few feet apart and I could see my own reflection in his glassy eyes, but I could not see any indication of what he expected of me, or what he was thinking. There was no perceptible emotion in his dry shiny eyes, just the coldness of someone very far away.

"The correction began when we met," he said, answering me with a calm coolness, "but the success of it depends upon your comprehension of what is contained in this book. I can only go as far as the script directs me, given where we are right now, so I am going to leave you now to read it, and then we will meet again. But be assured that all you will read is the truth, and there is no greater proof of this then the very existence of the book itself. It was written by a man of great integrity and intelligence, whose intent was the recording of events as they happened, as true to him as he could possibly understand."

"That's it, no other explanation," I asked, disappointed that there wasn't something more to the script, but also eager for him to leave so that I could begin reading.

"That is all for now," he responded, and asked with a wry smile. "Except for this," he said, pointing to an envelope on the desk. He said the concierge had sent it up earlier. I opened it to reveal a receipt from a bookseller—an antique book shop in Covent Garden. "Slip this behind the cover, you'll need it later."

I took it from him, and put it in my pocket, nodding in acknowledgement.

"Do you want me to put the robe back where I found it?" He asked, attempting some humor once again.

Before I could respond he simply disappeared, and the robe hit the floor covering up what I knew would be a small pile of silica on the carpet beneath it. I was left alone in the room with the book, an empty mini bottle of Jack Daniels, a bathrobe on the floor, and every intent still of ordering a room service hamburger and cracking open the book.

Chapter Four

inde Iesus venit in posserum
(Thence the Wounded Man Came into Power)

The st'rye of an embasy of a land from across the ocean. A true account by Robert FitzEdward, Duke of Cornwall, in the year 1481.

It is not a book in the ordinary sense. It is more of a manuscript, a handwritten first-person account by a man of some importance who held a place at the court of some long dead English king. The prose style is exhausting and at times incomprehensible. The author claims that he wrote the work in 1481 and so it is in a form of the written English that is so antiquated that I found myself having to look up every other word or sentence just to get through the first couple of pages. I had not read Chaucer since college, and even then, I had to rely heavily upon notes in the marginalia from previous readers of the used book I had purchased, so that I could make my way to Canterbury with the rest of the class. I had wrongly assumed that I would be able to set myself down for a leisurely read while enjoying mini bar liquor and a hamburger, instead I was faced with the daunting task of working through a hundred pages or more of Middle English text. So, what follows here is the transcription of my reading, and not a precise narration of a story hastily written by a man whom I was assured was of the greatest credibility. Although written in an English barely recognized today, I am presenting it here to the best of my ability in our common language. I was told it is all true as written, and the proof of its veracity is meant to be the very existence of this manuscript itself, and although I can yet vouch for this truth, all I can add at this time is what I have been told and what I have read.

The Ship

It was late morning on a clear day in June when without warning the ship appeared in the river, having moved to its place unnoticed on the morning tide. There was no evidence of a barge having towed it to its full stop dead on the Tower. It just simply sat motionless against the current without anchor or line. There were no sails on the ship, no mast, nor any visible means of force of movement. Although the boat sat high above the quays and dwarfed the caravels and cogs by its massive size the metal of its hull, like that of highly polished armor, was not visible beneath the dark Thames. The ship appeared to float on the surface without wave or wake. Crowds of morning merchants, laborers, and fishwives lined the banks on both sides of the river, staring silently in fearful curiosity and I among them just as awed staring down from a parapet. The ship had no visible ports or hatches, no rigging, lines, or visible anchor chain. Its shape was smooth and uniform. It sat silently in mid-stream, its massive size speaking its presence loudly.

Alarm had been slow to rise throughout the Tower. The sound of men at arms should have been ringing in the innermost ward and the water gates should have been shut at first sighting of the ship but they remained open. And why had no riders come with warning, I wondered? This ship should have been seen for miles off the coast and its progress up the river would have been noted along its entire length. A quick rider could have easily provided forewarning. Nonetheless, the slow alarm was not an excuse for my own tardiness. Summoning two warders I bid them stand with me and describe to me clearly, in their own words, what they witnessed floating on the river below. Once satisfied that they could tell a credible and similar story I sent them on a fast ride to the king at Windsor, advising him to stay put and to begin defenses.

The constable of the Tower begged instructions from me in my role as Primus Curia Regis. And as brother to the king, even if I was a bastard, it was expected that I would at least be able to confidently command a response to what we all assumed to be an imminent attack by a hostile invader. However, I was stymied by the unknown curiosity and paralyzed by a lack of precedent. If it was a threat, I had nothing to compare it to. Was this a hostile invasion? Where were the people on the ship? Who were we to defend against? Every aspect of its appearance was alien—wedge shaped at the front and wider at its stern, it had no forecastle or visible decks. It appeared wider too at the water line but tapered as it rose to where the deck and masts should be. It was half as long as the Tower was wide along the wharf, and its height rose higher than even the Brass Mount. I could not detect any cannon, nor a seam in its metal plating. Where armor has rivets and folds this ship appeared like a single piece of highly polished steel. It appeared to me as more blade than boat.

A call to arms meant all the cannons were placed and primed as quickly as possible. Without recent threat from Spain or France, and with no Lancastrian challenges to speak of in recent years, it meant the Tower was dangerously undermanned and under-armed. The yeoman was thusly charged with the distribution of weapons and a cry was sent out to all able-bodied men in Tower Hamlets to make haste for added defense. And while awaiting a response from the king, and what I hoped would be reinforcements from Windsor, I nervously inspected the munitions in a show of false brava—it was an attempt to appear in control of the situation when I had no understanding of the ship's intent, nor understanding of what our response should be given the alien object before me. Being the king's half-brother was insufficient qualification for the events of the day, but I still felt more able than Richard, his true brother, who was thankfully far away in the Marches.

Whilst the Tower guard gathered on the parapets stacking our lead and maneuvering our cannons the ship remained still and silent with no indication of malice or announcement of purpose. The only activity on the water was the mass movement of merchant ships and barges that had been nervously cut loose by their crews and floated down river in a tangle of ropes and rigging and away from the unknown visitor. The hours of the morning passed but without boredom as we fixed all our attention to our defenses and kept a continuous keen eye to any movement on the river. Crowds gathered on both banks in ever greater numbers and the Tower itself began to fill with guards, soldiers, and civilian militia confounding the constable who had great difficulty keeping out the rabble. More than one peddler, and lady of questionable intent, had made their way in, and the longer the ship sat in the river the larger the number of people gathered on both shores—a sure sign of the stupidity of the masses and their ever-present need for spectacle. I consider myself no coward and having ridden in France and the north with the king with as much vigor as warranted, however, and I hated to admit it, my first instinct in this case if given the chance was to flee as far from the river as possible. My position prevented this, but it did not lessen my fear that in the tension of the moment something terrible might be forthcoming. I greatly feared the idiocy of the crowd and the risk of a shot from the nervous hand of a yeoman. It was one thing to look upon a bear in a cage, it was entirely another thing to poke it.

The morning passed quickly and by late afternoon we had our cannons in place and some semblance of order had been applied to the battlements with soldiers lazing at the ready and ammunition stacked in ample quantity. As the sun began to set a commotion arose from the outer ward. The king had arrived with a great host of men-at-arms, and what appeared to be most of the council—led by Norfolk and Somerset no less, and all in full armor. I was dismayed to see that my recommendation that he stay safe at Windsor, our strongest hold, had been ignored but I also knew that his desire for battle—any battle—would outweigh any concern for his own personal safety. His arrival on the battlement seemed to smarten up the troops and paying no heed either to them or with a dismissal of my deference he began his inspection of the situation by excitedly pacing in agitation, captivated by the visitor upon the river with the same awe that I had done hours earlier.

"Have you fired on it yet?" He asked as his pacing slowed to allow me to catch up to him. It was not really a question, but I had been expecting it, nonetheless.

"No. I have kept a prudent watch to see what manner of people or arms it might present," I responded confidently, knowing that he might not agree but that he would be highly displeased if I had not presented a meaningful answer.

He acknowledged my response without agreement and looked about at my fellow councilors all gathered around like chicks to a hen. I noted that I was the least armored amongst them. Norfolk was so heavily plated he could not straighten his knees. He stood as if begging for a horse, while Somerset's prodigious belly seeped out of his side plate as if his middle was wanting to escape to someplace safer.

"My lords," the king enquired, "shall we fire a volley across its bow?"

Not that anyone could be certain of its bow, or its stern, its shape was so unusual, or so I thought to myself without jumping to respond. I waited for the others to add their opinions, but they simply murmured incoherently. None in agreement or offering a challenge, acquiescing without debate or opinion. I was thus compelled to interrupt the pathetic murmuring.

"Your grace, there's been no sign of malice. And there are no visible ports or hatches, but we cannot be sure there are not cannon on board," I said, pausing to gesture towards the ship. "I have yet to hear a sound, but I fear that is its intention. It has had all day to fire upon us, and yet has not done so. Its silence may be fearful, but perhaps it is not an indication of its desire to harm us. I believe we should be suspect, but would it not be prudent to row out an emissary? Perhaps a sign of *our* intent to parley."

The king walked away in thought and towards a cannon manned by two of the regular guard. Without any more counsel he directed them to fire a single shot, demanding they not hit the ship, but pass the ball across its bow or near thereof. So, the cannon was raised on its blocks, nervously so by the two men, at an angle that they assumed would allow the ball to fly over the top of the center point of the ship with the intent that it would land in the river and not hit any of the buildings or people on the south bank. My hopes for success were low. There had not been a cannon fired from the Tower with a live ball in any recent memory.

The fuse burnt quicker than I had anticipated and with a great roar, and kick of the blocking, the ball lobbed low across the water and struck the side of the ship just above the water line. The king lashed out catching the guardsman by surprise, striking one across the face with his gloved hand while the other shrunk back in terror saving himself from the king's wrath. My fellow councilors and I watched in astonishment as the ball simply bounced off the ship without noise and dropped into the river.

Even in the dimming late afternoon light we could see that it left not a marking or dent of any kind. We waited wide-eyed for a response, fearing that we would receive a shot back in response, but no response came quickly. Only as dusk settled into darkness did the ship provide an indication of life for the first time; remarkably, it came alight with a glow from what could only be thousands of candles from within.

Its illumination was greeted with an audible astonishment by the people on both banks. Where the light source was on the ship we could not tell as the entire thing seemed to glow through its metallic skin with a soft yellow light, like a flame through a pane of Venetian glass. But still, no sound or movement was detected. Just the glow of the ship reflecting off the water like a bonfire on the edge of a lake or a torch on a barge. But nothing else happened. No return volley or recognition of our presence.

The council spent the night on the wall in shifts, alternating between the king's bedside and pacing the battlements until dawn when the sun rose and the ship's lights dimmed, returning it to its original metallic form. The king, however, remained comfortably in his bedchamber relying upon reports and observations that remained unchanged throughout the night. Admittedly, I had grown weary of the watch and had little patience for my fellow councilors whose advice and desire for aggression seemed counter to the logic of a what was an undetermined threat. The discussions were heated at times and tedious in their banality. Prayers were offered by the king who implored the Lord for wisdom, when it was obvious that the only wise course of action should have been to remove the throngs of people from crowding the shore, end the carnival atmosphere that had pervaded the masses, and evacuate the city out of prudence. The aldermen had begged for an audience and were denied, so they too paced the wharf and ruminated along its shore along with the citizenry, while I secretly wished for a returned shot from the ship to enliven the very dull situation, or in the very least a raised banner and a herald of horns for a bit of entertainment.

The Cardinal's Entrance

The sound of the horse on the cobblestone of the Innerward broke the quiet of the early morning. A rider in the cardinal's livery had come from York Lodge with an earnest message for the king. Norfolk, Somerset and I brought him directly to the king's chamber where we found our own lord at prayer in his wardrobe. The rider produced a sealed letter from his satchel and attempted to hand it to the king, but it was roughly snatched away by Somerset. Edward bid Somerset to read it aloud with a simple raising of a royal eyebrow.

With great haste I write to inform you that I have been visited by an Embassy from a place We have yet not heard of. A princely lord and two attendants have begged an urgent audience and I shall swiftly follow this letter as it makes preparation for my arrival.

It seemed that no sooner had the note been read then the most reverend man himself arrived. He was his own herald and must have promptly followed his rider in certainty of his own importance, and with his arrival our council, by the numbers, was complete.

Although we had been spared his domination throughout the night, his arrival was certainly inevitable as was the drama of the hasty letter that preceded him.

As chancellor he held the court tightly in his grip but had little sway over the curia regia whose fraternity was held in thinly veiled contempt for both him and his office. The king relied heavily on his counsel since he needed Rome to retain his legitimacy, but even the king knew that the cardinal's vanity dictated his need for ceremony in all his movements. Acting as his own herald was the assertion of his own import of whatever he had learned of the embassy *We have not yet heard of*. Like the ship in the river that *We* had never seen before, but collectively understood that it was plaguing all and not just, unfortunately, the cardinal. True to form he was first to know of the embassy, and without coincidence *We* all knew—meaning the king and the remainder of the council—that the arrival of the ship and the embassy had to be connected as it was unlikely that two unknowns could be known in one day.

The cardinal's timing may not have been very artfully devised to follow the arrival of his letter, but I suspect he had not intended to follow his words so closely. His timing was usually more rehearsed, but perhaps the arrival of the embassy had thrown him off his game. Regardless, in his usual swirl of watered silk he charged into the king's chamber; comically, upon his head he wore a helmet of polished steel—as if ready for battle—emblazoned with his charge, the beaver, which *We* all referred to it as a water rat. Proportionally tragic as always, thin as a reed buried beneath crimson, his arrival brought some relief to the tension and an added level of curiosity with the collective supposition that the embassy might be attached to the ship. And whereas we might usually gather with reluctance to hear what he would have to say, we were all aroused by the possibility of some intelligence from the rat.

Bidding the cardinal to share his story, the king took his seat at the table, and we surrounded him, in no particular order of importance, which was purposefully done to distress the cardinal—unrehearsed, but well-practiced by all. The cardinal remained standing still at first, his usual lethargic pose, but when his story began to heat up his pacing of the room began with an ever-increasing intensity and animation that did not befit a man of his diminutive size and general lack of virility, whilst we listened carefully to the story, like an Arabian tale, of the prince and his attendants.

In the cardinal's words: Early evening of the night before his guard at the gates of York Lodge were surprised by three men on horseback. The usual crowd begging an audience was absent, not surprising since all of London was on the Tower wharf and the south bank watching the ship, but apparently, he and his household were unaware of the curiosity on the river. As the cardinal told it, the three men were described by his guards as riding fine destriers and dressed in the most expensive purple silks (the description we knew to be an embellishment of the tale since his guards would not know expensive silk from worsted wool) arrived begging an audience with the cardinal, presenting a patent of introduction rolled in a sheath of gold encrusted with jewels. This was brought immediately to the cardinal's chamber where he—so he claimed—was deep in prayer, or more likely deeply feasting or deeply lusting after one of his pages.

Interrupting the cardinal, the king enquired of the letter, which the cardinal brought forth from a hidden pocket in his ferraiolo and handed it to the king while begging forgiveness for having conveniently left the golden and jeweled sheath behind at the Lodge. Which he assured his majesty would be duly delivered of in the future.

The letter was written in common English, which challenged the king as his French was much better, so he handed it back to the cardinal who continued his narration without reading from the letter. He continued. The bearer was a Prince named David and his attending lords, who were nameless at this point, collectively represented the kingdom of Istoia which was located across the great Atlantic Ocean in a place that *We* had yet to know. The story seemed incredible. But so did the large steel ship afloat in the Thames not a hundred yards from us. The letter seemed to confirm our suspicions that the ship had brought the visitors, but only once the cardinal had granted an audience to the princely visitors did the entire story unfold.

The men presented themselves as representatives of their king. Led by Prince David, brother of said king, he was described by the cardinal as tall, youthful, of virilis proportions with a curious accent that was neither French nor English, and with a slight lilt of what he considered to be of possible Irish influence. The cardinal believed him to be about twenty-five years of age and having a light complexion with dark brown hair cut to a length well above his shoulders and naturally falling back off his face. His purple silk surcoat was long and lined with a fine brocade of black and silver, and beneath it his tunic was short in the style of Bologne under which his brais was of leather and tucked into boots of a similar fashion.

The description was uncomfortably precise, as if the man had been weighed for value, but the same could not be said of his companions. As lords, but not royal, they were accorded the most basic description by the cardinal as two men of similar age and visage as the prince, but varying in height and proportion, equally dressed in fine cloth, but he offered little more in the way of identity.

Tired of the cardinal's lugubrious narration the king interrupted him and demanded angrily to know to what the purpose of their visit was, and why had they brought their ship so far upriver without permission—to the very base of the Tower no less. The cardinal was unaware of the ship, having paid no heed to its presence upon his arrival. He, being so intently focused on his own part in his own story, had marched into the Tower having failed to notice the masses of guards, the yeoman running about, the cannon perched on the wall, and hundreds of curious on-lookers who had just awoken from their night's sleep on the wharf. Begging the king's forgiveness, and still not acknowledging the presence of the ship, which in the cardinal's defense was not visible from the wardrobe in which we were meeting, he continued his story.

The foreign prince had sought out the cardinal as a means to garner an audience with the king. This was not unusual. Most foreign embassies had the ability to approach the court directly via a message from abroad delivered through emissaries, typically from Rome, but it was more typical that there was a diplomatic relationship of some sort beforehand or means of trade that meant that either party was readily known to each other. Here the cardinal was approached to act as a first point of contact, but only after the foreigners had already landed on our shores. This was highly unusual and could be viewed as antagonistic in the simplest sense as if they had just landed on a Kentish beach and waded ashore, but in this case, they had come upriver and sat perched at the very foot of the Tower, the very center of military might and power in all of England.

There were so many questions of the cardinal that a shouting match, with much fist pounding, ensued around the table as everyone except the king fought to be heard. The cardinal relished the attention and sensing his mastery of the situation allowed us to shout over one another. He paced the room while we pondered aloud.

Why are there only three in the embassy?

Where are they now, are they armed?

How many more men are aboard the ship?

Where did they get the horses? Are there more on the ship?

Why is there no visible movement on the ship then, if the prince and his attendants are on land? Where, and what exactly is Istoia? Why have we never heard of this land before? Is it a Christian land? Why have they chosen to visit us? Do they know the French?

Is this a trap, a Trojan horse? Are the three visitors really from the ship or are they opportunists who are taking advantage of the fact that a ship has arrived unannounced? Perhaps they are Spanish, I wondered.

The cardinal yelled over us while the king relished the mayhem, explaining that that he had enquired of the visitors many of the same questions. As he told it, they had arrived in our waters some three or four days earlier and had entered the Thames at high tide having met no other ships to stop them. They had passed Hadleigh Castle and received no acknowledgement and therefore made their way peacefully upriver past Cooling where they alighted on the opposite shore with their horses and continued to London on land while their ship continued its journey on the water. He continued his story as we calmed down, which allowed him to speak in a more composed manner, which was pleasing to the king. Apparently, the three men had delighted in our countryside and the fine summer weather, and having foreknowledge of the cardinal's influence, and with much help from our countrymen, they were able to make their way to

London unmolested.

This seemed implausible to me. A large steel ship gleaming like a beacon arrives at the mouth of the Thames and gently cruises unaided upstream stopping unnoticed across from a defensive fortification to allow three men and their horses to alight for a leisurely stroll along the Kent Road, all the way to the gates of York Lodge? How could any of this go unnoticed on a river as busy as the Thames? And to a port larger than almost any other in Europe. With the immense traffic between Dover and Hadleigh alone, it would have impeded a ship of its size. Even traveling without light at night it would have been seen by eel men in the marshes, or any of our sentries along the banks.

What troubled me greatly was how eager the cardinal was to accept this story. His own role at its center seemed to me to be blinding him to the implausibility of all he was saying. Did we not have an obligation to be distrustful of the embassy until such time as it has proven itself legitimate? Instead, the cardinal was presenting as fact the story of three men on horseback, seemingly on the quality of a gold sheath encrusted with jewels and the fine cloth worn buy its bearers.

"Where are they now?" I shouted. "Where is this prince and his entourage?"

"The Lodge," he responded drolly. "In the presence of my servants and with great care as to their comfort."

The king rose from his chair at this news. As voices began to ring once again at the incredible news that the cardinal was giving comfort to these visitors rather than turn them over to the Crown as custom would dictate. This was a presumptuous act, even for the thin man. He had taken it upon himself to assume jurisdiction over an embassy which was an incorrect decision on his part. Even as chancellor his position had limits and he had stepped well beyond the norms of his office. The king's anger was evident as he lashed out at the cardinal.

"Do you not see the peril you place us in, you ignorant rodent!" he yelled as he moved towards the cardinal as if to strike him.

Somerset stepped between them attempting to intercept the king's blow as he has done so many times before. I stood back enjoying the outburst, hoping to see the king's fist get lost in the yards of red silk that enrobed the holy man. But alas, the king stopped short of actual striking anyone, and instead he checked his blow and paced the room in a dance with the cardinal who was kept nervously on his toes by the king's constant movement.

"We must see this embassy at once," the king continued with extreme agitation, "they must account for this ship that plagues our river. They cannot sit comfortably in York Lodge while we cower here. Summon them to the Tower, rat! Or better yet, bring them here personally. Ride back and return with your guests," he screamed, "and do not return without the gold sheath and with every jewel in place."

The cardinal fled the wardrobe, sweeping up his attendants who had been hovering behind the door. It was a remarkable scene in which the king dismissed his most loyal confidant and sent him fleeing like a page. The rest of the council was both pleased and unsettled. This comeuppance was long warranted, but it only added to the uncertainty of the moment rather than bring any calm or order to the situation. Our world was not as it should be, and I for one had very little confidence at that moment in the king and his ability to right the situation, and if I knew my fellow councilors well enough, they too would have doubts as to how the rest of the day might unfold in our favor. There was a carelessness at play by both the cardinal, and more importantly, the king. Rather than enjoy the safety of Windsor he had come to the Tower endangering himself and the entire council, and now he has sent for the unannounced embassy to attend him in the sights of what is very possibly the very same enemy ship that brought them to our shore.

None of this seemed logical or tactically appropriate given the unknown nature of what had unfolded over the course of a single day. In my bemusement I had to decide whether to offer counsel, or to allow myself to float along on the course that was unfolding like a comedy by Aristophanes. I chose to float with the express hope that blunder would not mean harm, but I had little confidence that would be case, and wondered to myself if hubris would bring tragedy rather than comedy.

Three Men in Audience

In the hours between the cardinal's exit and his pending return we made haste to establish the authority of the court within St Thomas' tower. This was not the king's normal abode and few of the trappings of his royal presence were in place. The king disliked the Tower and spent most of his time at Windsor or Eltham, so little attention had been given to the audience chamber for quite some time. Fresh rushes were ordered up and candles were lit in preparation for the embassy's arrival. The king usually bestowed an audience surrounded by hordes of courtiers and was now to receive this new embassy supported only by his privy council and the Tower guards. This distressed the king and so he sent a message to intercept the queen—who had been making her way to Eltham and was not far from London—to join him, which also meant that the usual court stragglers were also able to tag along.

The lack of ceremony had the potential to limit his authority.

His ego, born from deeply rooted insecurities of a once lost but since regained crown, and whisperings of his own illegitimacy demanded excessive trappings of majesty to bolster his courage—not unlike the thickened cushion that he had placed on his throne for added height when seated at court. The king more than anyone knew that majesty is neither inherited nor earned, but was achieved with blaring trumpets and colorful pennants, hordes of fawning courtiers, and one very thick cushion.

I had no sway over his decision to send for the courtiers, but I did take advantage of any time alone with the king, whilst the others feigned busyness, to express my concerns over the cardinal's lack of skepticism and my belief in the need for prudence in allowing this unknown embassy to enter the Tower. More importantly, I attempted to stress the hazard of the ship and its relationship to the three riders and how I thought it better that we arrange an audience at another place, far from the river. He did not necessarily disagree, and my comparison of our present situation to the story of the Trojan Horse was not lost on him, but his logic was that engagement within the stronghold of the Tower offered the greatest protection and hedge against attack. I deferred to his logic without outwardly disagreeing, which was my obligation, but inwardly I reserved my own doubts as to the soundness of the decision and worked quietly and determinedly to ensure that the Tower's defenses were readied and that the ambassador would clearly see the strength of our position.

The queen's arrival brought her immediate household and an extended entourage into an already crowded fortress. The king was achieving the reception he desired which now included the two archbishops and the ambassadors from the Emperor, France, as well as Spain and their secretaries and attendants, and their attendant's attendants. Curiosity had spread like a chimney fire, but as I would later come to learn the cardinal had sent word around court and so all manner of malingerers arrived in advance of the cardinal's own return, setting the stage for a very dramatic reception.

Every lord, no matter how minor, who was in earshot of the capitol seemed to have made their way to the Tower. A messenger had established the time of the cardinal's return with his guests— so delayed by the cardinal to allow the queen to arrive. At the appropriate time we arranged ourselves in the hall in due style and anticipation. The king and queen were seated, and his counsellors (me included) stood on their flanks along with the archbishops and other important members of court. The ambassadors from abroad and their cliques crowded the walls and columns, while the ladies of the court hovered in the shadows in a less conspicuous display of obvious curiosity. A trumpet heralded the group's arrival and the cardinal, once again swept in, in a blur of crimson satin—now trimmed with ermine. It was not lost on anyone that he had chosen that particular cloak. After kneeling to kiss the hand of the king he took his place alongside us, wedging himself in between me and an archbishop, pushing all others in the line just a bit farther down the flank. The queen turned a quick side-eye towards me as neither of us was quite able hide our mirth. My good sister-in-law could not contain her sense of humor, even under such serious circumstances.

The three men followed closely behind the cardinal having waited for him to make his affected entrance in what we all recognized as a bit of practiced drama. Approaching the king with deference, the gentlemen bowed deeply and one, who we would come to know as a prince by title, was beckoned forward by his majesty to kiss his ring.

The visitors showed no signs of being armed as there were

no visible swords or daggers, regardless, our men were on guard with their hands on their hilts, ready to draw at the first sign of any threatening behavior. It proved to be unwarranted as the king received his greeting and expressed a welcome to the embassy inviting them to present themselves and to the purpose of their visit. As if on cue, the cardinal pulled out the golden sheath containing the letter of introduction and passed it to me so that I could hand it to the king. I turned it over examining with an exaggerated affect to ensure that all the jewels were still in place. The king smirked, noting my insolence, acknowledged the sheath with a curt wave of his hand, and I knew to hold on to it in case it would be necessary to bring it forward later.

The leader of the group began speaking. His physical appearance as described by the cardinal was quite correct. Finely dressed, appearing no more than thirty years of age, he was much taller than most men and carried himself with an assuredness that seemed to confirm his royal stature. Named David, he claimed to represent his brother, a King James of Istoia (where that was exactly had yet to be established) and he was accompanied by two attendants, titled lords of some merit named Thomas and John. Combined they claimed to represent the entire embassy which could not possibly be true given the size of the ship on the Thames, and the obvious need for many men to sail her, if in fact it had sails, of which I was still uncertain. Prince David announced his intent to present the greetings of his brother and the desire for his nation and ours to join in friendship and mutual benefit.

This was a standard diplomatic greeting, and the king was quick to move on to direct questioning. Thanking the prince for his well wishes, he enquired of the health of King James and without waiting for an answer asked impatiently where Istoia was, and why he, or any of us, had not heard of it before their arrival.

"Your majesty," the prince responded in a clear deep voice, his English inflected with the slight Irish lilt detected by the cardinal, "Istoia is located due west of England, some 1500 leagues."

There was an audible gasp in the hall since to our knowledge no one had never ventured that far west before. There are many stories of our distant and past Danish overlords having traveled that far to lands that were covered in ice for most of the year, but they were thought to be tales with little truth to them. Portuguese sailors had talked of great sea banks in the far west with schools of cod so dense you could walk of them, but this distance seemed too incredible.

"We have known of you and your people for many years," he continued, "and have quietly visited your shores in the past. But our sovereign lord has chosen this time to now announce ourselves."

There was more than a collective gasp at that bit of information. There was genuine and audible alarm heard from the court. This was a break in custom and the admission of foreign agents of an unknown country having been on our shores for years undetected could not be left unchallenged.

The king hushed our murmurings and asked calmy, "How many years have your people been visiting our country, and why have you not previously announced yourself?" His tone was controlled, but there was obvious anger detectable in his voice to those that know him well.

"My deepest apologies, your grace. But I cannot say for certain when my people first discovered your island, but I assume it was several generations ago."

At this astonishing bit of news, the murmur of the crowed rose to an actual chatter, and even I found myself wondering aloud to no one in particular what manner of diplomatic failure this information was leading towards. The prince had used the word *discover* as if we did not exist before they happened upon us.

"I am certain we meant no offense, and our presence was to observe and not cause harm."

Turning to the cardinal, the king asked, "Did you know of this?"

The cardinal acknowledged that the prince had mentioned that they had sent unannounced visitors to England before, but he had not pressed them for further details. Saving the opportunity for the royal inquisition.

"So, you have been spying on us for some time?" The king asked angrily of the prince.

"No, your majesty. My brother and my father, and his father before him sent ships east to observe your country as well as those on the continent. We have visited both France and Spain, and many other places, but have chosen to observe in quiet rather than interfere in your affairs, or those of our Christian brothers abroad."

This alarmed the foreign ambassadors who, up to this point, had been enjoying the fact that England had been spied upon for generations. But alas, they too had been the subject of foreign visitations and therefore had been just as vulnerable as we had been and may possibly still be. If they could have manifested homing pigeons from their cloaks immediately, they would have done so.

The guards in the room moved instinctively towards a posture of assault. It seemed to all that at any moment the king may order the arrest of the three men, and even they seemed to sense the mounting tension as they inched closer to one another while remaining outwardly calm.

"What of this friendship then? The kind king continued angrily, "how might we be friends with spies? Should we trust your king now, or his ship that menaces my home? It is his ship that sits outside my keep, is it not?"

"I assure you, your majesty, we come in friendship. Our past visitations were meant to gauge our," he paused, as if searching for the correct word and finding it, "*approach,* to you and your people…and to those of Spain and France, and of course Rome. Not to menace you."

The prince turned to acknowledge the other ambassadors, which struck me as odd since he had not been introduced to either, but seemed to know exactly who they were—perhaps by the manner of their dress, maybe?

"We are here to bring messages of peace and hopes for prosperity, and for a sharing of Christian love."

I noted that the prince had mentioned the word *Christian* twice already and I was uncertain of its importance but sensed that there was some deeper meaning there that we would yet discover. Turning to me, the king beckoned I bend my ear and requested that I demand the removal of their ship.

"I am Lord Cornwall," I interjected loudly, hushing the crowd. "On behalf of the king I demand you remove your ship from its present anchor and remove it down river towards a more appropriate mooring away from the Tower."

"Lord Cornwall, we appreciate your request and assure you that the ship shall move in a few short days with our own departure. In the meantime, we intend to use it as our place of abode while we conduct our business with you and your king."

This response was impertinent and a direct afront to what was certainly not a request. My hand instinctively went to my sword, and the cardinal took the prince's words as a cue to leap, or lurch clumsily as it were, towards an intervention.

"My lords," he exclaimed "I think we are not affording the most gracious audience here to our guests. Surely, we might start with a more cordial parley and speak of why they are here and not of their departure so soon into their embassy."

His words did little to calm the tension. And sensing the anger rising in the room the prince dropped to one knee and begged the king for his forgiveness at any insult that had been proffered. His attendants followed suit and so we were left in a somewhat embarrassing moment of quiet as the king pondered what to say next.

From his seated position he beckoned me once again and asked for the sheath that I was still holding. Taking it in hand he turned it over in examination and removed the letter that the cardinal had previously read to the council. He pondered it briefly before allowing it to fall on his lap.

"Prince, shall we begin again." It was not a question. The king continued with clear authority, "I accept your apology and having read the letter from your brother I implore you to speak in earnest. Why are you here?"

The prince and his attendants got to their feet and conferred briefly amongst themselves before he responded.

"We are here to bring you the gift of enlightenment. To share with you what we know of bettering the health and well-being of your people, and to guide you towards a more benevolent kingdom. A kingdom that clothes and feeds its people, that ends hunger and filth in the streets of its capital and in every town and village. A kingdom that educates all its people so that all may read and write and know the words of our God having seen them with their own eyes and understood them in their own language. A kingdom that does not defer to the will of a church that enriches itself on the prayers of its people. A kingdom that does not tax its people into penury to fund wars on foreign soils only to capture land from people that mire in penury from taxation by their own king. A kingdom where free will and freedom of thought and conscience is the right of all people, whether they be born of noble blood or born from the soil of a humble farm."

What followed was an immediate and deafening silence as we all contemplated what we had heard. The prince's speech was an incredible insult. A direct attack on the majesty of our king and the state of our nation. The Crown was presented as failing its people, and we its highest born representatives were portrayed as negligent in the care of the people within its dominion. Upon hearing these words, the crowd grew even more restless and each man in the room made ready to pounce upon the visitors.

The tension was so great that the king stood and asked that everyone stand back and stand down but begging us all to maintain our pride with his express desire to continue this interview with the embassy. I was surprised by the king's even temperament as his blood usually ran hot and towards mistakes made in haste, but his command of the situation was obviously buoyed by the security of the room and the strength of our numbers. He sat down again and leaned comfortably on one elbow in the direction of the queen, as if he was in complete control of the conversation.

"Young prince, I suggest you elaborate on what you call your gift of enlightenment. And why do you judge me and my treatment of my subjects and the lands within my realm? I am assuming your brother, your king, has directed you to entertain me with such insults, but I ask by whose authority does one king have to judge another?

"Your majesty, it is by the authority of God that we are here. We are representatives of our king, but our message comes from God. Our purpose is not to stand in judgement of you. We are bound by duty to share the knowledge gifted to us by Him."

This was an unbelievable statement. He was claiming the authority of God in the presence of a man anointed by his very birth. Even the cardinal, who had been advocating for the embassy in some belief that he would be benefit from its success, was incredulous. At each response or comment from the prince in his short interview the court had grown angrier and more animated. My confidence was waning in the king's ability to keep the hall in his control, and I feared that someone might lash out at the three men and cause great hysteria.

Sensing the growing anger of the court, the king rose again and walked towards the prince stopping an arms-length away. The height difference between them was now quite evident. The prince and both of his attendants were a full head taller than the king, which meant that I, being the same height as the king, was similarly challenged.

"What is this knowledge that you presume I do not possess?" the king asked confidently, looking the prince clearly in the eyes.

"Perhaps it is best to begin with a parable of sorts since the knowledge we wish to share is complex and will require many hours of your time."

"Perhaps. But do not insult me further with your impertinence. I warn you that are close to being dismissed or locked away here in this Tower where the hours are mine to give."

"I understand, your grace. Let me clarify my earlier words.

We are not here to insult you, but it is an unfortunate fact that our time here is limited, and we feel courtly diplomacy does not serve our purpose. So, I shall speak in earnest, now given your permission, if even in parable which will best explain why we are here and what benefit we bring to you and your people."

The king returned to his seat, and I breathed a slight sigh of relief as it appeared that he had taken command of the situation. The prince seemed to recognize that he insulted all of us, and as he continued addressing the crowd this time his tone was much humbler, but not without confidence.

"Imagine, if you will, that you in all your majesty sends a group of adventurers abroad on a long journey and they happen upon a land filled with people who do not possess the same talents that you do. Think of your music, your art, the poetry of your court, the fine weave of your cloth, and your ability to forge iron into steel. And imagine that the people of this land have heard the word of God, but only know it in the context of their own existence. Their idea of God would be as unevolved as they are, it would be as if you happened upon a land that existed in a time different than your own. Like a period from your own past of one thousand years ago when you did not know how to make swords from steel, when you wore skins instead of cloth, when your court had but rustic music and poetry. Would you not look upon the people of this land with benevolence? Would you not share with them all you know of God and the gifts that time has wrought for you?"

I realized then, as everyone else in the hall did as well, that the prince was telling us that we were in the presence of those adventurers from his story and that we were the poor unfortunate souls in the animal skins.

"The knowledge we bring," he continued, "is greater than

just music and poetry, it is greater than you could ever possibly understand in this precise moment. This knowledge comes from one thousand years in your own future. And we believe you are deserving of the same benevolence that we believe you would bring to others, given a similar circumstance. We simply ask that you allow us to do so, unhindered and with welcome. Because failure to do so has consequence for your people and ours, as well as all the peoples of this earth."

It took a few minutes for the meaning of his words to sink in. We had just been called backwards, like heathens from some far away land, and that we had been promised enlightenment with specific knowledge from the future, but if we fail to embrace these strangers, we face punishment of some sort.

"You threaten us?" Yelled Somerset.

Followed up by the cardinal who added in anger. "Who are you to claim superiority over the most Christian king in all of Europe? This is not benevolence you speak of it is not a shared peace, it is an insolence never heard here before!".

With the cardinal's words the crowd seemed to take permission to move on the three men with the guards attempting to seize them without waiting for a command from either me or the king. Swords were drawn as the king yelled out to cease, but there was so much confusion that many in the room attempted to flee the hall following the lead of the queen and her ladies. The cardinal moved quickly to presumed safety behind the throne while I stood between the king and the embassy, my own sword drawn in defense and defiance. The king, to his credit, attempted to halt the chaos and jumped up to stop the guards from seizing the men. But before he could reach them, the guards, who were quick to act, lunged towards the men and just before they could grab them they were seemingly repulsed by an unseen force.

Their movements were suddenly halted before they could make contact, and like an explosive shock discharged when one walks across a woolen carpet and touches a metal object, the guards were soundly thrown back some distance. Still on their feet but badly shaken by the experience. There might even have been a sound like that of a crack of lightening in that moment, but in all the confusion I cannot be certain of what I heard.

The repulsion of the guards seemed to freeze the chaos of the room. If we had hoped to subdue the three men, it was obvious that we would be unable to do so. The king raised his arm and demanded quiet. Somerset followed by bellowing 'stand down, stand down' in support of the king. This seemed to work, and the crowd slowly drifted back to their original positions, while the king, the counsel and I remained standing. The cardinal still cowering from behind the throne.

"You have caused great pain and your embassy is a failure," said the king in a calm and determined tone. And now knowing that we seemed to have little power to forcibly subdue them, the king commanded them to surrender and accept confinement within the Tower until they may be peacefully removed from his kingdom.

Each of them nodded in quiet agreement and allowed the king's personal guard to lead them from the hall. They did so without protest and offered no apology for their actions. The insults and impertinence had been the only recognizable gifts bestowed by this embassy, but I was suspect that there was something more hidden in their parable. They were to be locked in cells and afforded some comfort, but the ship still menaced the Tower and if their words were true, and that they had come from a land that is somehow advanced one thousand years in 'talents' as they described, then I feared for what was to come next.

The prince and his compatriots were taken willingly to individual cells, so that they could not communicate with one another and locked in for their safety as there was some fear that harm may come from them from a courtier acting as a mercenary in an attempt to curry favor. The king dismissed the court sending them back to Eltham or Windsor, or wherever they had come from, and the council gathered in his private chamber to discuss the events of the audience. The queen joined us, which pleased me greatly since she always had a calming effect on her husband, since she was one of the few people able to prevent any violent outbursts which we all feared.

I am certain the cardinal was pleased by her presence as well as it afforded him some protection, which in my opinion was unwarranted. The cardinal had willfully allowed flattery to sway his judgment and his own sense of self-importance brought possible harm to the court, and at the very feet of the king. He had entertained this *embassy* without diligently investigating its origin. The shiny gold sheath that contained the patent had blinded him to his own responsibility as chancellor. By his very title he had an obligation to protect the Crown, and this should have started with skepticism and extreme prudence. Instead, we were treated to a spectacle of poor diplomacy by individuals whose entire introduction was impudent and insulting.

The king seemed resigned to the failure of the embassy and wanted to put an end to the entire enterprise, but we could not do so with the three gentlemen locked away and their ship sitting on our doorstep. There was great debate amongst the members of the council about what to do next, but without much agreement. It was posited that the men should be executed. Another suggested torture to teach them a lesson. It was the queen who suggested that the men be given a private audience, after a night in their cells, with the king, me, and the cardinal. Of course, we would have guards present, but she reckoned that they deserved another opportunity to express their purpose and to provide a greater explanation of their statements. She described the parable as unfortunate, *I would say insulting*, but as she explained, it had a clear purpose and even if it was overly simple it suggested that they had some knowledge that might benefit us, and would we not be advised to press this further?

It was a sound argument and one that would allow us to question them with some informality. It would also allow us the opportunity to dismiss them entirely if we found their responses wanting. We were under no obligation to accept their desire for diplomatic relations, and I had real doubts that this was in fact a genuine embassy. Only through further questioning would we be able to establish whether they were fraudsters and whether there actually was a country called Istoia. I had my doubts and assumed the others of the council did as well.

We retired for the night with agreement that a more private audience would be granted in the morning. There was some relief that a course of action had been decided and I fell asleep from exhaustion without waking once during the night. My peace was broken by the warder barging into my bedchamber in extreme agitation. He had just been awakened himself with the news that the guards had found the cells of the visitors empty when performing their morning rounds. Each of the cells had been locked and there were no visible signs of escape. All that remained of their confinement was the clothes that they had been wearing, dropped on the floor in layers as if the wearers had simply vanished into the ether, and strangely, a fine film of powdery salt-like crystals covered the floor.

Grabbing my cloak, I sped to the ramparts to see if the ship was still in place as I was suspect that it too had departed. My suspicion was correct. I gazed out on the wide river at its morning tide and saw it empty in all directions. Stopping a guard, I enquired of its departure and was told that no one had seen it leave. Apparently, the ship had been visible at dusk, although it had not illuminated as it had the previous evening and with no moon last night it was barely visible from the Tower anyway, and at sunrise it simply was not there. The embassy and its ship had departed as mysteriously as it had appeared.

Chapter Five

Discite
(Learn)

David sorely underestimated my ability to comprehend Middle English. The book was not in a narrative form recognizable to me, its punctuation followed no discernable pattern, and words appeared randomly in French and in Latin. Thank god, again, for AOL. The simple act of reading required constant translation which required me to cut out passages in bits and pieces and paste into AOLtranslate and then cut and paste the result into a standalone document. Reading became an act of rewriting the manuscript using online software and this left significant gaps in the translation. I was forced to search phrases and words, and cross reference them against other documents on the web. Even with that I was barely able to parse complete sentences, but it did enable me to weave together the conversations that ran on the vellum with some understanding of who said what, and to whom.

After considerable effort, I found myself identifying patterns in the language and sentence structure, and so after several hours of laborious translation I was able to craft a version of a discernable vocabulary from the first few pages. It was like codebreaking. Once I had created my own dictionary of words, and a list of common word orders, I was able to develop a translation process and establish a work rhythm that allowed me to apply my own weak attempt at modern grammar, making what, in a sense, was a foreign language legible to me and perhaps eventually to another reader. However, it did not take me long to figure out that the exercise would require me to retype the entire manuscript into modern English, complete with legible dialog between the characters contained therein. I realized that it was going to require many more days than I had left in London.

The night passed entirely with me sitting at the hotel room desk, which meant I was forced to abandon my labor and return to the office without having slept. If I could have, I would have taken the day off from work, but even as I contemplated calling in sick I knew that this would raise an alarm with my superiors. If I had been in Austin I could justify a workday from home, but not while I was here in London. So, as tired as I was, I packed up my bags, put the book in my briefcase, and headed to Whitehall knowing I could sleep on the airplane later that evening.

I was tempted more than once during the day to take out the book and continue my translating. As tedious an effort as it was it was also intriguing, and I was very keen to see how the story was going to develop. However, there was no way that I could pull the book out at work and not have to explain to my colleagues what it was and what I was doing.

From the first few pages I had discovered that David and his colleagues had managed to project to 1481 and by harnessing whatever low-tech they were able to manifest a ship in the Thames, right out front of the Tower of London. This was a remarkable feat to say the least. To craft a router in medieval England took talent. The prep work must have taken considerable time, but certainly possible given the availability of base materials. Metal in form of steel was available to them, and of course there was plenty of gold that they could access as Hollows. And of course, silica. It was everywhere.

The idea that they could manipulate medieval peoples into helping them craft the tech to project a Solid was fascinating to me. But, as David had explained it, the ability to do so was purely transactional. Just like now, money then could buy you anything or anyone's labor. The promise of reward, whether in the future or in the present, makes people blind to their own best interests. But understanding precisely how they managed to do this successfully would have to wait for further discussion with David.

I had been impressed by the quality of David's caste and so I knew that there was no possible way that anyone in 1481 could suspect that David, and his supposed embassy, was anything than what they appeared to be, and certainly not that they were interacting with a couple of guys on the moon 747 years in the future. But what I knew of him and his current mission now, in 2028, made me exceptionally wary of his intentions in 1481, and so my desire to continue reading and translating was really about getting to the root of what he wanted from me. My future, or at least one version of my future, was somewhere in the book and if it seemed confusing it didn't matter, I had to continue the translation if I was to be able to (rationally) meet the challenge of whatever part I was to play in the correction.

What disturbed me the most, and from my very first very interaction with him—and perhaps I had always known this but was unwilling to admit it to myself—was the fear that I had little control over how things were playing out with David. I feared that I was deceiving myself in thinking that I was making any choices for myself. Even my willingness to participate in the correction, which I wanted to believe I had some control over since I had not yet agreed to fully cooperate, was delusional on my part. I was already participating—even thinking about him and the correction was a form of participation. The algorithm anticipated all my moves before I did, and fed them to David, so in fact my free will was being managed in such a way that I could not control the result of any of my choices. It was like being half-conscious when you come out of dental surgery. You say things you wouldn't normally say, you tell your legs to move and then you are surprised by the motion they make, or don't make. Even my eagerness to continue with the transcription was a managed act by David and whomever he represented.

I was beginning to suspect that the parallels between myself and the king's half-brother, the duke of Cornwall, was purposeful and not in a very subtle way. It was becoming quite transparent to me that he and I were being guided by the algorithm to intersect somehow and somewhere in time, and for what purpose I didn't yet know.

And to my dismay, I had been so busy treating this translation as an academic exercise and so I wasn't really learning anything meaningful. I suspected, but had yet to find, something in the duke's interactions with David that might help me with my own dealings with him, but I was certain that it was not enough to simply read and retype the words in modern English. The translation was meaningless without understanding the deeper context of the story and characters therein and this is what drove my desire to continue the task. I was anxious to continue reading if only to learn more about myself, possibly somewhere in the manuscript.

Chapter Six

An Embassy of One

In the weeks since the sudden disappearance of the embassy there had been little discussion of its importance. I appeared to be the only one with a sense of unease at the possible return of the ship and the three gentlemen from Istoia, or wherever they purported to be from. The king had been highly alarmed by their sudden departure, he even said so, and yet he was persuaded by the council to dismiss the event as a charade or possibly some mischief most likely instigated by the French, or worst, the emperor. Collectively they did not allow the event to dictate any fear since the spectacle came and went so quickly that it seemed easiest for everyone to accept the entire event as just another day at court. I, on the other hand, held a completely different view and had hoped the king did as well. But I was wrong in thinking that our defenses required strengthening or that the cardinal needed beheading, for the king seemed pleased with the council's decision to let the event pass without further discussion.

I had raised the topic of further defense of both the Tower and the castle at Windsor against future embassies but was rebuffed by Somerset and Norfolk. When I pressed the cardinal on how the event might play out in Rome, since the ambassadors of both Spain and France had been present during the now forgotten audience, he just shrugged it off, claiming to have written to the Holy See explaining that the court had been victim to a hoax of no consequence and that the jape had been relegated to the dung heap.

I knew that the cardinal's explanation was more wanton than the truth and that he was surely sweating the stories that would be swirling around the Vatican. He had brought the failed embassy to court, and it was his reputation that required salvaging, and to do so meant that he had to put the metal ship and the false embassy as far behind him as possible. He obviously felt it best render the event harmless, and in the past. Time was his only hope for favor again with the king—the only person he cared to please, other than himself and to some degree, the pope. The king hoped time would erase the embarrassment of being challenged by three seemingly defenseless individuals who had called him and his entire realm barbaric and ignorant, and worse, when physically challenged they were able to rebuff an armed advance without raising a hand.

However, I could not easily forget that a metallic ship of the strangest proportions appeared suddenly in the river not but a few yards from the Tower and that it glowed with the light of thousands of candles. It was silent and took the shot from a cannon as if a rock had been lobbed at a pile of hay, noiseless and without any harm. And furthermore, the three men—two of which were basically mute during the entire encounter— vanished from their cells, leaving their clothes behind. How could my fellow councilors not be alarmed by the thought that three naked men seemingly evaporated from their cells? And along with them the largest ship, metallic no less, that anyone has ever seen.

If the king and the rest of the clod pates at table were willing to allow this event unanswered it was to be at their own peril. I was not going to do so and began my own plans for defense which would require greater intelligence.

Over the proceeding weeks I took every opportunity to pry the members of visiting embassies at court for any news. The Spanish ambassador employed the loosest of retainers, made up mostly of his own nephews and cousins, each more dimwitted then the next. They offered little or no information and seemed to think the whole even had been a jest by some rather bold opportunists. The French ambassador was far wilier and kept his people from court for the weeks following the event. This raised my suspicions as to their possible participation in the prank, but in direct pressing of the ambassador he admitted that he was keeping his people from court in fear of a return of the ship and had been making plans for a quick departure from Rye. Even going so far as to purchase his own cog. His candor was unorthodox, but well taken and confirmed for me what he must have been reporting back to Tours.

My repeated attempts at engaging with the king on the topic was fruitless. He had committed the season to hunting and had left London on a procession to York taking most of the court with him. I begged to be left behind, which he welcomed since he was tired of me discussing the strange embassy, with the caveat that I would make my way north in time for Michaelmas. This gave me several months to work on a strategy to combat any future nonsense from the likes of Prince David and his so-called embassy from Istoia, and to perhaps dig deeper into its origins.

I began by engaging scholars from Cambridge. Staying at my own estate at Madingley, not far from the university, I could easily summon them without raising suspicions amongst the stragglers who remained at court, or amongst the clergy in Cambridge who were known to be in the pocket of the water rat. The trip up the Cambridge Road was easy enough for them and an evening at the table of the king's brother, legitimate or not, was readily accepted to those offered, but unfortunately I learned very little and spent several weeks engaged in endlessly tedious discussions which always danced around theology.

I was interested in metallurgy and the possibilities of crafting a giant ship out of polished plate and one that would not sink under its own weight. But of course, Cambridge was not the place for such investigations, and I would have been better off inviting a shipwright from Blackwell to dinner than a priest who claimed to know the God-given properties of iron and the miracles to be found in Christ's nails, if only he could find them. I was also interested in certain things David had said, for instance, the name of his brother's kingdom. Istoia. No one had ever heard of this place, but interestingly I did learn that the word was not unknown and that it was actually a common Greek term denoting the history of mankind. This would make it a curious place name or a subterfuge, but at the same time it showed a knowledge of the classics that only the most learned could access. The belief that the three men as presented acted alone in some sort of hoax was not plausible, and yet I had little evidence otherwise.

David had said that they possessed knowledge that we did not, as if they had leapt forward in time. He even seemed to challenge our place on God's earth, describing our time here as backward or primeval, as if we were less just or righteous in our daily lives than him and his brother. He certainly challenged our king's authority over his subjects, questioning his benevolence, and of course by extension our own nobility.

David had said that Istoia was some 1500 leagues west of our own island, and yet no maps, or so I had been advised, existed that showed land that far west, or even beyond the northern ice. There are rumors of such lands, and word that Spain was planning an expedition after Portugal's refusal, but we had no intelligence of the expedition's actual existence.

He also said that his people had been visiting us, and France and Spain, for several generations and had chosen to do so in secret. If this were true, then why had they chosen now to announce themselves and why at a simple challenge of a night in a cell did they choose to abandon their embassy? They said that they had come to give us the gift of enlightenment—a new word for all of us. Enlightenment. Light. Knowledge, I suppose for the purposes according to David, of bettering the well-being of our people. A kind thought, and one that begs the question again. Why did they leave so abruptly if they had so much to share with us? Why invest time over generations, and the manifestation of such a massive ship to simply vanish in the night?

My time at Madingley left me certain of several things: the priests and scholars of Cambridge know nothing, the embassy was not a jest or jape, and that it had likely not been abandoned.

Proving these certainties would only be possible from London and by seeking out those who know all the movements and happenings along the river and those who had been to the far west by sea. I, myself, was unable to make direct contact with such folk having never ventured too deeply into the shipyards in my entire life. But employing a few trusted guards to make their way to Blackwell, and along the Kent Road, proved fruitless as well. No one had reported seeing the ship make its way upriver and all tales of land to the west was deemed fantastical, or in the very least the stuff of very old Norse stories from the dark days after Rome had left our island.

Any continued outreach to the foreign courtiers was fruitless since those that had not gone with the king on his processional had returned to the continent for a much-needed break from the tedium of diplomacy. My own correspondence with Rome, and even my friends at Frederick's court in Vienna, was empty of intelligence or went unanswered, so I resigned myself to carefully taking stock of our munitions at the Tower and soliciting inventories of Windsor and as far north as Warwick. But even as I told myself that the threat remained, I too began to slowly dismiss the event as time passed. By the second month of the embassy's disappearance, I was ready to proceed north to join the court for Michaelmas and leave the memory of the embassy behind me with the knowledge that London was possibly, but not assuredly, and most likely not sufficiently, protected. Nonetheless, the Tower, and the city and all its inhabitants, blissfully ignorant of any remaining danger.

Preparations for my own journey were simple and with only a small retinue I planned to leave in the early morning on the day of the Exaltation of the Holy Cross. It seemed an auspicious day to begin a journey and if I had been reluctant to travel with the court in early summer, I was ready now for a change of scenery. The regiment of life at the Tower had grown bothersome and my head had been clouded for months with the problem of the failed embassy, and I was in much need of some sport, and the entertainment of the court. The travail of the journey would not be hard and so on the morning of my departure I awoke to say my prayers with a light heart and promise of fine weather. I left my bedchamber to attend the king's chapel (the benefit of a shared father), alone as usual, and was surprised to see a hooded figure kneeling at my usual place in the chancel. An empty court meant a lazy clergy and even my own confessor had gone north months prior, so it was a great surprise to see a monk in such a private space.

Approaching loudly from the nave I called out to the figure

demanding that they rise and identify themselves. I was not opposed to an individual's right to prayer, but I was highly suspicious of any person's trespass in a space reserved for my family alone. Admittedly, it would not be unusual to have one of the cardinal's men poking about, lurking behind a screen attempting to hear the private prayers of any one of us but, with the court abandoned this individual was highly suspect and so it was with great surprise that the monk stood and turned to face me revealing himself to be the errant prince.

To be clear, my surprise was not born from fear, but more so from incredulity that he had chosen to reappear alone and in a place of sanctuary. I had entered the chapel unarmed and without guard and was too far down the nave to retreat safely and needed to decide quickly whether to flee down either side of the transept when he called out to me.

"Robert don't be afraid," he yelled out. "I am unarmed, and alone."

He could sense my alarm and raised his hands to remove his hood and to show me that he was in fact unarmed, but I could not trust that he did not have a knife or sword hidden in his cowl.

"Open your robe," I demanded.

I could tell he was reluctant to do so, and this gave me pause again to consider fleeing to retrieve a weapon and return to run him through.

"Of course," he responded. Opening it to reveal nothing beneath but a simple tunic.

"What impertinence brings you back?" I cried out angrily.

The fact that he was able to access the Tower and to make his way into such a private space, so deep within the Tower, without notice by anyone, was a blatant failure on my part to have properly secured what should be the most secure place in all

England.

"I have come to speak with you," he responded cautiously and in a slow soothing tone, as if he was speaking to a mad dog or unruly child.

I realized then that my own tone gave away my alarm and that a more rational voice was warranted to take some control of the situation, or in the very least to level the field of battle.

"I repeat myself, sir. What brings you here again where you are most unwanted?" I asked again, this time in a more certain tone. Slowly, and as calmly as he had spoken to me. "Are you truly alone?" I continued my query.

"Yes, most assuredly. And you have nothing to fear. I apologize for our hasty departure from our last encounter and beg your forgiveness."

"I am unafraid…most assuredly, and your apology is not necessary for you are neither wanted nor missed by your departure," I responded with confidence and continued, "why have you returned? And please tell me how you got in the Tower this time, and while you are at it, tell how you departed unseen the last time?"

My questions were most earnest and possible too many. I feared it betrayed my nervousness. But I wanted to know why he was here again and how he seemingly manifests himself in and out of the Tower unseen. And yet, my intent of appearing confident was failing by my own ramblings.

We were now standing no more than a few paces from one another, and the tension had subsided slightly, but not enough to warrant a closer approach and yet he deemed to move a few steps towards me. My hand instinctively went to my waist as if searching for the hilt of my sword and noticing this he assured me once again that I had nothing to fear and that he was unarmed.

I stepped back and he halted his movement towards me.

"I have come back to speak with you directly, to press upon you the importance of what I shared in my audience with your king. We know you are alone at court and that the king is now in the north, and we also know that you have his ear and that you have the ability to get us another audience."

I pondered what he was saying for a moment, wondering who the 'we' is he mentioned since he reported to be alone. He also failed to answer my questions I had posed directly.

"How did you get in here today and how did you leave your cell last time, both unnoticed?" I repeated myself.

"I can explain and I will, but it is part of a much bigger discussion that will take some hours, and now is not the time or place as I require your attention and yours alone for other reasons. That is why I am here today. To speak with you in confidence and to seek your assistance in securing another audience with your king."

"Why not approach the cardinal again?" I enquired dryly.

"That was a mistake, we know that now. We assumed that the protocol was correct, but we were unprepared for his...his lack of diplomacy," he responded candidly.

"You were unprepared for his ego. He serves himself first, the king second and then the pope," I added, "and, if you have been observing us for generations, as you claim, you would have known that the cardinal was not your best option for access to the court, would you not?"

"I suppose the closeness of our observations was limited to outside the workings of the court," he answered, with what seemed a poor excuse to me.

What supposed embassy prepares so weakly for such a complex game of diplomacy? Either he was naïve, inept, or he was lying.

"You are very bad at this game," I added.

He did not answer my challenge right away, but rather paused to think about his response.

"I suppose we were confident in our eventual success, not really caring about first failures since we are armed with something you are not."

"Ah, yes. Knowledge? What you call enlightenment" I parroted as proof that I had clearly heard his message the first time.

"No," he answered emphatically. "Time. We have the gift of time and our ability to manipulate it whenever and wherever we may be. I think you are beginning to realize that now, are you not?"

He was very confident in his answer, and this alarmed me, but I tried not to show it on my face. He had mentioned during his last audience that he possessed knowledge that came from a thousand years in our future, was this what he meant by *time*?" Our time was measured in present hours. We could neither move forward nor back except in our minds, so what did he mean by manipulation?

"I did not think that," I answered emphatically. "And I do not understand what you mean when you say you can manipulate time whenever and wherever you may be."

"My apologies, I thought that you might be quicker than you are and that you might have suspected that my presence here was by some method that was alien to you and perhaps of nonmaterial form," he responded cryptically.

"My suspicion, sir, is that you are a liar. And that your intentions are of ill will to me, the king, and his realm."

"They are not," he responded with a smile that was bereft of either kindness or humor.

"But perhaps you may be correct in some regard." I interrupted him before he could go on. "I do suspect that you possess some alien methods for appearing and disappearing. But I know nothing of any nonmaterial form and do not even know what those words reference. Perhaps you mean to tell me you are a ghost? But what I do know for certain is that you were dismissed from court and yet here you are again asking me to arrange another audience with the king. But how and why you come and go remains a mystery to me."

"I said that I can explain and will do so with your agreement to continue this conversation in a place that is convenient to both of us outside the Tower where, we might be unheard and unseen by others," he answered, posing another question, avoiding answering the questions that *I* had posed to him.

I was very reluctant to continue the conversation, and with my immediate departure north for Michaelmas it was unlikely that I would agree to his request. But something compelled me— curiosity or perhaps the thrill of the challenge—that weakened my resolve.

"I am to leave today for the king at Warwick," I answered.

"You can postpone your departure, you have plenty of time until Michaelmas, and I believe our continued communication intrigues you enough to do so. I need nothing more than a few days of your time, alone. That you have, correct?" He asked.

"I do, and I can. Where and when do you propose to meet again?" I enquired with more than a little trepidation, but hopefully well masked.

"Let us meet tomorrow, same time, outside Bishopsgate. Do you know the ancient cemetery at Spitel Fyeld?" He asked, proposing the strangest of locations to meet.

"I do, but tell me why such a place, why not some place more convenient, perhaps where we can ride? The deer park at Windsor, perhaps?"

I was uncomfortable with the location he proposed and was reluctant to agree and begged the question why Spitel Fyeld? A wet and ponded landscape just north of the city gates, and certainly not suitable for a meeting place for noble men. He explained that he needed to be close to the city walls and that it suited him better. That the area was free of most people and was pleasant enough and not on royal lands. I suspected that perhaps this might suit an ambush of sorts in which he had prepared in advance the scene of my demise. But I also questioned myself why he would go to such trouble when he had the element of surprise having appeared and disappeared at will. If he wanted me dead, I would most likely be so already. And so, I reluctantly agreed.

"We shall meet alone. And I shall be unarmed, I promise," he said upon my agreement.

"I too shall come alone," he nodded in acceptance. "And unarmed," I continued, but received no further acknowledgement.

"If it pleases you," he responded belatedly, seemingly unmoved by my own promise and sensing my dismay. He continued, "bring a weapon if it makes you feel safer, but you will have no need of it."

I was surprised by his last remark and wanted to query him further but decided to let it stand rather than present any more questions for the time being. I had received unfruitful, but intriguing, answers to the questions already posed today, and so I felt it best to simply offer to escort him from the chapel and see to it that the yeoman remove him from the Tower properly. My offer went unaccepted and before I could insist, he walked swiftly away from me, almost in a run, and passed behind the alter screen and out of sight. The speed at which he had departed the conversation was surprising and it took me several seconds to register what had happened. By the time I began to chase after him he was nowhere to be seen. Like the morning after his audience and the empty cell; save for his clothes and a small pile of sand, he passed behind the altar and did not come out the other side of the ambulatory. Instead, all that remained of him was his robe and tunic in a neat pile on the floor as if he simply stepped out of them and alighted unseen to an unknown place.

Searching through the clothes I found a small mound of sand beneath and rubbing it between my fingers I noted that it was more like powdered glass than coarse sand and that it was warm, as if it been close to his body. How very strange, I thought.

Amongst the Roman Dead

The delay in my departure confused my guards and generally perplexed my household. Those that were to travel with me were disappointed that I had given them no excuse or alternative day to leave, and those that were to remain were disappointed to have to attend to me further. I cared not because my mind was preoccupied with thoughts of David, once again, and the matter of his disappearance. I knew that no rational person would agree to meet him as requested, and furthermore, the possibility of personal harm was very great given the mysterious nature of our meeting in the chapel. A more superstitious person might see an explanation as the work of the devil and given the preponderance of witchcraft as an explanation for everything unexplainable, and I might be forgiven for thinking the same, but I was unafraid.

The belief in wizardry and sorcery, miasmic fevers, and

superstitions of all sorts fed the hysteria of the masses and provided explanations for simple unknowns, like a salve for the many ills that the church cannot fix. I believed in none. I had seen enough blood, guts, and misery in my lifetime to know that everything in this world can be explained through a rational belief in the certainty of life and death and nothing else. God does not create ghosts, save the holy one. So, I was not afraid of what I did not know, and I did not fear David and the mystery of his arrivals and departures because I did not believe in witches, magic, or sorcery, and I did not fear death.

The road to Spital Fyeld was well maintained and having passed through Bishopsgate it was a short ride to the cemetery. I had not actually visited it before and was not certain of its precise location, but I knew I could seek directions as I got closer. I had chosen a horse of no distinction and dressed myself in the simplest manner to attract as little attention as possible. I had left alone without my usual accompanying guardsmen, and this required significant subterfuge on my part. Having saddled the horse myself, I left the Tower early receiving a perplexed nod from the yeoman at the gate at Cradle Tower. His confusion at seeing me alone was not enough to cause alarm as all were accustomed to my coming and going at will, but I took the opportunity to let him know that I was riding north to Spital Fyeld and should return before nightfall. I took some comfort in knowing that I left some trail of myself in case of need, but with the knowledge that no one dare follow me so I could proceed alone as promised.

The cemetery was readily marked by the clear remnants of an ancient stone road passing through a bramble of blackberries yellowing in the late summer sun. Christian burial markings could be seen on some later graves, but most appeared to be pre-

Christian, and the oldest of crypts lining the road had been stripped of most of their marble revealing darkened interiors that gave the appearance of vacant, miniature, ramshackle houses. The cemetery was more fallen city than open ground with smaller stone paths leading from the main road lined by crypts of various sizes and shapes in all form of disrepair, but still, it had a calmness and pleasantness of nature overtaking the place with a wildness of vines and birds of every type. It was obvious that the cemetery had been abandoned many years before, but there was evidence that it was still frequented by some—perhaps locals— and any stone or metal of value had been stripped. None-the-less, it was not a fearful place, and if it ever harkened as a place of death, it did not do so anymore.

I kept my horse to the main path and followed it until the pavestones gave way to barren earth and finally to a simple dirt path. The crypts and graves grew smaller and less grand as the path narrowed until I had passed from the cemetery entirely and entered upon a small clearing bordered by yew trees and towering cedars. David was in the center of the clearing atop a black charger of enormous size, with a stirrup and pommel made of silver, glinting in the morning sun. Whereas I had chosen to be as inconspicuous as possible wearing well-worn brown leather breeches and a tunic of simple wool, he had arrived in full splendor with a cape of black velvet draped across his one shoulder and high boots of the shiniest black leather that I had ever seen. On his head was a peaked hat of the same velvet, certainly too warm for a summer morning. I assumed his costume was suited to his native Istoia, or I might even suspect Navarre, but here in the fields of outer London he appeared a fool.

"Curious choice for a place to meet," I said as soon as my horse was close enough so I would not have to shout. My eyes surveying his curious clothing choices as well, everything he was wearing looked so new and unworn.

He nodded in greeting and turned his horse indicating that I follow him as he rode out of the clearing. I was suspicious of his intentions but followed anyway, but first I surveyed the perimeter looking for signs of anything untoward. Noting nothing in particular, I followed his lead as we passed through the dense yew hedge and into a large fallow field. We stopped, remaining on our mounts, beside an old, wattled barn, its sides leaning heavily beneath the weight of its partially collapsed roof.

"No need for alarm," he said. Sensing my discomfort at having moved so far away from the cemetery proper. "The place has many visitors, mostly the local villagers collecting blackberries and bits of rubblestone for their hearths. Here we can talk freely and without interruption.

I nodded in acknowledgement, while furtively scanning the barn for any signs of others and found none except for some alighting pigeons who had made the old structure their home.

"Thank you for coming. I wasn't certain you would," he continued, "but I am grateful you did."

"I am here," I replied with some agitation. "So get on with it."

"I will speak frankly," he began in a calm, conversational voice. "Your king and your noble class are cruel and ignorant to the kind treatment of the common man, the people you claim to govern with love. Your cities and towns are filthy and ridden with disease and your church is exploitive selling lies to the people while it grows rich. You claim to govern with benevolence, but you are violent, and ignorant of the general need and want of your people, while all the time building wealth for yourselves at the expense of those who have nothing. You wage endless wars over lands that are unproductive because they are war ravaged, and through all of this you claim allegiance to a God and his son who spoke of nothing but peace and kindness. On Sundays and feast days you command great services to be performed in cathedrals of stone, where you sing of love and forgiveness and then the next day you starve children, lop the heads off enemies and fill your pockets with stolen monies you call taxes."

He paused for a moment, looked around at the open fields and the distant hedgerow before continuing: "As a people, you have not progressed in thought or deed for hundreds of years. Your wattle and thatched hovels and your stone castles are no better built today than they were in the time of Alfred. You burn candles and weak oil for light like the ancient Romans, and yet your nights are no brighter than they were a thousand years ago. You are neither regressive nor progressive, and you show no talent for thoughts greater than what is already known as if you believe there is nothing more to know, and I assure you, there is much to know."

He paused again before finishing his sermon. "Your world is doomed unless you amend your behaviors, immediately."

I listened attentively and watched him carefully as he labored over this lengthy beration, imagining me as a surrogate for my brother and the others of the court and clergy. Our horses faced each other, their necks touching close enough that I could have lashed out at him, but I also knew that what he said was all true and so I refrained from striking him. It took great restraint not to, and so I too looked out at the fields and hedgerow while collecting my thoughts and tempering my anger before responding to his lengthy tirade.

"You ask a lot of us," I responded, my anger controlled, having collected my thoughts. "Great change, much different than the norms and customs of our people, our church, and for all peoples of Europe for that matter. Have you considered speaking to Rome? Or France perhaps, our cousin Charles might appreciate such a message as delivered to me. Why us, and why now?" I said, with some unmasked amusement.

I further explained that his delivery was very poor and under no circumstances would I support another audience. Especially if he were to say the same things he said to me to the king, the cardinal, and my fellow noblemen. His sermon was insulting, but it was also a challenge that would only be met with violence in the exact manner as he described was our usual behavior. I said I agreed that the leadership of the church is corrupt, that they sell indulgences with impunity—granting absolution while committing the gravest sins themselves. I told him that our armies are led by noblemen who seek enrichment and favor with the king who in turn seeks enrichment from the very same nobles who wrench it from the poor and the landless. I told him that our very existence is but a series of circular transactions that grind the poor and hungry deeper into the muddy lands that are meant to sustain all of us. I also told him that I was powerless to change any of this, and that his request for another audience was pointless. He had nothing to offer us and there would be no willingness to listen.

He explained that they had not made any requests to meet with any other sovereigns, nor had they made any requests of Rome. He said that we are the closest lands to theirs and with a shared common language, which I had yet to understand how this was possible, and that there existed a kinship that was earnestly desired. He said that they genuinely felt that they had a goodness to offer and that it was born from Christian kindness.

His continued explanation sounded insincere and

unbelievable. My skepticism was born from pure pragmatism as I had never met another man, noble or not, willing to enrich another without requiring something in return. It was simply not natural for a man to give and not receive. I pressed him further to explain why he thought I might be of assistance when I was very much at the root of the ignorance and violence he spoke of, that as son of a duke and half-brother to a king, I was most guilty of the sins he hoped to cure us of. His answer surprised me.

He said that they had noted my furtive glances to the king, and to Elizabeth at the first meeting which indicated to them a distancing from others at court, particularly the cardinal. They had also noted my intimacies with the king and that my lack of royal birth, albeit acknowledged by my father, set me apart from all other nobles—meaning I was of some value and sufficiently non-threatening to keep around. He described me as having the ear of the king, but no real power. I could rise no farther than I had and would always have a place at court until I did not. Which meant until I lost my head.

They knew I had no known heirs of my own, and that it would be dangerous for me to produce any, and that I had shown no indication of amassed wealth beyond the lands granted by my father and brother. Most importantly, he said that from their distant observations, that I was not unaware of the common people, and although I might have been born to great privilege I was also born from a common woman.

I was not really one of *them* and that my place at court was tentative at best and held by grace and favor, and therefore they risked this contact with me as an assumption of my perceived pliability.

It was a truthful reading of my place at court. I did enjoy great privilege, but always with the knowledge that it was fragile and that my title, could be snatched from me in an instant, along with all my lands and my life. My brother's sons were the only true and rightful heirs, and my other princely brother, Richard, and his distaste for me and refusal to recognize my legitimacy meant that my life was reliant upon my support from our brother the king, and his heirs. If something were to happen to them I would not be long for this world and any allegiances I had at court, or elsewhere in Europe, would die with them. In short, this prince of Istoia was offering me his allegiance and protection. A bold and treasonous offer, but one I was not quick to dismiss.

We continued our conversation while we exercised our horses, but curiously, he requested that we remain in the fields adjacent to the barn, which I found suspicious but not alarming and therefore agreed. I suspected he may have hidden accomplices in the barn, but I was careful in our traversing to remain on the protected side of David. If there was to be an arrow shot from the barn it would be difficult to hit me, and my proximity to him meant that I could draw my hidden dagger at any time if necessary.

We discussed the workings of the court and I pressed him further to explain his sudden appearances and disappearances. He could offer no explanation other that in time he would explain more fully and that I would understand. He said that he did not want to lie to me and asked that I accept his explanation and that in good time I would know more. I protested lightly and demanded to know where his ship was since no one had seen it enter or leave the river, and although he promised that it was not hidden is some marsh in Kent, nor was it within firing distance of the coast. I accused him of not being truthful when questioned earlier at the audience and he admitted so and begged my forgiveness promising to be wholly truthful from that moment on but asking me to be tolerant when he refused to answer a question rather than lie to me.

I reluctantly agreed and as we rode the hedgerow, I pressed him further on Istoia and its location and the whereabouts of the other members of his embassy. I found it incredible that he had returned alone to London, and he corrected me saying that he had not returned but instead that he had never left. He claimed to have not been present over the past two months, but that he had maintained a close observation while his attendants had in fact departed and would not return until later. When I questioned him on the value on an embassy of one, he simply laughed and said that he possessed all the diplomatic powers necessary to convey the message he needed to, and that if granted another audience, that I would come to understand what he meant.

This was a boastful and evasive claim, and I felt that it was nonsensical to continue my conversation with him. He talked in parables and half-answers, providing no real intelligence to any of my queries. However, I remained intrigued and although my better judgement should have had me ride away long ago, I continued for several more hours until the sun grew quite hot, and I became tired of sitting on my horse.

We parted with the agreement to meet again the following day in the same location, and I left to return to the Tower and to give thought to the value of meeting him again. Even through his vagaries and evasive answers to my questions I was able to glean some intelligence about Istoia and even about the man himself, just enough to keep me interested in the conversation. His descriptions of Istoia seemed quite aggrandized, or even utopian—a word Thomas More had been using as of late— meaning almost too perfect to be true, at least to my way of thinking. As he described it, Istoia was a center for learning with all children being taught to read and write from a very young age. And he talked of something he called *science* which seemed to me to be different than but related to the Latin word *scientia*. A word not in our common usage but meaning a type of *knowledge through experience*, perhaps like his earlier use of the word enlightenment.

He talked of science being at the root of both health and religion, and surprisingly, that it defines their idea of religion— claiming to have borrowed much of this philosophy from the Mohammedan. How this was possible?

I did not understand this connection between health and religion, and besides, he stated, the discussion of which would have required many more hours and he was reluctant to elaborate, even with my prodding. Instead, he offered a simplified explanation by claiming that all faiths had a common God, and although he and his brother professed to adhere to Christian tenets, like ours, they also sought the wisdom of Mohammed and the children of Moses, seeing no value in judging the conscience of any man or woman. Taking from each religion that which suits them best.

He seemed particularly focused on the health of his people. Stating that science, his word again, helped them to prevent diseases and to treat common ailments. He reminded me that London once had clean running water and the cloaca maxima to carry waste away from the city and to the river, but sadly it had collapsed or run to complete ruin like the cemetery. He talked of health as the basis for all happiness and that his people judged the value of their own governance by the ability to provide for a healthy life, one that included a right to an education and a free conscience. This philosophy, if I can call it that, is completely at odds to our own beliefs. We possessed a God-given right to govern and enjoyed the blessings of our birthright as a reward for our Christian piety. We are certainly not blind to the pain of others and can see the poverty and the excrement running in the street, but we also give alms, pray for those that need help, and give generously to the church.

He laughed when I told him this, calling me naïve and ignorant. I should have taken offense, but I had grown used to his slights and thought perhaps it was an issue of culture, like the French and their damned use of irony in lieu of humour.

Of the man himself I learned that he was one of three brothers and no sister. He claimed to have a close connection to his God, whom he assured me was the same as mine and even went as far to claim to know Jesus. This was mentioned in the most off-handed way so that I allowed it to pass as one might allow the ravings of a madman. He openly shared that they had been observing us for many years and that they had done so similarly with other courts in Europe. They had traveled as far east as Cathay and the spice islands but remained aloof there too, having no need of any trade.

The fact that they did not look for trade with the richness of the orient was highly discouraging. What then did they want of us when we were in no need to purchase their piety or benevolence? I stressed repeatedly that their notions of health and happiness, and their version of Christianity, was of no value to us without something tangible in return and yet he continued to rebuff this logic.

We concluded our conversation with one important question on my part. Why would I want to assist him in securing another audience? Besides the painful truth of my precarious place at court and my need to hedge a bet for my own preservation, what actual benefit would I gain from doing so? He answered by saying that it was a matter of life and death. Whose death he did not say, and that we should continue this discussion at our next meeting. This was not an encouraging answer, but rather than debate yet another enigmatic response to one of my questions we departed the same way we met. I turned my horse back to the path leading to the cemetery, leaving him in the field where I found him, and began a leisurely ride back to the city, all the while enjoying the late summer sun. I felt no more enlightened than when I had arrived, and not less better for it.

Chapter Seven

A Matter of Life and Death

My return the next morning to the cemetery, and the field beyond, was not done with any great urgency. I returned with some reluctancy having given great thought to what I had and had not learned the day prior. In many ways I had gained insight into the purpose of their embassy, but I remained skeptical, if not completely distrustful, of its intentions. I do not believe that human nature lends itself to the benevolence David claimed, no matter what the scriptures implore, since men simply do not abide by any canon other than self-preservation. Except maybe in the collective when warranted—such as war or crusade. David's sermon on health and science did resonate with my own thoughts on what rights all men should be entitled too, particularly the idea that one's conscience should be free of persecution. I, too, would like to see an end to war and poverty, but I did not believe in the possibility of utopia for England, or anywhere for that matter. It was simply not in our nature, and so I was not yet convinced of the truthfulness of his purpose here.

I had made a mental note of all the oddities in his stories, and even in the strange presentation of himself; he possessed a commanding presence and a genuine air of confidence. He was tall, and from what I could ascertain, well-formed and, I suspected would be a formidable opponent in battle. He had a handsome face and his once long hair had been shorn since his first audience and now was in the fashion of a convict rather than a prince. His garments, once again, were of the finest cloth and the leather of his boots, as well as that of his saddle and bridle, showed no sign of wear. His appearance in general was too perfect. He, like his stories, seemed contrived as if he fit the description of prince better than the look and comportment of an actual prince. He rode well, but not with the ease one might expect. He spoke of things as if he had simply read of them rather than experienced them, and even his horse seemed unfamiliar to him, or rather the horse seemed disconnected from him in some way. If I was to describe him to another I would do so as an imposter, or in the very least someone uncomfortable in his own skin.

On the day prior, I had questioned him about his use of language, and why, as he stated, he believed there was a commonality of languages between our two countries? Truthfully, I knew little of the origin of our own words, but I knew enough of our history to know that our language was unique to our island. While France, Savoy, and Spain all had related words from their Latin language of origin, we had adopted so many Danish and Celtic words that when married with our early Anglo-Saxon and subsequent Norman tongue it created a language not spoken anywhere else in Europe. Of course, we knew our Latin and some of us our Greek as well, and we spoke French at court more readily than English, but David gave no believable reason why he and his people spoke English.

I had also questioned him about where he was presently residing, and he had indicated a manor near Hackney, but proffered nothing more than its name which was unknown to me. I asked him how he knew of the cemetery, and he said that he had scouted it earlier, which begged the question of why he was so certain that I would agree to meet him after our encounter in the chapel? When pushed on this point he again answered affirmatively that he was simply confident that I would.

It was this mix of self-assuredness coupled with the lack of fit of his appearance that drew me back to the cemetery. Curiosity and intrigue. But this time I came armed with a level of intelligence and a clearer head than I had the day before. I was now prepared to be more forceful in my interrogation; whereas yesterday he had the upper hand having led me to a place and time of his choosing, today I was wiser and more determined to get genuine answers rather than just more questions.

I arrived early hoping to be there before he did. I was not able to do so, but not for lack of trying. I had intended to scout out the barn to see if there was anything of note contained therein, but David was already in the field when I arrived, in the same position atop as his horse as he had been the day before. Upon my approach he dismounted, leading his horse to one of the old oaks on the perimeter, and I joined him there alighting from my horse as well.

This was a much friendlier start the second day two of our conversation and it was very much welcomed on my part. Yesterday I had been unprepared for a lengthy parley and had not brought anything to eat or drink and so on this day I had with me a skin and some fine cheese and bread, and therefore was more prepared to engage in a profitable discussion, even if took the entire day.

His greeting was friendly, as was mine, and I did not have to inquire whether he had been uncertain of my participation again, since my arrival had now established a level of trust that extended in the very least to our agreement to meet if nothing else.

We allowed the horses to wander in the field and enjoy the

fallow turf while we took some refuge in the shade of the ancient tree and began our conversation where we left off the day before.

"Tell me, David," I began. "How is it that you expect me to advocate for another audience when your answers to my questions yesterday were so evasive? Have you come today with the intent to be more fulsome in your responses to my queries?"

I meant this as a condition of our continued dialog. I was emphatic in my ultimatum without being dismissive. He was quiet for a moment before responding, both of us watching the horses graze in the haze of the morning sun.

"I understand, and you have my assurance that I shall be as *fulsome*, as you request," he responded earnestly, sitting down in the duff of the oak, and inviting me to do so as well, I continued my questioning.

"Yesterday you talked of an urgency to your embassy, saying that it was a matter of life and death, and yet you are here alone which does not lend credibility to the seriousness of your threat. What reputable embassy is a single person, especially one that begs a wholesale commitment to a change in our manner of governance, and under threat of death no less?"

This leading question was direct and to the point. He lacked credibility and therefore so would I if I approached the king about another meeting.

"Once again, I understand. Our embassy will be complete, and of the utmost credibility, if so granted. It is our intent to present to your king and his councilors the reasoning behind our initial approach, and we will do so with great humility and without insult."

"And of life and death?" I asked once again.

Pressing him further, I asked him to carefully explain to me the precise purpose of his embassy. If not for trade, then what in return would they receive for our accepting their benevolence? And was this a threat or a warning?"

It was then that he began a long and fantastical explanation of the intent behind his warning. He begged my indulgence to allow him to start at the beginning—before he first approached the cardinal.

According to him, their previous forays into our kingdom, and those on the continent as well, were done only to observe and there had not been an intent to meddle in our business. He stated that it was common to spy on one's neighbors and he was blunt in his accusations that we too undertook such games of intrigue and therefore our taking of offense was at best feigned, at worse ignorant. I had to agree.

When I asked him why he chose us for first contact, he once again stressed the importance of our shared language. I asked for him to elaborate on how this was possible. He said that it was assumed that we had common ancestors but clarified that our language was similar and not quite the same and that he had taken years to learn our manners having been tutored by his spies from their years of observation. This was an insufficient explanation, so I pressed him further.

He said that they were pressed to make a choice between us and those kingdoms on the continent, and that they had weighed an embassy to Rome, but believed that they could build a relationship more readily with us than with the others. He talked of our importance to the future of the world and their belief that although we had not expanded our sphere of influence much farther than our own island having lost France not so long ago, that we were destined to be a great power.

This was obvious flattery. I told him that we had no colonies beyond our traditional holdings in Ireland, and even Scotland had rebuffed us, holding the border to our constant pressures. Portugal had put forth vessels that had followed the African coast and south, with talk of islands far out in the Atlantic, and our own spies told us that Spain had been entertaining for some time a major expedition to the Indies. We were not as important as we thought ourselves to be.

So why would I believe that they thought otherwise? Why did they feel pressed to contact us now? These questions were particularly troubling, since his statement implied that there was an outside pressure of some sort bearing on him. He admitted that they had intended to proselytize and that they understood that we might take offense, but they believed there was a Christian imperative to do so. Precisely because Spain and Portugal had entered the Atlantic, or soon would, and that Rome was surely at work behind them both.

Of course, there was a certain intrigue behind their motivation, how could there not be! When he spoke of the gifts they would bestow upon us what they expected in return was a front to their own borders and an ally against the expansionist desires of our Latin neighbors. This gift of enlightenment they promised would come at a heavy cost. If there was going to be war in the future, and this was a certainty, it is us who will bear the loss of men and fortune.

When I questioned him further on this, he admitted that war was a likely outcome and that there was no way to avoid many future conflicts. Feeling confident in the success of my interrogation so far, I proposed a break before continuing. I had taken the wineskin and the pannier from my horse before setting him free to graze and brought out the small amount of cheese and bread. I offered the skin containing a fine madeira to him, but he declined. I cut a piece of cheese and offered the bread so that he might break off a piece, but he declined this too. I was not offended, but surprised. It was offered in good faith, and quite frankly, a gesture of friendship. Sensing my concern, he quickly explained that he was in no need of anything to eat or drink, but that he was deeply grateful for the offer. I accepted his explanation but noted this breach of manners as yet another example of the peculiarity of his person.

We lay back for a while as the sun had now risen high enough to be completely blocked by the canopy of the tree and talked of small things. I learned that by title he was not really a prince, not in the sense that we understand. This was a revelation, but it lent some credibility to my own suspicions about his mannerisms. He informed me that he used this term to describe his elevated position as a means to relate to our understanding of the hierarchy of his people, based on our own social structure. He explained that the governance structure of his society had evolved over time to a representative form with the dissolution of individual rulers and the appointment, in a more collective sense, where responsibility was shared through direct participation of individuals by their own choice.

He explained that he had not intended to mislead, but to ease into understanding our differences. He clarified, upon noting my surprise, that they were not without leadership, but that self-determination of all men and women, and the elevation of any one person over another was by merit and not by birth. There was no absolutism in their governing structure, but rather a shared belief in common wants, and through a shared ownership of equity with the expectation that the needs of all could be met through collective efforts.

I was not ignorant of the democratic Greek traditions and the influence over own governance, however weak. I was also unconvinced of what he described might work in our society without chaos ensuing. Knowing one's place was the keystone to the bridge between all levels of our society. And when I explained this to him, he laughed and said that was the difference between he and I. He said that our acceptance of the divine right of one man to rule lacked reason and perpetuated our failure to grow intellectually, spiritually, and even physically. He described us, in comparison to himself and his people, as stunted like a plant lacking light and water, even though we had all the dung necessary for it to thrive.

He described our kingdom and those of Europe in the most unflattering terms, and all the while assuring me that we did not have to be this way—rather that there was an alternative and that proof was found in the Bible, not the Old Testament mind you, but in the teachings of Jesus. The proof he said was most clearly in the beatitudes, specifically instructing me to reread Luke and the Sermon on the Plain, and to pay particular attention to the woes. There, he said, I would find the enlightenment he promised, and not in the church of Rome or in the court of my brother, but in the recognition of my own hypocrisy and perjury. It was a harsh indictment, comparing me and my fellow nobles to the pharisees and worse, the lawyers!

He also talked of places in the far east, places I had never heard of, where the people believed outlandish things including the worship of idols with many arms and even many gods, saying that they too were more *enlightened,* his word again, than us. He talked of something called a lens, like an imaginary piece of glass through which he and the people of Istoia viewed the world— claiming that it provided a focus that reasoned more clearly the rights and obligations of each of them towards each other.

I understood the analogy, but I did not feel compelled by it.

I also wished for the health and well-being of all people, or more truthfully, I did not wish harm to anyone, but I did not see the need to make us all equal. Most curiously, he said that he was assured that we were capable of such reason and that he knew emphatically, without explaining how he knew, that we would one day come to view our world through the same *lens*.

I pressed him further on the governance of Istoia. Stating again my dismay for having been misled about his true status, he was still unbending in his justification for having lied. He repeated that he believed we were incapable of understanding the formation of his society at our first meeting, and that the purpose for seeking me out was to have me prepare the way for another audience once I understood better their purpose and intent. He believed that if he could win me over then I would agree to be his advocate. There was some logic in this approach, but this logic assumed that I could be sufficiently convinced of the benefit to me for to me to do so. I could agree with his view that we were corrupt and selfish and at the same time admit without shame that I enjoyed the privileges of my birth, even if my place at court was perpetually tenuous.

His explanation of the representative nature of his government led to a discussion about the capabilities of the common man and woman and whether they had the ability to comprehend what is best for them. I argued that people needed the wise guidance of those more learned than themselves, and he countered that this was self-serving and that it underestimated the intelligence of people who should be given the proper tools to reason for themselves. Once again, he used the word *reason* as if it was some inherent mental capability that everyone possessed, regardless of rank, arguing that all men and even women, had the ability to make logical decisions that went beyond their own self-preservation. When I disagreed, stating clearly that no kingdom or city state existed with any form of equity, he agreed and laughed while doing so, but countered that this fact was the precise purpose of his visit.

The question of what I would achieve by helping him further hung heavy all morning, and I was surprised to note how high the sun had risen and how quickly the day was passing. He had talked of my position at court, and I had to agree in his assessment even if I found it difficult to admit it to myself, but this was something that I had dealt with my entire life. None of his admonishments would change what I already knew about myself. What then, did he mean when he said that his mission was a matter of life and death? What precisely did he mean?

He readily responded that the answer was complex and that there were only a few people he could name with some confidence that were in immediate danger, but that ultimately the lives of millions of people were at stake. This was a fantastical statement and required a lengthy explanation, but he assured me his response was factful. Although it seemed to me more fantasy than plausible, again I questioned why I had given my time to this man. But what held me was his unwavering confidence that he knew things that we did not, and although I was apt to call him a charlatan, I had seen enough of the mysteries around him to wonder if there was some truth to his tales. And more importantly, when pressed again on who's life was in danger, he emphatically iterated what he had previously intimated. It was mine.

A Seer

In questioning myself what I had to gain by assisting David, I had considered rightfully that it was my own survival. When I asked how he could be so certain of my probable demise he confidently responded that he knows what will happen in the future by applying what he called 'reasoned thought and basic supposition'. I was skeptical of the idea, but I remained interested and encouraged him to continue his explanation. I had heard of mystics who professed to be able to predict the future and I knew that the common folk sometimes consulted the fairies, but the church frowned upon this, and you were just as likely to burned as a witch for seeking to know the future as you were for pretending to be able to predict it.

What I found strange about his claim was that he had yet to differentiate between knowing the future and his earlier claim that he was from an advanced society that had already achieved this enlightened future. It seemed reasonable to me that just because they had evolved to a particular state, that it did not necessarily mean that we would too. I could accept that Istoia had achieved more in terms of education, health, and even politic than us since I only had to look to the Irish to see our own advancement in a similar light. But to know our future assumes that he could predict the minds of men, and in particular, our most noble men. And that he was somehow able to contrive from them a rational logic that assured a particular outcome—these men who could barely sit around a table together without stabbing each other in the eye. This did not even consider the vagaries of the church, and irrationality of the women at court—who held more sway than was usually given credit.

He held firm to his statement, claiming that his people had used mathematics to create what he called an *algorithm*; an indescribable mental perambulation which assigned a number to each and every possible outcome in any problem. I did not understand what he meant, but I listened attentively, nodding along as he spoke. Numbers, he claimed, specifically the number one and something he called a zero (which was less than one, if that was even possible) were the key to viewing the future—that when arranged in an order that divided or multiplied (I could not comprehend his logic) they could thus be arranged to determine the probable outcome of any circumstance or query. He said that this philosophy of arranging numbers originated in the East and could be employed to near accuracy, but not perfection. This sounded like prophecy to me and perhaps something closely akin to witchcraft.

By their arrangement of the numbers, he said, it was a near certainty that the king would shortly lose his crown and that the lives of his sons were to be ended by their uncle—my own half-brother Richard—and my life was to end along with theirs. This was his immediate prediction, and that in the not-so-distant future there would be war after war in a manner so continuous that it would appear in hindsight as being endless. But, in the very distant future there would be periods of prosperity and peace; however, our want of avarice, hypocrisy and lustfulness for violence might ultimately lead to the destruction of all mankind. He talked of death and disease and raging wars that would render the land useless, and yet, he also said that it need not be. That the future could be altered by correcting behaviors in the present time, and that by rearranging the numbers they had been able to make choices that would affect profound change so that any near certainty could be avoided.

I played along with him, asking if it would be possible to prevent my death and that of my nephews by making corrections to our behaviors as he described them, and he said yes. This gave me some relief, but I still doubted whether the man was sane. I asked for some proof, as it seemed warranted given the fantastical nature of his claims. He said none could be given that would be convincing. Predicting the future, he said, presented a possibility that introduced a probability. Meaning, if you say it, you may do it and therefore make the possibility a probable reality. So, proof of the future is impossible, according to him. He said that by the same rational process of using numbers that he could observe the most private and secret actions in the history of any person. Although it was not the same as predicting the future it did prove, or so he claimed, that the algorithm worked.

I asked for this *trick* to be shown to me and he agreed, telling me without emotion that at my birth my father had sent all my mother's attendants and midwives from the room soon after I had been brought forth. Once they had departed, he took a pillow from the bed and smothered my mother until she died. He then took me, still wrapped in bloody linens, out of the room and handed me over to be given to a wet nurse. This was a shocking revelation and one I had not heard the slightest whisper of in all my years. I knew my mother had died while giving birth to me, but I had always assumed it to have been a natural death.

I did not respond immediately to this accusation, as in my astonishment I had no meaningful response to give. However, I did want to know how he thought he might prove this, but before I could ask, he informed me that one maid had remained in the chamber after all others had left. Rather than cross the duke she had hidden quietly, alone behind a curtain, too frightened to even make a sound. She had witnessed my father take the pillow and quietly and efficiently smother the mother of his child; a woman too weak from childbirth to put up a fight. Surprisingly, this maid was alive and still at court, watching me from the shadows for my entire life. Her name is Evelyn and although not noble, still held a place in my own sister-in-law Elizabeth's household. Old now according to David, but she could prove the accusation.

"You know her, you have heard this from her directly?" I asked.

"No, but I know she was there, and I know what she saw. We observed it too."

"But how?" I demanded angrily. "How could you observe when you said she was alone with my father and my mother?"

"You asked for proof of the algorithm, and this is the proof I have to offer, and the only one you are able to understand," he responded with the same smug assurance that he gave to all my queries. It was the only answer he was willing to give.

Elizabeth was on procession with Edward, so all her attendants including Evelyn would be as well. I would not see them until Michaelmas, so I asked David for the time to approach Evelyn and seek the proof he mentioned. He agreed and believed, as I did, that we had exhausted our dialog for the time being and agreed to part, but not before confirming our means of future communication. For my part I had not committed to press the king for another audience, and I would not do so until I had spoken with Evelyn. He said all messages could be sent to Temporal Hall in Hackney, the former manor house of a long dead Saxon family whose name I did not recognize. He assured me that I could easily find by riding to that part of the country, and so we parted amicably, but not without suspicion. I was certain that I was in no want of enlightenment, but I was in want of my head.

Chapter Eight

Normal

I was not far enough along in the transcription to draw many conclusions, but I was able to see the parallels between the king's half-brother and myself, and I recognize the shared skepticism and Robert's wariness to commit to accepting the so-called truths that David claimed to share. What was becoming evident to me, and perhaps to the young duke as well, was that not telling the truth and lying are the same thing, even though we try to believe it is otherwise.

David's arrogance did not mask the fact that he judged both the duke and me incapable of understanding the whole truth and therefore felt justified in giving us only bits and pieces of the story. I really knew very little of the correction—the *why me* or the *why* in general, and I suspect the duke knew nothing of the same. If I had learned anything so far it is that time is the same as distance to David; little has changed in human nature in seven hundred years. The duke and I are both viewed by David as ignorant rather than intellectually incapable, simply because we had not accessed the same knowledge that he had, through no fault of our own. I was no different to David than the members of the tribe in South America that I, myself, had experimented on.

My distrust of him was not because I didn't believe he was telling the whole and complete truth, which I was confident he was not, but because I think he is an asshole.

While contemplating our past conversations, I realized that he disregarded my confusion about his correction because he was certain that he was always a step ahead of me. Perhaps it was, because I originated the technology that he took for granted, that I would participate in his correction no matter what. My curiosity was always my undoing. I had to accept that this was most likely true, but what I wanted to know, and perhaps the book was the key, what was his motivation for the correction and more importantly, what the actual benefit was to me?

He had only given me vague references to death and destruction. Which, in my mind, was inevitable anyway, given the realities of our past and the politics of our current time whether I participated or not. Because of this I found myself living in a process flow-diagram with some unseen mind asking: if *this* then *what*? And what troubled me most was that he had advanced knowledge of the *this* as well as a program that gave him all the *what* at the speed of light. I had neither, except the fact that I knew what I didn't know, and I hoped the duke did too, but only the continued translation would tell.

It was no surprise to me, then when shortly before my departure from the office for the drive to Heathrow, that I was visited at my desk by two suits from upstairs. I knew my activities over the last week had exhibited some strange behavioral patterns that wouldn't go unnoticed. I lived my everyday life as if on camera and therefore I knew the risk in agreeing to meet David again in London. This meant that I would be seen with him, just as I assumed that I had been observed with him at the farmer's market in Austin. We had now met in public on two occasions, and it was most certain that my interaction with him and Sarah in the Hoxton bar had been closely observed.

160

Furthermore, I always presumed that my phone was monitored and that all my emails and texts were read by others, so the bosses had to know that Sarah and I had broken up. Any change in personal relationships warranted a questioning. What I couldn't assume was whether any of my conversations with David had been heard.

Assumption and presumption are not the same thing. We monitored all our staff's personal texts, emails, and calls, and therefore I presumed the same was true of me. What I did not know for certain was whether my personal space was bugged or if I was being surveilled, but I assumed for my own peace of mind that I was, even when I assured Sarah otherwise. It may be that I had never given any cause before for my superiors to suspect me of anything that would compromise our mandate, but I also knew that's not how it worked. They didn't wait for cause, they had too much invested in me and my lab to wait for me to fuck up.

The two MI8 guys came right to the point. They said they had me on CCTV entering the broom closet on the mezzanine and that I was in there for nearly forty minutes, and they wanted to know why.

I was prepared for this.

"I needed a place to be alone," I answered, knowing that they would press me for more details.

"Why the closet? And right after lunch since you had just spent an hour or so alone already?" One of them asked, giving away that I had been tailed.

"We're just trying to understand why you would spend forty minutes alone in a closet. And you were alone, were you not, sir?" Asked the other suit.

"I was, as you already know," I said, putting them on notice that I understood how this line of interrogation worked. "I just needed a quiet place, where I wouldn't be seen," leaning into them as they hovered over my desk, attempting to be discreet, "a place where I could be alone to have a bit of a cry. You see, my girlfriend and I, well, we had just broken up and I was struggling yesterday to control my emotions. I didn't want anyone to see me struggling in the lab. You can understand that, can't you?" I said, turning a question back on them.

They both stumbled to respond, put off guard by my drawing on their empathy.

"Wouldn't look very manly, would it?" I continued, "me crying at my desk."

I could see that they were made uncomfortable with my answer by their telltale grimacing. They were British after all. Any display of emotion or admittance to such was troubling to them. But more importantly, they most likely already knew that I was telling the truth about my breakup with Sarah, and they would already have inspected the closet and chances are they found nothing too suspect. I had cleaned up the mortar dust, and they would have had to carefully inspect for any noticeable changes in the stonework, and the amount of graffiti scratched on the walls would have made that unlikely. My embarrassing admission would be chalked up to yet another example of Yankee overfamiliarity. But just when I thought I was in the clear, they brought up David.

"And, so then, who was the chap you were seen with at The Hoxton?" The more composed one asked. "You were also seen with him in Austin, a couple of days before arriving in London."

My only hope of diffusing the situation was to draw them in with a bit more uncomfortable familiarity.

"Well," I said, "he's the reason we broke up," I replied, followed by a lengthy and affectively thoughtful pause. "You want more, or can we just leave it at that for now?"

It seemed to work. I could tell by the resignation in their faces. They were reluctant to press me any further to not embarrass me, or more importantly, them, any further. But I had been put on notice, which was the real purpose of the interrogation. We had to report changes in our relationship status and so I assured them that when I got back to the US that I would file the proper paperwork. But, in the meantime I begged their indulgence to let my fresh wound heal a little, requesting that they not embarrass me in front of my colleagues. The fact that others in the lab could see them at my desk was now reason enough to raise alarm. They agreed and left me to consider my next moves.

I knew that the only way to get out of the country, and safely back to Austin, was to act as normal as possible. I could do this, even with the added pressure of knowing that I was being closely observed for any changes in my behavior, movements, or communications. So, I kept my head down, concentrated on wrapping up paperwork, kept my interactions to a minimum and only left the lab to pee, and then doing so in the toilet located in my section of the lab. My training had prepared me for this, I could control everything about my actions today but the one wildcard was David, and I could not predict whether he would manifest and throw everything off. The fear of him projecting kept me on edge, but I couldn't show it and when I found myself looking around the lab furtively I had to make a mental correction. I was certain I had checked my watch a thousand times hoping the day would pass quickly, but at five pm I was still surprised to learn that my car was ready and waiting out front to take me to Heathrow. The day had, in fact, passed.

I left the lab and went through security, meeting the driver at the curb, and it took everything in my power not to look around and scan the street for David when I handed the driver my bag. It was imperative that I maintain an air of normalcy, and I knew that if I caught sight of him lurking on the pavement it would register alarm on my face, and that the CCTV cameras focused on me would pick it up. I remained calm, and without emotion. I slipped in the backseat, my briefcase in hand, and looked straight ahead while the driver stowed my bag in the boot, as they say in London.

Both the drive and the check-in at the airline counter was uneventful, and only His Majesty's Customs and Excise posed some concern when passing through the security gates. My briefcase was flagged for secondary inspection. This was common for me since the protocol was that we were always subject to extra scrutiny as a reminder to us that we were being watched. What was different this time was that my briefcase contained an old manuscript and not just a laptop and some papers. The secondary bag check consisted of them rifling through my carry-on suitcase, which had nothing but my dirty clothes and toiletries, but my briefcase was another matter.

The export of genuine antiquities required permits that were rarely granted except to museums and reputable dealers. This was not just for art, but for important manuscripts as well. Agents were typically used to clear customs on both sides of the pond, but David had already considered this when he presented me with the receipt from the bookseller in Covent Garden. There, in writing, on the receipt was an official stamp authorizing the sale of a fake, a non-genuine manuscript sold with the full knowledge of its worthlessness, purchased for a mere one hundred British pounds.

I had done as instructed and placed the receipt in between the cover and the first page, its official customs stamp clearly visible. Of course, this too could be a fake, but it didn't matter. The agent was not interested in complicating his day and an attempt at antique book smuggling would do just that. He was not interested in escorting me over to the Custom's desk for a lengthy chat about the validity of the receipt, or the reason why I wanted to purchase a fake manuscript. He was only interested in getting through his shift, and so I was ushered along to my plane with my bags and towards my exit from the UK.

I now had a singular mission, to complete the translation of the book and to find out what the correction was to be, and hopefully, why I had a role to play in it. I now knew that I was not the only one who was subject to an elaborate projection, and I was quite certain that David and his kind had been interfering in the future of mankind for centuries. But where in the history books does it mention this embassy, or a place called Istoia? David claims that the contents of the book are true and that it is the key to a correction that will prevent untold deaths. But again, I was most puzzled by what my role in all of this was.

I didn't understand the *how* completely, and the *why* was almost irrelevant given the realization that if they could do it to me, they could do it to anyone. It horrified me to think that the interference could be on an infinite scale, but I was heartened a bit by the opposite thought, that it could also be surgical and limited, but I had no way of knowing for certain, either way, at this point. What I did know was that that the technology my colleagues and I had developed was now being used to manipulate human activities at different times in our history, and this wasn't some sci-fi time travel bullshit. It was the harnessing of energy in its purest form to alter reality. I was hooked. I committed myself to completing the translation even if it would tell me things I didn't want to know.

Chapter Nine

Michaelmas

I caught up with the court at Warwick, having missed my intended departure date by no more than the two days I spent with David. The ride north was pleasant and dry, and it afforded me the quiet time to process the events of the past few months without worrying about my daily labours at the Tower. I departed with a limited number of my household and with the understanding that after Michaelmas the entire court would return to Windsor, and thus remain put for the yule season and the entirety of Twelfthtide. It was custom that as the autumn progressed that we resigned ourselves to hunting and generally getting fat, so this break beginning with Michaelmas was usually the happiest time in the calendar; however the court was never without politic or intrigue. Michaelmas was to be celebrated again this year at Warwick in yet another spiteful display by my brother of his dominion over the Lancastrians. Add to this the mystery of Evelyn and the quest for another possible audience for David meant that I had set for myself a decidedly challenging autumn, which was promising to stretch my ability to remain in favor worrisomely beyond my assumed capabilities.

The king's mercurial response to even the slightest perception of disloyalty was well founded. His crown had never sat tight upon his head. I may privately lament my own place to my detriment, but my brother properly wallowed in suspicion and retribution. So much so that our other brother Richard remained away from court and ensconced at York for most of the year. I, too, remained aloof as much as possible while quietly squirreling away a fortune with bankers in Savoy to support my own exile, if ever necessary. Edward had no such luxury as he had nowhere to go, and by his own admission had not married well enough to properly secure his throne.

So, how was I to approach him with another embassy, even if Evelyn was able to give credence to what David had claimed about my mother's death, without angering him? He had not suffered too great an embarrassment when the last embassy whisped away like the smoke from a snuffed candle, but David's arrogance and self-assured superiority had been unchanged in our subsequent meetings, and I had no confidence that it would not be the same if he was presented to the king again.

Establishing a reason for the next audience would have to wait until I had met with Evelyn and discovered the truth of David's claim. If, in fact, she had witnessed my father murder my mother, she might be able to provide some intelligence on David. Perhaps he had made appearance back then as well. Finding her was not difficult. Elizabeth's household was by far the largest at court and her ladies were constantly floating about. So, after a few short words in the right ear I was able to locate Evelyn in one of the wardrobes, in what was now the queen's apartment at Warwick Castle, having recently been abandoned by the earl's family when they fled to France.

She was now quite elderly and had been relegated to needlework, which I found her doing by the late afternoon light of a leaded pane, in a dimness that would tax even the youngest eyes. She rose as I entered, but offered no greeting, not even a curtsy. She knew exactly who I was and had an air about her as if she had been expecting me for some time.

"You know me, Evelyn?" I asked assuredly.

"Of course, my lord," she answered, her voice strong and without fear. She had survived long enough at court to know a genuine threat when one approached.

"Do you know why I am here?" I enquired while moving towards her, taking up a small stool and motioning for her to return to her own seat at the window.

She didn't answer right away but squinted her eyes as if to focus on me better before responding.

"You need something mended, my lord?" She asked with a smile, not trying very hard to hide her mirth.

"Not with your needle," I said, laughing a little myself while pretending to inspect my cuff, "but I have a small hole in a story that needs a patch."

"I see, but I only work thread my lord. Stories are for bards and those that jest."

"Perhaps so," I replied, recognizing that this was going to be a bit of a game. "But this story is not a tale or a eulogy, it's more of a recollection from a long time ago."

She looked at me quizzically, her eyes squinting again as if I had gone out of focus.

"I have many recollections at my age, things I've heard, things I've seen."

I could tell that my usual abruptness was not going to win over Evelyn, and although I had very little patience for verbal games, especially from servants, I had warmed to this old woman's attitude almost immediately.

"I am told that you were once in attendance to my mother, is that true?" I asked a leading question rather than jumping right in and asking whether she was in the room when I was born.

If she was present at my birth, she might be one of the last connections I might ever have to my mother because none of her family is known to me. Since her place at court, as it was told to me, was that of a very minor lady in the household of the duke's rightful wife. She left no mark or trace of her existence. Once found to be pregnant it was more than likely that she would have been whisked away to give birth under the watchful eye of some menacing steward. Her only hope for a future tied to a convent somewhere far from the duchess' view. All that I know of her is from the taunts of my half-brothers when we were younger, and so my approach to Evelyn was with some faint hope that I might also learn more about my mother's life, and not just her death.

"Ay, I knew your mother for a short while," she offered, not taking much of my lead.

"What can you tell me of her?" I pressed lightly.

"She came to Windsor whilst heavy with child, for her confinement. I attended her along with some other of the ladies. She was not much more than a child herself when I knew her."

I didn't know my mother's age at my birth and cannot say that I ever even considered it. I had no likeness of her and had never heard her described other than as a whore and the devil's bitch by my half-brothers, as boys are wanting to do when scrapping.

"What did she look like, if you can recall?"

"Fair," she responded. "Like you, but ever so slight. Pretty, Too pretty for her own good," she responded while simultaneously crossing herself, as if in atonement.

"And her nature, was she a kind woman?" I asked, hoping to coax a bit more from her recollection.

"Woman. She was barely a woman, as I said. She could not have been more than fourteen when she arrived. And she came to us under some threat, and of course there were rumors, but it was not by my business. You ask of her nature? Well, her nature got her a baby. So, you tell me."

I pondered that for a moment while Evelyn pretended to continue with her mending.

"How did you know to find me?" She asked, without making eye contact.

"A ghost told me," I answered with some truth.

"Is that so," she responded without alarm but with a definite register as she lifted her gaze from her needle and looked at me while making sign of the cross, again, with her free hand.

"Do you believe in ghosts?" I asked.

"Ay, I have seen many myself," she answered, continuing "and what did this ghost tell you?"

"Very little, as ghosts are wanting to do, but he did say that you were kind to my mother. And that you attended my birth." I lied; I had no knowledge of whether she or anyone was ever kind to my mother.

"It was a He, this ghost? I know of no manly ghosts that might know of your birth," she responded, a slight hint of irritation in her voice. Her eyes were now fixed intently on mine.

I pressed her again to confirm that she had, in fact, attended to my mother. She admitted so since such knowledge might be unspoken of but not unknown. I also asked her about the circumstances of my birth, and who else might have been present. Her responses to my questions were evasive, and rightly so. I could appreciate her wariness to talk with me since the success of her long life was based on her ability to avoid traps like the ones I was setting. This interrogation may have been unrecorded but every answer she might gave to my queries might lead to treason if she even as much as whispered a slight against my noble father or his long dead rightful wife. My own mother's mention was of no concern to her.

She danced around the issue of whom else might have been present, naming some ladies whom I had not known and perhaps were real or imagined, or perhaps retired from court or dead. I needed to get more to the point but risked frightening her further with talk of ghosts. I had no other means to convey the mystery of what only she could know If in fact she was the lone witness in the room. So, I pressed on.

"Evelyn, you are safe with me and whatever you say here will go no further than this chamber," I assured her. "But, I must speak of some deeply troubling things, things I have been told but cannot know if they are true, however I am told you can."

She crossed herself again.

"A ghost of a man, you say?" she repeated herself.

"Yes, or at least what I know him to be," I answered, wishing I had chosen a different plan of attack as this conversation seemed to be mired in ambiguity.

"Might it be the ghost of your own father?" She asked and I was thus certain that she knew where I was headed.

"No, I am certain of that," I responded, "another man, one that says he too was in the room when my mother died, hidden too, along with you as you hid behind a heavy curtain, silent and watchful."

"It cannot be. It cannot be," she said incredulously, her voice raised slightly but not enough to attract any attention from those passing outside the door.

"I also cannot understand how it can be, but I am assured that you were there and this ghost, unseen himself at the time, told me that you saw something terrible. Is it not true, Evelyn?"

Her hands were trembling and her brow beneath her wimple

was furrowed with fear. I knew then that I need not press her any further. I had my answer and tried to assure her that she need not respond anymore. I told her that no answer was necessary, since none could be given that would explain how I knew to find her with any plausibility on my part, and that her secret was safe. She may have had no reason to believe me, but she also had no choice. Her life meant little to anyone and one word from me and she would be removed from service or sent to the Tower, and both meant certain death for her.

I felt terrible for having inflicted such pain on an old woman and attempted to draw some more pleasurable conversation from her, but it was too difficult. She was now wary of me, and I could see that I had caused a great worry for her. I had hoped to know more of my mother, but I was resigned to the fact that she would not share any more of her and talk of ghosts and murder would not bring forth any more information. Evelyn was visibly distressed and pretended to continue her stitches while I excused myself, departing the chamber resigned to the fact the my very own father had in fact murdered my mother.

This did not countenance to my own memories of him, in which he was mostly kind and always benevolent in my safe keeping. I had few protectors in my youth, but the duke's acknowledgement of my paternity ensured that in his lifetime I enjoyed similar benefits of his natural sons, and upon his death I gratefully gave fealty to Edward in exchange for further protection; I received no threat and gave none. He himself may not have been a king, but he raised his sons as princes with all the comfort that afforded. I can say that I have wanted for nothing in my life having understood and accepted my place in the family, and this too was a form of resignation.

But the question remained. If David, as he claims, has

proven his ability to predict the future by showing me the truth of my past, was I then obliged to arrange another audience for him? I believed that the threat of my own imminent death was not reason enough to compel me to do so without investigating further the precise messaging he hoped to convey. But if his second audience failed, I was also doomed. It was plainly evident that I had only one hope for survival and that was a successful second embassy. The terms of which remained to be determined, but they would have to be to my benefit.

Temporal Hall

A letter was sent by rider. It was plain and to the point. I acknowledged that Evelyn, without naming her, had confirmed to my sufficient reckoning some truth that might warrant my support of another audience. I stressed that this non-committal offer required a complete accounting of the exact messaging that he intended to convey to the court prior to any formal agreement on my part. This commitment demanded a detailed explanation, in writing, of all that was to be said and more importantly, what was going to be requested of the king. Only once received by me would I give my final ascent. I believed that I could not be clearer in my opinion and had committed to myself that I would be unwavering in my decision.

One benefit to sending the message was that I was now able to spy on the manor in Hackney where David lodged. I had given the rider instructions not to tarry, but once arrived in Hackney, he was to scout the area and without raising suspicion and find out from the locals all he could about the manor's occupants. Only then should he proceed to deliver the message, requesting of David that he remain until a response was readied for his return delivery. It was my intent to gather as much intelligence as I could—given the limitations of time and distance while the rider waited for a response.

It was just a few days after the rider's departure from Warwick that he returned empty handed, but not without some intelligence. From his scouting he had learned that the manor and surrounding lands were mostly unoccupied, with few retainers except for the farmers who paid rent on the surrounding fields, and a steward who along with his wife and young son maintained the house in what was described as 'managed disrepair'. The rider learned the home was Saxon in origin and had changed little over time. No additions had been made in living memory, and much of its exterior retained its original timber and plaster, but with a front façade of stone which had been added in the time of Henry Bolingbroke. It too showed great wear.

The rider was able to confirm that the manor's lord was thought to be away in the Low Countries, and because of that he was rarely seen, but he often received deliveries of all manner, attracting much attention by the farmers who were willing to speak on condition of anonymity and coin. The steward was particularly apt to gossip with his neighbors and had let slip that great quantities of steel plate had been delivered recently, as had copper skein pulled thin and wound about great spools. Items of cloth in varying sizes, which was thought to be very expensive was kept in the wardrobes, but little other furnishings were maintained except the basics. Few visitors were reported, save for a handful of craftsmen who had been seen about the place a few months back. Rumor had it that they were Frisian, and master armorers at that.

The rider had been able to enter the manor to deliver the letter and although he had passed no further than the hall, he had noted that the space was clean with fresh rushes on the flagstone, but no fire burning or evidence of a recent one was visible in the hearth. The steward claimed, firmly, that there was no reason for the rider to wait for a response since he had no knowledge of his lord's return, but that he could assure him that all messages that were received were delivered but offering no explanation how. The rider had no alternative but to return empty handed, but not without first scouting the outbuildings and noting that the barns were well kept and that the horses were of rare quality. There was ample straw and good feed, and that the yards were not short of fowl, although he did not see any oxen. In all, his assessment that the lord was absent, which was not unusual, and that the manor was kept as best as could be expected given the limited number of retainers present.

I was pleased with his report but sorely disappointed at not receiving a direct response from David. I now suspected that the confidence I projected in my letter was misguided, or in the very least naïve given what I already knew of the man. My bravado was reliant upon him being there to receive it, and his absence rendered the immediacy of a response null, and consequently my bravado was neutered in the most abrupt manner. Which was not unlike all of our conversations to date.

This left me to wait, and to use the time to gauge the king on his willingness to entertain further conversation about Istoia. He had chosen to ignore the past embassy and not even question the departure of the ship or the disappearance of its envoys. I knew him to be a man of little curiosity, but to not investigate either made me think that he was more confident in his own ignorance than he was able to admit the embarrassment of his own failed diplomacy.

It was not that the embassy had been forgotten completely, but rather it had been relegated to just another entertaining court interlude, one which showed more poorly for the cardinal than for the king. I imagine that there was some comfort in this for him, and very little for the rat. It was a certainty that every court in Europe, and of course all of Rome, had heard of the prank and was delighting in the cardinal's comeuppance. But this quick dismissal of the embassy did not erase the very real memory of our own guards being repelled by some unseen force when they tried to apprehend the prince and his attendants. Nor did it erase from memory the giant steel ship that menaced the Tower. Although the court feigned a short memory it was a certainty that all were wary that it might reappear. The king would be as well, even if he cared not to show it, and it was this wariness that I hoped to target. This was of no real consolation to me, since my responsibility was in defense and not intrigue, but they were not exclusive of one another. The cardinal, and to some extent Norfolk, had a greater responsibility than me for diplomacy, which was in fact a form of high intelligence, but neither had shown any capacity for it. Our brother Richard also showed interest, but only as much as would benefit him, and although I had seen him at Warwick we had not spoken and we would not, unless compelled to by Edward, which was unlikely. So, this left me to ponder alone the next possible steps for the renewed embassy given the fact that I had not received a reply from David for some weeks.

A smarter man might have concluded that I was on a fool's errand, having broken my own commitment to receiving an explicit description of David's messaging before proceeding. But Michaelmas was ending and with the winter creeping in we were soon to alight to Windsor, and any hope of a diplomatic mission would have to wait until spring. Granted there was no hurry required here, except that which was compelled by my own curiosity.

Court happenings were very prescribed and often time consuming due to the constant ceremony of state. Council met daily and the bishops were always in need of attention. But with all the daily business there was still time for sport and merriment, and this kept the court occupied as the weather began to grow colder and the days shorter. Edward was not a man known to feast, but he enjoyed the hunt, which gave me opportunity to spend time with him alone. We rode together most days while at Warwick often using the quiet interludes between the chase and the kill to talk of business. We had spent our childhoods together at Rouen, and although six years older than me we had kept close company for most of our lives, and this ease of confidence allowed him to speak freely of his troubles when we were alone together.

He also relied upon me to speak frankly with him, something our brother Richard was incapable of doing. I think this trust we shared since childhood alienated Richard, and led to the discomfort between the two princes that grew from a normal boyish competitiveness into genuine animosity in manhood. I felt neither for both men, and where Richard simply dismissed me as a non-threat, and therefore had little interest in me. Edward kept me close, perhaps as a buffer to Richard, and certainly as a buffer to his council.

I used our rides together to ease the conversation towards the embassy. Finding him occasionally, but cautiously, open to the discussion I asked one morning if he gave it much thought. He admitted that he and Elizabeth had discussed it, and in particular the circumstance of the disappearance of the prince and his attendants. When I questioned him about his thoughts on the ship he grew agitated and turned the conversation back to me, demanding that I explain what I had done since its departure, to prevent future encroachments on the Tower. His deflective posture was normal and although accusatory in tone, it belied his true feelings of confused apprehension.

Elizabeth believed, he said, that the three men were tricksters or magicians of a sort, and that they had tried their luck at gaining favor in some scheme to enrich themselves. I acknowledged that I too had considered that, but that the whole event was too clever and if, in fact, it was a fraud it smacked of a higher intellect. Perhaps one that should not be so easily dismissed simply because of personal discomfort with the truth.

This conversation did not come easily, and my summary here hides the protracted nature of it, as well as the reticence of the king to engage in the topic. I had no intention of proposing the second audience at this time, but I was aware that I might need to establish a reason for bringing the idea up later, and so any steps I might make in preparing his mind towards such an event was eagerly taken. I was careful not to cross him or press him to deeply on the subject, but I did get him to acknowledge that it might be beneficial to be proactive in securing some greater intelligence on the matter, and when he finally agreed I admitted to having some knowledge of the manor at Hackney and its possible connection to the embassy.

He was surprised to learn of this but not alarmed since I was obliged to protect the crown by whatever means. This gave me an opening to advise him of a plan that I first began to fashion when David failed to respond to my message. I shared with Edward that I had sent a scout to the manor and learned that it was empty save for some servants, and that it was my intent to ride to Hackney on our return to London and interrogate them myself. I did not mention that I had met with David now on three more occasions and that one had been in his private chapel, nor did I mention the letter I had sent. I knew that sharing this with Edward was risky, since if he wanted to supplant my efforts and have his own men ride to Hackney, it was possible they would find the letter, and then I would have to come up with a plausible excuse that would allow me to keep my head. But I also knew that his own embarrassment prevented this from happening and my offer was accepted on the condition that I go in secret, adding that he would share this with Elizabeth and no one else.

The court's withdrawal from Warwick began on the Nones following Michaelmas, I too followed suit, but broke away at Oxford with two members of my own guard for company. Riding east at a much greater pace than the weighted train of majesty that was snaking its way to Winchester for at least several more weeks before it would arrive at Windsor.

My own journey was a hard ride with little rest except to change horses and to break for sleep and sustenance. Arriving in Hackney in just a few days, we immediately set about to locate Temporal Manor having only a vague notion of where it might lay from the information provided by my messenger, luckily the local farmers were more than willing to share its location without my guards having to menace them too greatly. We set upon the house and found it just as described, perhaps less well managed than I imagined, its grounds overgrown with blackberry, but it seemed sturdy enough.

Upon entering it was evident that, as the previous rider had found some weeks earlier, David was not in residence and the only occupants were the steward and his family. Having announced my presence, the guards beckoned the steward, his wife and son, into the hall and bade them attend me with all the fealty a bastard son of a Yorkist duke warranted. They had no reason to recognize me or my ducal authority without being told to, but they were schooled enough in the recognition of rank to assume the correct posture.

The steward proved himself quite stubborn and although he was sufficiently deferential to my status, he provided little insight into his lord and feigned ignorance of most of my queries. The wife, a plump woman with a sturdy countenance, was more forthright and admitted without cajoling that they served an absent master who paid them well. He kept them in some comfort with a promise of land of their own in the future if they were keep the manor well and maintain their distance from the other farmers and the nearby village.

She proved herself more garrulous than her husband and I could tell from his visible unease that he was displeased with his wife's loose tongue, but this did not stop her from talking. She was right to assume, without having to be told, that her present circumstance in my company required as much honesty on her part as she could muster. My questions were not too taxing, and I attempted to query with an air of friendliness since I had no intention of harming these people. Having won her confidence, or at least with her practical reading of the situation, she soon offered more than I expected to receive.

They had been in service for no more than two years, coming from Billingsgate, and having secured the position randomly from one of their master's retainers. They claimed to know little of the him and even the history of the house was vague to them. They kept to themselves, as directed, admitting that the low rents kept everyone happy and inclined to respect the privacy of their master.

I had had the rolls checked and the manor had not been in arrears since before the fourth Henry's reign. I also had noted that no noble family had been at court from this area since perhaps the conquest, and this was likely given the unimportance of the place; it was small by noble standards and the lands held by grant from the crown did not come with any title. Since the present court cared nothing for the gentry in this small corner of the realm the manor and its occupants were nearly invisible to those that mattered.

She described the landlord as absent and was corrected by her husband who had suddenly warmed to the discussion sensing rightly that my present favor was better warranted than that of his master. After seeing no harm had come to his wife for her loose tongue, he too joined the conversation. I immediately pegged him for a coward. Nonetheless, he corrected her by saying that the man they knew as David Temper was not *absent,* but away on business, most likely in the Low Countries, and that he made himself present with some regularity and always without warning.

According to the wife he arrived, often alone, at night and not on horseback. When questioned about companions or other attendants she made it clear that it was rare for him to travel accompanied by others, but not unheard of, and she was usually glad of his arrival with companions since it gave her some labor. It bothered her that the master never seemed to eat what she prepared, and the ale she left always went untouched. Amusingly, she said he even emptied his own chamber pot—claiming never to have found one full.

This was surprising to me as well, but it followed logically what I knew of the enigmatic nature of David. During the times we had spent together he did not partake of any sustenance when offered. This contrasted with the dutchmen that the steward said arrived unannounced several months ago; armorers of great size and appetite who set about the steel plate they had brought from Rhineland, producing a large rectangular coffin-like object containing copper, and small glass pieces that had come from Venice some weeks prior to their arrival. The purpose of the coffin was unknown, even to the dutchmen, but well-illustrated for them and their manufacture with drawings on vellum left for them by the master.

The wife was particularly intrigued with their appetites, which held no interest for me or her husband. When I questioned them on their speech, I was assured that they were from the lowlands across the channel, since the steward pointed out having been raised in Billingsgate, he knew all manner of speech by ear.

I asked to be shown the steel coffin and was told it wasn't at the manor. When questioned further, the farmer admitted that it had been loaded on a wagon and pulled to an abandoned farm also owned by the master, not but a half day's ride. When I asked if the farm was near the old Roman cemetery, he said with some surprise at my question, that it was. According to the dutchmen, the coffin had been left in a barn, or shed, on the edge of an abandoned field. Thereafter, the dutchmen left the manor and had not returned, nor had the wagon carrying the metal coffin they had constructed.

When questioned about their master's recent visit they confirmed to me that it corresponded to my latest encounters with David. When I asked if they had seen and spoken with him since his departure, they said they had not. When I asked for my letter back, having explained that the recent rider had been sent by me, they were visibly disturbed and grew quiet. To my surprise, it was the young boy who offered an explanation for their reticence, having not spoken a word during the entire interrogation he seemed eager to add to the story. He explained with great conviction, perhaps sensing the danger for his parents of a missing letter from me, that the parchment had been burnt, but not by any of them.

Curiously, he informed me that all papers left for David were always placed on a table in an anteroom off the main hall, per strict instructions. There they remained until they didn't any longer. This was a confusing explanation, but the boy continued, adding that the remnants of paper and vellum could be found some days later in the hearth, burnt to ash but still discernable as the correspondence I had mentioned. Since they never lit fires in the anteroom it was assumed David came and went unseen. It was evident to me that they accepted this unusual activity as a condition of their employment, and although strange and perhaps unnerving even to me, it affirmed my belief that people were capable of the accepting the strangest of circumstance given the right reward.

At the conclusion of the interview, I was left feeling that I could not even have thought to ask the questions that derived such a strange tale. Metal coffins and burnt messages? It was like a ghost story told at Christmas. But I could see it was very real to the servants and sharing their story with me had intimidated them to the point that even the boy had felt it necessary to talk in defense of his parents. I did not want to burden them any further. So I departed with the intent to return to the Tower, but not before stopping at the field where I had met David to confirm if, in fact, the coffin was in the shed. If so, what purpose did it serve?

Chapter Ten

Christmas (Twelfthtide)

The ride to the field did not prove entirely fruitless. The shed may have been largely empty save for the remnants of an old cow crib and some moldy hay, but upon inspection I noted the faint footprints of several soft soles visible in the dried mud of the floor, as well as tracks left by a wagon. Of course, there was no way to know if the foot and wheel prints coincided in time with my own visit to the adjacent field. But I had my suspicions that they were from one in the same. The description provided by the steward of the dutchmen, and their transport of the coffin seemed too coincidental to be unrelated to why David had selected this location to meet me. I added this bit of information to what I knew of the man already, and although the picture was growing larger it was not growing much clearer. In summary, he arrived and departed as if he was a ghost, he had some power to repel when being apprehended, he had some relationship to metallic objects, he burnt his messages, he never seemed to eat or drink, and he was consistently evasive and yet all the while claiming to be truthful.

He is an enigma to be sure, and yet he is *not* unknowable; he had revealed some, but not many, personal details of his life and he had spoken candidly of Istoia. He had talked of his most-Christian mission, and he had admitted that the altruism he proffered on behalf of his country was really in exchange for a defense treaty of sorts, or at least that is what I assumed he had intimated. I surmised that at his core that he was no different than all men and as such subject to the same needs and wants that dictate every man's actions: avarice, wantonness, pride—these were the characteristics that truly defined a man, and I was certain that he was no different. But, I didn't know was when he would reveal himself again, and so I set about preparing myself for the eventuality.

Edward had shown himself cautiously open to possibly receiving David a second time, but I believed it would need to be a private audience, perhaps with just myself and Elizabeth and of course some guards in close proximity. Just as Elizabeth had proposed once before.

I had requested, no demanded, that David give me a written response to my message, so I might know what he intended to say, and I was determined that I would not proceed too deeply with my plans until I received it, but since David had a habit of appearing without notice, I couldn't risk being unprepared. This meant that I had to stay close to Edward at court, although I relished the independence my residence at the Tower provided me, I found myself, reluctantly, with the court at Windsor well before Christmas.

I had not discussed David with Edward since Warwick, and no one on the council mentioned him or his embassy, and yet I found myself constantly looking over my shoulder for any sign of David. Whenever I entered the newly renovated St. George's chapel, I felt compelled to search the shadows for any sign of him, and even in my own apartment I worried that he might be hiding behind a tapestry or a bedcurtain. I even found myself peering behind cupboards for no good reason. The quiet portended nothing, and yet as much as I worried about when he might appear again, I found myself wishing for him to make himself known. The suspense was torture, and no amount of feasting and music could temper it.

I was not idle during this time. I had the Exchequer search the rolls for the full accounts of Temporal Manor and was surprised to learn that the estate dated back to the eleventh century and had once been prominent in the region of Hackney. The Saxon family that owned the place had died out, but not before the crown had pocketed it for neglect of its levies. I suspect it may have been more political than that since our Norman forefathers were not particularly kind to their Saxon subjects. The crown then let it by charter, and for a significant amount, to a family named Temper—the surname that the steward had used for David. This was well over one hundred years ago, and yet no other court record appears in the years since. All taxes were paid in full and had been done regularly and without any recorded debt or late payment. It was if the manor and its occupants existed in obscurity, no easy feat in a land so challenged by intrigue and upheaval.

A spy had been sent again to Hackney and reported no unusual activity, with only the steward and his family in residence. Further attempts at engaging with the tenant farmers brought forth no new information and it was not for lack of coin being dropped. I was assured that there was simply nothing to report, but I kept the spy in place anyway, with the hope that David might make an appearance.

It was thus a week or so before Christmas, when the hunt had all but stopped, that I finally received my response from David. My spy returned with a sealed parchment and admitted that he had been sought out by the steward and presented it for delivery to me. Apparently, the spy was not a very good one, and the steward had no difficulty locating him lurking in the blackberry thicket. He returned directly to Windsor and found me, along with the others, in full festive spirit. Our days had been full of drink, masquerades, and feasting even though Advent had not ended, and I had even allowed myself to temporarily relax my mind of thoughts of David. This ease was broken the moment the parchment was placed in my hand and when I noted the seal script and name of Istoia clearly imprinted in the wax.

The excitement of having received the parchment was almost too great for me. I immediately retired to my chamber and set upon it in earnest, not stopping to light a lamp and used the dim winter light from, the oriel by which to read it. It was in French this time and it began with some typical diplomatic verse that held no interest for me. It spoke of brotherhood and Christian peace and of the need for an allyship to combat common enemies—name unstated—but enemies nonetheless, and the request for another audience the terms of which were clearly spelled out as I had requested.

David, on behalf of his king, would candidly and without pretense of malice speak of a shared allegiance and offer specific gifts of knowledge for improved health and politic, all for the preservation of a common love of God and his son Jesus Christ. It mentioned, once again, enlightenment. But not as the vague idea offered before. But specifically in terms of intelligence about England's place in the world, and our relations to our brethren across the channel, with the intent to provide competitive benefit to us. It concluded with assurances of peace and truthfulness with no injury to the king's majesty.

Admittedly, the reply was short on specifics, but it provided the assurances that I had asked for. My return response was drafted immediately and sent the next day by the same rider as the previous delivery. Knowing that the king would be tired of the festivities by the sixth of January I proposed that David attend court at Windsor with some haste, but to not come directly. I gave him the location of the parish church at Boveney and the name of the priest that could be found there. He was to wait at Boveney for an escort who would bring him to meet the king with the express understanding that his audience was not an embassy and that he should bring attendants for legitimacy. All must come unarmed, and with the full knowledge that he had no diplomatic standing. I stated further that he need not respond by return rider with the unwritten understanding that his arrival would be made known to me by the priest, and conversely, as would his failure not to respond.

This left me some days to prepare the king for David's arrival, and I began by requesting a private audience with him on the feast day of Saint John, knowing that he would be ready for a break from the festivities of Twelfthtide. He had low tolerance for extended feasting, and in particular, a distaste for excessive drink and gluttony, but he knew the power of the circus to keep court happy and free of treason. He maintained a level of reserved decorum not often shared by his predecessors and Elizabeth followed, dutifully, his example. With the court otherwise engaged in music, plays and drunkenness I believed I could successfully arrange a private audience unnoticed by the council, and most importantly, unnoticed by the water rat.

I sent a message to the priest at Boveney telling him to expect a visitor and to give him comfort. I requested notification of the visitor's arrival and for the priest to detain the visitor until an escort arrived to bring him to the castle. I gave strict instructions that this was all to be done in secret, knowing full well that this part of the directive was not required. The priest had the finest communion plate of all the surrounding villages as gifted by me and it had been well earned over the years for similar favors.

Edward's agreement to meet David again was given reluctantly—as I suspected it would be—however, I had enlisted the help of Elizabeth who softened his resolve with the promise of participating herself. I was confident that between the three of us we would be able to engage in an intelligent discussion with David, and precisely ascertain his true intents. Without the noise of the court, we would be able to parley without ceremony, and perhaps set the stage for further engagements. I had not set much hope of Edward's formal acknowledgement of Istoia, but I was confident that without repairing the damage done earlier that any future dealings between the two nations would be impossible. Edward had been humiliated previously, even if he chose to pretend that it never happened, and so this meeting required humility on David's part, and I was intent on encouraging him to beg forgiveness at the outset.

I had made a personal investment in this meeting as a hedge against a bet in a game in which, admittedly, I had a minimal understanding of the rules. I am not naturally a gambler. It is not that I am opposed to the occasional wager when I believe the odds might be in my favor, but my general reticence to gamble is well known at court, so much so that I am rarely invited to cast dice with the other men. But in this case, I had been told by David that the success of his audience might guarantee my own survival, and that of Edward's family. Which, if he is to be believed, the present odds disfavored. I could not know this to be true and the talk of his algorithm seemed too fantastical to have any genuine plausibility, but I needed this hedge against the uncertainty of the wager.

I had a genuine fear of re-introducing David to Edward. I worried that he, once again, would speak these things in an insulting manner. If I had learned anything in my dealings with David so far, it is that his self-assuredness could easily be mistaken for condescension. It was not an endearing trait, and although I had accepted the tone of his delivery as amusing, I knew Edward did not. I was also fearful that he might share his predictions of Edward's death and that of his sons, which would be treasonous. His rationale for this prediction was not comprehensible; his use of numbers in what he called an algorithm would sound insane to Edward, and I could not explain my own belief in its validity as confirmed by an unseen witness to my mother's murder—by our very own father. This too sounded insane.

My apprehension had manifested into genuine worry as the day approached. I had contemplated sending a rider to stop David from coming, and yet I allowed the time to pass without doing so. I told myself I could always refuse his escort to the castle and have David sent back directly to Hackney upon his arrival at Boveney. I took some solace in having at least this card in my pocket, and yet I was robbed of this solace on the morning of the sixth of January when the guards of the Lower Ward awakened me with the news of a strange coach having entered the castle— unimpeded any way through the Norman Gate no less!

Thankfully, the castle was mostly asleep having partaken too greatly of the last and final evening of the season's festivities. Having been awakened by a yeoman, I rushed out onto the cold cobbles still in my bedclothes, but sufficiently sensible to have grabbed a fur cloak for some protection from the chill of the winter morn.

It was as I had suspected as soon as I had heard the news.

David had arrived without stopping first at the church. I should not have expected otherwise, and once again my naivete had proven me a fool. He, along with the same two attendants, had driven a coach of the most curious form right into the heart of the castle. A large crowd of guards and knights had surrounded him out of curiosity, apparently in some deference given the magnificence of the coach, and negligently not out of the need for possible defense.

Upon first glance one might be forgiven for thinking the coach was of French design; its box-frame being narrow, and made of shiny metal plate, and hooped in a luxurious tapestry of rich brocade woven with gold thread. It was pulled by four driving-horses, each with a luxuriant black tackle, also trimmed in gold. At a second glance I noted, to my surprise, that the spokes of the wheels too seemed to be made of the same steel as the box-frame. I did not understand David's fixation with metal embellishments. Perhaps it was some form of armoring, but it just served to make the coach that much more conspicuous.

His arrival was exactly what I had planned to avoid. The success of the audience required secrecy, but it had been shattered by the conspicuous arrival of David and his entourage. My anger was not to be restrained. I lashed out with the cord of my cloak at the guards, who had surrounded the coach admiring its craftsmanship, and demanded that David and his attendants alight immediately. They readily obliged and David approached me with some ceremony, bowing in greeting and removing his hat with a flourish. I had little patience for such spectacle and bade the grooms, who lazed about in awe, to lead the horses and coach away and to keep it, along with David's attendants, in the stables while demanding that David follow me back to my chambers.

He dutifully followed as we moved at a clip through the castle corridors. I had much to say to him but did not want to raise any further alarm with harsh words that might be overheard. My anger was restrained, but only until we had reached my chambers and the door was secured.

"How dare you parade into the castle when you had specific instructions to wait at Boveney!" I shouted, not caring that one of my grooms might hear.

"I understand your anger but it is not possible. Time is of the essence, as always," he responded, with the self-same arrogance that so befuddled me.

"Not possible!" I yelled in reply, "I decide what is possible, not you!"

His calmness unnerved me, and while I marched around the room in anger, searching for the clothes I had discarded the night before, he simply sat down on the stool in the light of the oriel and watch me fumble with my wardrobe.

"You were told to wait for an escort so that I might secret you into the castle," I continued, "my message was clear, did you not receive it, did you not read it?" I exclaimed in frustration.

"Yes, of course I read it, but I had made other arrangements for my coach and thought it best to arrive a bit early. What is the harm done?" He asked.

It was plain to me that he was ignorant of the political machinations of the English court, and that he was purposefully manipulative of my time.

Having found my hose and tunic, I managed to dress myself without the help of my groom, and once again wrapping myself in my cloak, I set myself down on a stool to ponder my next steps now that the original plan had been ruined.

Edward had agreed to meet on the condition of secrecy and

yet, David had entered the castle proper, along with a retinue and in a coach of garish fashion pulled by four white horses, with metallic tackle glinting in the morning light. He might as well have brought a herald or a trumpet to announce his arrival. The courtiers may yet be awake, but it will not be long until they are, and word will spread throughout the castle of the arrival, once again, of an embassy from Istoia.

I knew that I had to get to Edward as quickly as possible and that I would need Elizabeth's help to avert another disaster. With any luck I could get David in front of Edward and out of the castle before word of his presence had spread. Elizabeth would be the key to accessing the king since his morning ablutions, and morning appeals to God, were not to be disturbed under any circumstance. He kept the council at bay until he had his potage, which included me, and which usually I found quite agreeable, but just not so on this day.

I roused my own groggy grooms from the wardrobe in which they had been hiding and directed them to keep David hidden in my chambers until I returned. Advising them that under no circumstance was he to leave, and when I returned if he was not present, they would both be thoroughly whipped. They sensed my anger and frustration as contrary to my normally good countenance, so they dutifully stood over David as he rested on his stool. I left to rouse Elizabeth and implore her to assist me in getting David before Edward.

I found her maids sitting outside her chamber door and demanded they open it and let me in. This was highly unorthodox, and although I was intimately known to both, they were reluctant to obey. Only once I began to force my way past them did they relent. I entered the queen's chamber and found that she was not alone—Edward was with her. This was a fortuitous turn of events, but highly unusual. The king slept alone and although the queen had birthed some eight children from Edward they were not known to lay together for some years. Seizing the opportunity I quickly closed the door behind me and dropped to one knee begging forgiveness for my intrusion.

The surprise at the site of me in Elizabeth's chamber was evident on their faces, but our actual familiarity precluded hardly much more ceremony than that. I dutifully bowed, and they both sat up having not been asleep and not fully roused either. It was not the first time I had seen them in their bedclothes.

"What do you want, brother?" Edward demanded.

"I beg your majesty's forgiveness, but I have some news."

"Requiring you to invade my bedchamber?" Elizabeth interrupted while drawing her furs about her as she sat up on her pillows. Edward doing the same.

It was not as much a question as an admonition.

"Yes, sister," I responded with humility, hoping to lessen the insult of having barged in uninvited. "It is about David of Istoia."

"Oh? Why such a commotion about that clod pate!" Edward exclaimed, "what about him warrants this intrusion?"

"He is in my chamber having arrived earlier this morning unannounced. I *had* hoped to spirit him into the castle unnoticed, but he took it upon himself to appear, once again, at will. I beg your indulgence, but I am hoping we can conduct the audience now and the have him retire to whence he came...before the entire court is upon us."

The king pondered my proposal for a moment and glanced over to Elizabeth for her advice. She simply nodded in agreement and waved me away in irritation for encroaching on the bed curtains as she alighted, all the while yelling for her maid's attention. I was glad that she understood the necessary haste and required no further prodding. I had not prepared her directly for this day, but it was clear Edward had. His own reluctance had obviously been tempered by the possibility, however slim, of a possible alliance with another king who might assist us against Louis, or better yet, Isabella and her ever-pious husband Ferdinand.

I had not talked with Edward about the precariousness of his own head, or those of his sons as David had mentioned, and so I made haste back to my chamber to preface the topics that could not be broached with Edward. The king asked that we meet in St. George's, so I stopped briefly to advise the yeoman of the need to prepare for our arrival by securing the chapel against any visitors, other than those brought by the me or the king. The only additions allowed to the group was to be David's two attendants, who were presently housed in the stables, and of course, the king's own guard.

Returning to my chamber I found David still sitting in the morning light and my own grooms still in their nightshirts, barefooted on the cold flagstone, comically hovering en garde over David. It was an absurd visage since David and I both knew that if he wanted to leave, he would have found his way out either by force or by *magic*—such is his way.

In preparation for the rushed audience, I had my grooms prepare my toilet and afterwards I quickly changed into more courtly attire. All the while I gave instructions on what David could and could not say to the Edward. This included no treasonous talk of the king's death, or any member of his family. He was not to speak of the algorithm because it seemed like nonsense to the uneducated ear, and he was not to mention my own mother's murder; the king had no need of such proof of David's veracity, none such as painted the king's own father in such a terrible light. He was to speak only of treaty and the wantonness of our European cousins and focus on the benefits to this realm and the prosperity that it could bring to Edward and his people.

David nodded in agreement, asking few questions, or requiring few points of clarity, while pacing observantly about the room. He seemed to be listening carefully and watched me with some intent while absently thumbing through an old volume of Chaucer's bawdy tales that I kept on the table next to my bed. I wanted to take this as a good sign of his compliance to my directives, but I was aware from experience that this was not likely to be the case. Before leaving my chamber for the short walk to St. George's, I pressed him one more time on the need for respect and civility and asked that he give the king the deference his majesty warranted.

David agreed, and touching my arm he said that the king will receive exactly as he deserves.

The Chapel of St. George

The chapel had been hastily prepared for our arrival; candles had been lit and two alter chairs had been set up in the empty nave. A fine Anatolian carpet had been placed at the foot of the chairs for some warmth against the winter chill. Braziers had been lit as well, but they had yet to create any warmth, so I took David to the vestry to await their majesty's arrival. Guards had been posted to all the doors and it was not long before long we were joined by David's attendants. I returned to the nave leaving the men from Istoia under the watchful eye of the guards. I was pleased that the chosen setting was sufficiently removed from the castle proper, and although the proximity to the knight's lodgings risked a curious eye or two I was quite confident that the king and queen taking their morning prayers in the chapel would not arouse much suspicion; to the courtiers who were more attuned to the king's movements this change of normal venue might seem strange, but I remained hopeful that the early morning hour meant most of the more meddlesome nobles were tucked warmly in their beds.

It was not long before Edward and Elizabeth arrived, and I was quickly dismayed to see that he had brought along his chamberlain and a scribe. Elizabeth brought two ladies of her own and curiously, their daughter also named Elizabeth, but whom the family called Beth. At just fifteen years old, and quite plain, she had already been promised in matrimony to the dauphin and she has already ascended to the Order of the Garter some years earlier. However, I believed she had no legitimate place at this audience. She was often at her mother's side, and although I was fond of her as one should be of their niece, I never found her particularly interesting. She rarely spoke in the presence of others who were not family and was given to long periods of silence that I, and others, perceived as a form of simple-mindedness. But I really wondered whether it was just a sign of general disinterest on her part.

My dismay at seeing her, and the expanded company arrive, was not easily masked and yet I could neither scold nor ask any of them to leave. I had committed to this audience, arranged its timing, and so far, and to my disappointment I had failed in most respects. Any hope I had of its success was quickly waning.

The king and queen took to the alter chairs while the others stood back in waiting. I approached and bowed again, begging their majesties approval for the reintroduction of David and his attendants when I was interrupted by a loud commotion from behind the alter screen. Before the king could respond we were assaulted by the sound of a familiar voice as the cardinal pushed his way past the guards in a flourish of self-importance. I would like to say that we were shocked by the interruption, but alas, it was now inevitable that others had heard of the embassy's arrival if the cardinal's bold entry was anything to go by.

Sure enough, whilst the cardinal impertinently demanded of the king an explanation of why he had not been informed of the audience, Norfolk and Somerset arrived in the accompaniment of their wives and demanding the same answers of the king. The forcefulness by which they all had entered was typical of their perceived place at court. One that Edward had allowed to fester out of his own insecurities and the not unfounded belief in the instability of his crown.

I was angered to the point of bluster but was hushed by the king and further calmed by the queen and bade to have the enlarged group now stand in attendance immediately behind them, with their backs to the alter. The tableaux was far from grand, each of the new attendees had rushed to dress and the ladies had not tended to their hoods properly so that errant hairs were visible beneath the velvet; the men were disheveled, particularly Norfolk, who had grease marks on both his tunic and jacket—remnant evidence of last night's feasting.

I took my place to the right of Edward and Elizabeth while my niece stood to the left of her mother, the queen. Having resigned myself to the group as it was, but not before admonishing the captain of the guard with a promise of pain of death if anyone else entered uninvited. The king agreed reassuringly since I had no such power to give whilst in his presence.

David and his attendants were then fetched from vestry. I presented them all with a re-introduction requiring little to be repeated from the last audience. Everyone knew who they were and where they claimed to be from. If any of the court had chosen not to acknowledge the happenings at the previous audience, they were now confronted once again with truth of their willful ignorance. David had returned accompanied by the same two servants and he stood before us, once again, in similar attire and under similarly strained circumstances. The crowd was thinner this day with no foreign dignitaries and most of the court absent. However, those most important to the king were present and my own reluctance to allow their attendance was moot.

The three men had bowed deeply when presented and as David stepped forward the other two receded, just as before, to a position of subservience some distance back. The king bade David to step closer so that their conversation would not echo throughout the nave.

"What business brings you back to us?" The king asked, choosing not to admonish him for past insults and instead greeted him with a wan smile.

"I humbly beg your forgiveness, your grace, and ask that you allow me once again to bring greetings from Istoia," David answered with all due respect, and to my immense relief.

"And do you bring enlightenment, again?" The king responded without humor, "somewhere about your person, perhaps in your surcoat, or hidden in your hose!" Adding to his response, this time with true humor.

We all chuckled at the remark, including David.

"Even if it could be so hidden, I would not do so, your highness," he answered, and continuing, "but yes, I shall enlighten you, as directed by your brother Robert, and as to why I desire another audience."

"My half-brother, you mean, and yes he has already made it

known to me," Edward interrupted, "that your king has want of a treaty that might be of mutual benefit. One that might keep our European cousins at bay." But the king had gotten straight to business.

David paused for a moment before responding.

"More of an agreement and a revelation than a treaty. One that obliges Istoia to share information we possess that might preserve your realm and expand its influence elsewhere. In return, you would be obliged to improve your kingdom, such as it is, and in doing so, ensure its preservation. Quid pro nihilo."

"Robert, help me with the Latin," Edward commanded.

The cardinal jumped into the conversation uninvited, not being able to contain himself any longer: "Something for nothing, your grace," he interrupted.

"Quiet!" The king yelled back at him. "You gnawed your way into this audience, you will not gnaw your way into this interview."

"He is correct," I whispered to the king, without adding anything further.

"You want nothing in return from us?" The king asked, with unmasked disbelief.

"Nothing of tangible benefit to us, or rather nothing you might recognize as such," David answered cryptically.

I could sense that the interview was going nowhere with such vagaries being offered by David. So I stepped into the conversation and asked him to expand upon our previous conversations about the health and welfare of our people and his plan to share certain knowledge that might benefit England. While saying this I attempted to catch his eye with my own intense gaze to impress upon him the need to speak concisely and to not be capricious.

David took my cues and talked calmly, and at some length, without any reference to what he considered to be our barbaric nature, and explained once again that Istoia had been gifted, by virtue of time, certain knowledge of medicine and science that would preserve and protect life in ways that we did not quite understand. He did not talk of Greek equality or offer any egalitarian notions like he had done in the past but did offer that this knowledge was based in the traditions of a common faith.

This was an acceptable approach to all in the nave, and Edward seemed engaged without showing any disfavor on his face. The assembled nobles also listened intently, and the cardinal kept quiet, but I could see that he was straining at the bit to challenge David.

"Last time you spoke of the health of my people, as if I had no love of them," the king finally interrupted David's homily. The queen nodding in agreement.

"I did not speak of lack of love, your grace. I spoke of neglect. One may love a dog and chain it in a yard. One may love a bird and keep it in a cage," David responded bluntly.

The company released a collective groan upon hearing this, since David had kept the conversation on the high road up to that point, and now we had crossed over, once again, to a direct insult. But the king was having none of it. He chose to ignore the response and asked another question.

"You spoke of war and taxes and soil bloodied by avarice, did you not?"

"I did, and did I not speak the truth?" David responded with a challenge.

"I know of soil bloodied to preserve the sanctity of my realm and to ensure peace between kingdoms," the king answered, an uneasy banter now developing.

"And what of the blood on your own soil, between brothers and cousins?" David challenged. "What of crops that rot in wet fields while men make games of death?"

The king turned to me, a look of puzzlement on his face.

"Robert assured me that you would not cast insults at me, did you not, Robert?" Edward asked, instructing me to take some control of the conversation and bring David to heel as I had promised. Before I could say anything to calm the situation, David responded.

"Yes, it is true your grace. I did promise to be respectful and to provide deference to the majesty of your position, and I speak in earnest when I say I mean no insult. But we are here today, in this place of God, with a small company of your kin and supporters and you are correct to demand that I speak with frankness and without banality."

"Agreed, go on then," the king acquiesced, agreeing to David's tone. "But your repetitive stories of health and peace are tedious, and your mention of science belittles our own superior minds. I have consulted our scholars at Oxford, and they know nothing of Istoia and believe all that can be known of science, as you call it, is already known."

This was news to me. I had not heard that Edward had undertaken any intelligence, and it was highly possible that he was lying here to keep David on edge. A kingly trait that Edward excelled at. Lying was one of his greatest talents.

"We are aware that your scholars do not know of Istoia," David responded calmly and without a trace of antagonism in his voice. "Just as they do not know that the mold on an old piece of bread can save a life from a gangrenous wound, or that the rays of the sun can light a room even at night. All that *you* know is certainly known to *you*. I do not doubt that is true."

"Pray, tell us then. What do you know that will benefit us?" The king continued, answering David's volley, "tell us what will light our nights as you say and the bread that will heal our wounds that we get in battle."

"I am not here to deliver a manuscript or a sermon. I am here to tell you that Spain, and shortly France, shall embark on voyages of great discovery that will grant them wealth that will dwarf that of this island. This wealth will embolden them to war and persecution of many people in their quests for even greater wealth, and you shall suffer for it."

This statement was of little shock and required no proof. We had heard that a ship's captain from Genoa had been visiting various courts seeking a sponsor for a great sea voyage. Our spies told us that he claimed to have ancient maps showing that the spice islands and India were located across the Atlantic, exactly where David claimed Istoia to be.

"You need us to defend your land across the sea from the Spanish?" The king asked what we were all thinking.

"No," David responded with a smirk. "We do not need your help. I am not here for military assistance."

"Ah, yes. Quid pro nihilo," the king's said, his own smile less wry than contemptable.

This conversation was not making much progress, so I interjected myself, asking David to speak frankly about his intentions, if, in fact, he was not here to deliver a sermon as he claimed. If not, then to provide us a codex, or the like, with the precise intelligence he had spoken of repeatedly.

I could tell he recognized the confusion of the group and the growing impatience of the king and so he asked, politely, if he might talk of his observations of England in the vein of his first audience, and the king reluctantly agreed.

David reminded the group that Istoia was ahead in time, meaning it had progressed to a point where they had largely eliminated hunger and poverty, their population was mostly all literate and education was provided freely to all without concern of station, and that the general health of all their peoples enabled them to live long lives free of disease. Thankfully, he did not mention again the egalitarian nature of his government and I had not told Edward that Istoia was not in fact a monarchy, as that was certainly too complicated of a message for this audience.

David wisely did not point out that England enjoyed none of these advances; he did not have to since by implication we were aware of his judgement in this regard from the previous meeting. He did, however, bring the conversation to religion, informing us that the advantages they enjoyed were a product of centuries of adherence to values adopted from the great religions of the world. He talked of a reformation of sorts, one that aligned all words of all faiths into common laws that benefit the rich and the poor alike and formed the basis for a more representative governance. This last comment was bordering on seditious talk, but David was careful to keep the England free of the analogy.

But what of Spain, and France? It was not immediately clear why David used those two kingdoms to lure the king into this conversation. Once he had laid it out plainly did we begin to understand that our future prosperity was dependent on the nature of transactions between peoples, both at home and abroad. That religion, like commerce, was based on covenants that promised reward but required trust in the relationship between parties, between God and His church, and between His church and His people.

David explained that trust required agreement and agreement required faith, such as can be found in trade, which

Spain was certain to master. He asked us to consider that when a farmer buys a cow in trade for coin, the farmer has faith that the coin has the agreed upon value equal to that of the cow, when, in fact, it is but a small shiny object with a king's visage stamped upon it. The coin is tiny compared to the cow, but the cow gives milk that farmer's wife uses to make cheese and butter, which begets more coin. In truth, the coin does nothing but exist and imply a value that is accepted by both parties. This, David explained, is the true nature of faith. Claiming further, that it is no different than a sinner's confession to their priest. The sinner trades his sins for forgiveness with the belief shared by both him and his priest that the word of God, as spoken by the priest, is of sufficient value to buy the sinner's place in heaven.

We all understood this analogy and the cardinal, once again, attempted to intervene as the ecclesial expert but was hushed by the king. Any interruption was not to be tolerated as he was now fully engaged in a philosophical discussion with David.

It was the perception of *value* that David said was most important in any transaction, and the idea that the greater the perceived value for both parties, the greater the chance of a successful transaction. Without insult, he shared that by his observation that the king provided little value in his transactions with the ordinary people of his realm. He asked for fealty in the form of labor and taxes and even their blood in battle, and in return he provided little in return. He did not directly feed his people, he did not clothe them with wool from his stores, they received no state sanctioned education, and even their prayers were not said in their own common language. David claimed that, in his direct experience, that the greater the value placed on the ordinary person the greater loyalty they showed, and the greater the populace grew in strength—physically, mentally, and spiritually—the greater the prosperity of the country.

Conversely, the exploitation of any peoples, according to David, placed a finite limit on prosperity. He said that they knew from their own experience that Spain would achieve great benefit in exploiting their advantages for a very short time, but ultimately Spain was doomed to failure and obsolescence. England, on the other hand, could assume dominance in Europe if it took its cues from the city states of Italy. There, thinking men were creating new art and music, and putting great thought to rational philosophies that challenged the church and the superstitions that kept its followers mired in darkness. He spoke again of enlightenment, but this time in terms that we could easily understand. Enlightenment, he said, was the rationalizing of the unknown as a means to bring order to chaos. Something we, as Englishmen, did not do, or had not done, since the Roman occupation.

The king listened attentively to David and allowed him to speak uninterrupted until David's speech came to its conclusion. Only then did the king ask directly what concern of it was his if Spain exploited its people if they were doomed to fail as David expected? Why, the king asked, would he care to deny any of his princely cousins their own success, however fleeting, when all he asked of them was the same right to rule without bother? And why should the king care if the bankers of Florence had any particular philosophy, or new work of music when his gold could readily buy the very same *rationalizing* from Florence or Flanders at will?

I feared that the audience was failing again, but not through insult or lack of interest on the king's part, but because David had truly nothing to offer Edward. Of course, I knew of David's algorithm and the prediction of the king's death, but this would not be sufficient reason to warrant any further or future engagement with the kingdom of Istoia. In the brief hour given this current audience David had committed heresy, and danced around insult without retaliation or agreement, and so I feared that he was treading upon a possible charge of treason.

David suspected this as well and begged one final indulgence since we could all see that the audience was coming to its natural conclusion. David asked if the king might allow one additional visitor to join us in the chapel, and although I was inclined to deny the request, the king gave his agreement out of amused curiosity, or perhaps as a reward for David's tenacity.

Once permission had been given, we all looked around in some wonder at whom David was talking about since I had forbidden anyone else to enter, and we had not heard any knock or received interruption from the guards at any of the doors. It was then that we heard the faint sound of distant voices in song that seemed to grower louder with every second. It was as if a choir of young boys was walking towards us at a rapid pace, but we could plainly see in the dim light of the chapel that no choir had entered. The melodic voices seemed to come from above and yet it sounded as if the choir was all around us, their voices echoing from the arches and the walls of the nave.

It was the queen who first noticed the light coming from the ceiling. She pointed to a single bright ray that shone down from above, illuminating the stone floor not far from where David was standing, then another appeared, and another, and as we all gazed up as the sweet voices of the unseen choir grew very loud. Next a roll of dark clouds appeared on the ceiling as if a great thunderstorm was about to break through the vaulted roof, but strangely, from the inside. And then the clouds began to part revealing glimpses of a brilliant blue sky where the ceiling should be. The roiling choir continued, a hymn without words, and we all cowered beneath the rolling clouds and multiple beams of sunlight that now illuminated the nave, as if in an Florentine painting.

We were frozen in fear and awed by the spectacle. More rational heads would have fled the chapel, but we all felt compelled to remain, our feet frozen to the ground. If the king and queen had bolted, we would have followed, but they remained seated, their eyes raised to the ceiling in awe of what was transpiring before us.

The clouds then parted, fully framing a circular opening in the roof, and I noticed the head of a child peak down and my alarm grew to wonder as it appeared to fly across the sky…and then it was quickly joined by others; remarkably, cherubim as described in the Hebrew bible had emerged from the ceiling of St. George's chapel. They appeared to be heralding the arrival of someone or something else. A small speck in the distant blue of the sky was descending at a rapid pace, and it was quickly revealed to be a man with his arms spread wide and his legs crossed at his ankles. He dropped through the ceiling as if cast on a gentle breeze, stopping his descent just as his unshod feet landed effortlessly on the rug that lay before their majesties.

It was a truly remarkable sight and my immediate thought was whether everyone else was seeing what I was; a man in a simple woolen robe had floated down from the heavens, heralded by cherubs, his hair long in a fashion not usually seen at court, his face clean shaven and of a darkened complexion, his eyes blue and piercing and his overall countenance was of a calmness I had never seen before in a man.

Upon his touchdown David dropped to both knees, his head bowed in reverence, followed by his attendants who cowed while the rest of us simply gawked in stunned silence. The man crossed over to David, his feet not seemingly to tread on the flagstone, but gliding as if on ice, and he raised David up in an embrace begging him in a soft, yet firm, voice to not prostrate himself but to join him in an embrace.

They appeared to exchange pleasantries of some sort but unheard by the rest of us, before turning to face the royal tableaux directly, the sunlight still shining from above illuminating his spot on the rug in a brightness that rendered the rest of us in shadow.

'Your majesties," David began, "you asked what benefit we might bring you, and you seemed reluctant to accept my message of prosperity, instead seeking a tangible reward for indulging in our gift of enlightenment. Your ignorance is understandable given your naivete. For this reason, we have asked for help in convincing you of your obligation to your people…and to God."

Edward was speechless, but not the cardinal. He stepped out from behind the king to assert his place before the visitor, dropping to one knee in his hands clasped tightly in prayer and exclaimed: "My Lord, as your representative here at this most Christian court we welcome you in humble worship and seek your blessing."

The visitor gazed down upon the cardinal and beckoned him to rise and began to speak, first directly to the cardinal, and then to the general company.

"Rise cardinal," his voice firm and melodic, his accent unknowable but without ambiguity, "and be blessed with the knowledge that you are not my representative here or anywhere. How could you even believe so as you wrap yourself in silken robes, while I wear the humblest of wool? I have no rings on my fingers," he held out his hands to reveal holes in both palms, wounds without blood or scab, "and yet you have rings of gold and shiny stones that surely are of great value, and I have nothing of material value about my person. No rings, no gold, just these well-worn hands and this garment woven by my mother."

There was a collective gasp as we all noted, for the first time, the wounds on his hands and on his feet.

"The only representative I have in this court is my friend David," the man continued, as the cardinal skulked back behind the king, his hands now hidden now in the scarlet of his robe.

"Not this man of Rome who enriches himself on the simple and yet taxing offerings of the humblest believer. And not you," he offered the king to us with the wave of his upturned palm, "who earnestly believes he rules by right of birth, as if our father would choose you, of all people, from all the goodness here on this island."

The queen's ladies began to weep, and the visitor took note that the queen too had begun to cry too.

"Do not cry, Elizabeth."

He knew her by name.

"You should not fear me. I am just a man, or was a man, who once asked that you," he said, while looking about the group, "do unto others as you would have them to do unto you. Nothing more."

This did not stop the queen's tears, or those of the others. My own eyes welled in shame and fear, but not the king who stared dry-eyed directly at the visitor who had challenged his right to rule.

"Am I not the king here in this country, won beneath your banner?" The king asked, his voice cracking to reveal the falsity in his bravado.

"I believe you are a king amongst these people here, as well

210

as others, who accept with willing fealty your governance. But know this, you are a man like all others, you have no special claim on any God or any earthly right except those shared universally by all men and women."

"What might those be?" the king said, challenging the visitor. "These universal rights you speak of?"

"Is your person not inviolable?" He asked the king.

"Yes, by right of birth," Edward answered.

"Do you enjoy liberty in all actions?"

"Yes, by right of birth," Edward answered, again.

"Are you free from oppression by others?"

"Yes, by my own strength of character, and the loyalty of the swordsmen who defend my will," Edward answered with confidence.

There was a short pause before the visitor continued, and although he did not move from his place on the carpet. He seemed to grow larger as he continued to speak, as if his whole presence was expanding.

"How many kings before you believed the same, and yet their bodies bled and then rotted in the ground as all men do? How many of those lords and priests who supported those kings lost their heads to the executioner or perished on a field of battle in defense of a king's presumed rights? Many...many and not just here on this island, but in all the world. For I assure you, not only are you not special, you are less than any one person who hungers for righteousness, because righteousness is a gift you, as king, have the power to give, but by your own actions you have chosen not to."

This speech was shocking and held true for everyone in the nave. We all, by our own place at this very moment in time, and in this very chapel, knew we were as guilty as Edward. Even the cardinal was humbled by the visitor's words and yet none of us had the courage to utter his name.

"Do I not build churches in every parish, and toil to construct great cathedrals to honor our Father?" Edward continued, challenging him in defense, but only confirming his willful pride.

"Our father has never asked for a great house to be built in his name. He only asks for humble prayer from pure hearts," the man answered, drawing a quick comment from the cardinal.

"But the bible commands a temple be built to the Lord, such as here, with this great chapel built to worship him."

We all stared at the cardinal in shocked silence, and even the king seemed taken aback by the holy man's impudence once again. But the visitor was nonplussed and simply turned to the group and continued to speak calmly and without anger.

"The bible is but the word of man. But there are many men in this world, as there have been many men in the past and there will be many men in the future. And therefore, there will be many more words spoken and written."

"So, you say the bible lies?" The king asked accusingly.

"I say men lie and the bible is written by men," he answered.

"Is the bible not the basis of all law, did Moses not receive the commandments directly from God?" Edward asked, again, challenging the visitor to defend his theology. "When the bible says that you must not mingle linen and wool, does God care about the garments of man, or is this the care of coin by the shepherd and the cotton merchant?" he answered and continued sternly.

"When the bible says God only wants sacrifices from the physically perfect, does God care whether a man is crippled or maimed, or is it the priest who wants to preserve his place in a church which so hates the disadvantaged? And what God needs words written on parchment or carved in stone when what is right and true is known by all men in their own hearts."

There was much murmuring amongst the group at hearing these words from the visitor. It was plainly evident that the cardinal wanted to enter the debate, but he knew better than to speak again. The king was defending his own right to rule in complete ignorance of the message that was being presented to him. At no time did the visitor say the king should not govern, he only suggested that the king should govern with the basic needs of his people as his first concern, and not his own importance.

"But does the bible not also speak of turning the other cheek and offering forgiveness for those who harm us? Does it not also speak of kindness of love for those less fortunate? Were the hungry masses not fed from a single fish and a single loaf of bread?" The king asked, attempting to turn the visitor's own logic against him.

"Do you feed the hungry, king? Do you turn the other cheek when slighted or do you hang and quarter your enemies for treason? Do you tend the sick or allow them to fester in the streets to die and be buried in pits outside your city walls? I ask this because you have proven that in your heart that you know that the will of God is otherwise…and so your bible says, and so you are able to recite to me as taught by this man here swathed in red, and those others like him."

The visitor once again pointed out the cardinal's presence and reminded us that it was the hypocrisy of the church that we used to justify our daily actions. We did not have to question our own conscience against the truth of disease, hunger, pain, and filth that defined this realm, when the church itself gave us the forgiveness we desired and cleansed us of our sins with every coin we dropped on its plate—allowing us to sin again and again for the price of a penance. We have been told that the meek and the pure of heart were the blessed ones and yet we were neither meek nor pure of heart.

"I see by your faces," he continued, "that my words seem hollow and that you are unable to examine your own deeds by the sound of my voice alone. I understand. My words challenge your very survival in this earthly reality, so I shall offer you a vision, before I depart, of what lies before you if you refuse the gift of enlightenment as presented by David. But, please know that I wish you the wisdom to know your own heart."

As he was speaking, his final words the clouds above began to roll again with a rumble of thunder that echoed throughout the chapel. The blue of the sky disappeared, to be replaced by a darkened and tortured sky. The sound of the choir had long since ended without our notice and now, where the flagstone floor once stood solid, the ground began to blacken and appear to liquify into a torrent of water. The vastness of the empty chapel seemed to grow smaller as we pressed ourselves back towards the columns of the narrow nave trying to escape to safety the rapidly liquifying floor. Even the king and queen were forced from their stools, joining us as we cowered against the walls while we watched the liquid of the floor open to reveal a black hole filled with hundreds of skeletal bodies writhing in a sea of agony. Only David remained in place, seemingly floating above the horrors.

The sight was terrifying. It was, as we well knew, a glimpse into the hell that we all faced if we did not heed the words we had just heard from the visitor. These were the words of Jesus that we had heard since birth, the words we swore at every sacrament, and the very same words we took to our graves in hopes of avoiding what lay precisely before us now in the hole in the chapel floor.

There was much yelling and wailing in terror from our group as we crowded against the walls of the nave. The horror proved to be short-lived as the black hole closed as quickly as it had appeared and with it the writhing bodies disappeared from our view leaving David standing alone in the center of the nave. The beams of light from above ceased, the dark sky had disappeared and the visitor was no longer with us. What remained was all as it had been before David begged that we indulge him one more time. The candles were still burning, and the braziers stood surrounding us now in warmth, but the room now seemed dimmer, and we were faced with the reality of having born witness to eternal damnation.

Chapter Eleven

Finitione
(The Final Act)

The clouds had receded and the sky had given way to the timber of the roof again, and we were left to ponder what actions were warranted by the blatant warnings offered us. I believed prayer and self-reflection was immediately required, but the collective relief of having endured a glimpse of both heaven and hell seemed only to embolden the king's resolve to challenge all that he had heard. While even the cardinal was humbled, and the queen's ladies inconsolable in fright, the king stood defiant and stiff in front of David and demanded to know what was now expected of him.

There was now a standoff of wills between the two men, and the king stood alone before us without fear. Norfolk, Somerset, and the cardinal—his chief advisors—remained silent as the king asked David to give him specific instructions on exactly how he was to accept enlightenment. Was it given in blessing? Should he perform a sacrament of some unknown sort? Did it require penance, perhaps a new baptism? Would he need to make a pilgrimage or wage a crusade? None of these questions were asked with any demonstrated understanding of what had just occurred; rather, they were asked in the tone of a child lying defensively when caught stealing a apple. The king's defensive posture revealed him as a weak man. We now saw him naked before us all, and with some shame it was his own daughter Beth who led him away from David and back to his stool. She exhibited the calm courage that we all lacked, or perhaps her love for her father allowed her to see him in a different light than the rest of us, including his own wife. Perhaps she was not courageous, as much as forgiving in ways that we are not. In that moment I hated Edward, and I know I was not alone, save for Beth.

The king now had a decision to make, and yet he could not make it without guidance and so his questions of David, although sarcastic, had some merit. What could he legitimately do to change the fundamental structure of his authority? And more practically, how could he clothe and feed all his people? There was not enough treasure in all the realm to do so. How could he heal the sick and educate the lowest of men when he could not heal himself, nor even adequately read and write in the English language of his own people? We knew this is what ailed Edward's mind, and even the lowly scribe who had scribbled furiously during the audience could now see his king for what he truly was; just a man who held his place by the faith of others, and nothing else.

The king was struggling with the realization that he now risked losing the mastery of even this small company. If he did, it was certain he would certainly lose his crown. I believed he had only one option and it was to seek David's help and to show some humility before all of us, his most trusted allies.

"What would you have me do?" He asked David earnestly.

"I would have you do as you have been told," David responded, with little sympathy detectable in his voice.

"With just *these* hands and *this* heart?" The king asked, responding weakly to David's presumed sympathy.

"You have the loyalty of those here in this chapel. A wife who has heard and seen today what you have heard and saw, yourself. She knows your heart and what you are capable of. She may be of help to you. You have your brother here," he pointed to me, "whose shrewd mind brought me here today. You have your loyal council of dukes who have tied their fortunes to yours, and you have your daughter Beth here too, an observant child with a courageous heart."

Tellingly, he had not included the cardinal in the king's company.

"And…most importantly, you have the wisdom of many people who have lived before you," he continued, "and their writings kept locked away in your own libraries. You have at your disposal the bible, the Torah, the Quran, the books of ancient Greece, and the words of the books from the very far east, and the men at Cambridge, Oxford, Padua, and even Al-Azhar are all at your disposal. But only you can know what to do with the knowledge they bring you."

Edward sat in stunned silence, with Elizabeth's hand resting reassuringly on his arm and giving some comfort to his confused state.

"But *He* said that the bible was not to be believed, *He* challenged me directly on this point," Edward responded pitifully.

"No, man. Did you not listen?" David reprimanded. "*He* said the words of the bible come from men and nothing more; certainly, these words have meaning and truth, but only in context of the time and place in which they are written. Surely you can understand this point, can you not?"

David looked around at all of us and shrugged. We all saw what was obvious and David needed no response from us.

"These people here understand this," he continued, "and you are obliged too as well, because you have been shown your own fate and the fate of those you love."

"You mean that pit of hell that opened in my very own chapel? Is this my fate, prince?" Edward exclaimed, still not understanding that nothing he had been shown was fixed. Either eternal damnation or eternal paradise, they were options open to all of us. He held the key to his own future and yet he was too self-absorbed in his own importance to recognize that a gift of time had been given to him. He could correct his behaviour if he so chose.

"Edward," I found myself begging, calling him by his first name, which I never did unless we were alone or just with family.

"You should not expect to receive anything of substance from David, nothing that you can hold in your hands, no book or manuscript, no lesson to guide you except the universal truths that all men know in their hearts…I ask you, when you see a starving child, do you not pity her and seek to end her misery with sustenance? When you see one of your own liegemen cut down in battle do you not weep for his mother or bride? What I think you have been told today is but a spark of what is already inside you, and it can be nurtured into a flame found in the written word, if you look for it!"

There was a long, thoughtful pause from Edward, and we all stood in silence, waiting to hear his acceptance of this most elementary counsel.

"And?" He asked pensively. "If I perform all this Christian kindness, will I go to heaven?"

There was an audible gasp from the company. Elizabeth let go of his arm in quiet resignation, and in probable confirmation of what she already knew of her husband. No comfort could improve his childish vanity. Her touch could not give him wisdom or humility.

"Yes, Edward. Yes, you will," I lied for David, rather than subject the king to another insulting lecture. Although it was clear that it didn't matter either way.

It was still early morning, and yet it felt as if we had endured hours in the chapel. We were all emotionally exhausted by the revelatory spectacle, and although having witnessed a miracle of sorts, I did not feel any more strengthened in my faith than before.

I suspected that my fellow courtiers were similarly weary. The audience ended abruptly, without any treaty or agreement for continued parley, and any attempt at ceremony was simply discarded along with any sense of accomplishment on my part. I had hoped that we could forge an ongoing relationship with Istoia and perhaps even extend an invitation to David to reside at court, but Edward was having none of it. He had seen a path to his future, a path which unfortunately was only known to him. So, with great efficiency he dismissed all of us and summarily commanded David to vacate the country.

I was greatly disappointed at the abrupt conclusion to the audience, but I knew that any additional efforts to engage with Edward would be fruitless. Interestingly, David did not object to his dismissal and was seemingly accepting of the command to depart England, begging the king that he might return to Hackney to gather his things before departing and offering no other objections. The king reluctantly agreed, instructing that I attend him in his journey and witness his departure, to ensure that he made his way to the coast from Hackney and leave our shores on the first available boat. Adding that under no circumstances was David to summon that great hulk of a steel ship that had first brought him to our shore.

I was more than happy to accompany him to his manor as I could then evade having to meet with the council and partake in the endless discussions about what we had witnessed in the chapel. I needed my own time to process all that I had heard, and seen, as well as plot my own escape from the blame that would befall me. I was certain now, having witnessed Edward's obtuse response to the warnings presented to him, that he was incapable of entertaining any substantive change in his thinking. What was asked of him was to open his mind to the possibilities of a more rational approach to governance and to surround himself with men of a reformed philosophy, nothing more, but I suspected that all he heard was that some Christian charity would buy him a place in heaven. The events of the day had confirmed for me that if I was to ever have any peace of my own, I would need to quietly retire from court and move far way.

The guards had been summoned to return David and his attendants to the stables to retrieve their coach. I set out to change into my traveling clothes, but I was stopped by the king and bade to remain in the chapel. Once the embassy was out of sight, Edward admonished all of us for our insolence, and me most profoundly for allowing him to be subjected to such a theatric and humiliation in his own chapel. We stood in stunned silence and allowed him to berate us one by one, save Elizabeth and Beth. The dukes and their wives and the cardinal were scolded for nothing more than having born witness to the king's humiliation, and I was reprimanded for having permitted the audience to have taken place at all. Edward projected no sense of humility nor acceptance of the admonishments the visitor had laid upon him. Instead, he projected an air of victimhood, that he had suffered for having his true self revealed before all of us, as if we didn't know his failures already. He made no mention of the extraordinary visitor.

Before allowing us to vacate the chapel, he swore us to secrecy. If any of us present even uttered a whisper about the morning's activities, we were to lose our head. I wasn't certain his threat was meant for me, Elizabeth or Beth either, but I had already committed myself to keeping it as quiet as possible. I could trust that the dukes and their wives would follow the king's instructions, but the cardinal was another matter since he was the biggest gossip at court. Figuratively, not literally. We all suspected that Edward would try, and fail, to reform himself rather than reform his realm. He had a singular vision of his own importance and had not heard the visitor's admonition of all the other kings and tyrants that have come and gone before him.

While the others were gathering their wits about themselves, the cardinal had begun to make his way over to the scribe in an obvious attempt to secure the notes of the audience. I was able to intercept the scribe before the cardinal could and gathered all his vellum into my possession for safe keeping. I noted with interest that he had recorded very little of the morning's events, probably too stunned to do so. He had arrived with a very large stack of the most expensive vellum; all neatly cut and carefully incised in preparation for recording the event but left unmarked. I took all of it.

Veritas (truth)

By the time I had changed into my riding clothes and gathered sufficient provisions for the ride, David and his compatriots had made considerable progress on the road to Hackney. I had briefly considered using a barge and the tide and pick up horses at Richmond, but instead I secured two of my usual guard and some fast horses from the stables at Windsor and caught up to their coach at Langley. I had not intended on engaging much with David over this half day's ride, but once upon him I felt compelled to challenge him on his performance, in particular what he intended to do next. Would he in fact vacate England entirely? It seemed unlikely, since Istoia had been sending spies here for decades. Would he then pursue further contact with Edward, perhaps after the king had time to cool down, or at least collect his thoughts? This was an unknown and required a warning from me. David needed to know that Edward was completely done with Istoia and enlightenment. Both parties had gotten all they could from the audience. David had said his piece and Edward had heard very little. Would he then continue to visit in the clandestine manner by which he had always done? If so, would he want to continue to parley with me? Would it be to any benefit, I wondered?

Tying my horse to the coach I begged permission to ride along inside with David. He said that he was grateful for the company, and so I joined him beneath the shelter of the hooped cloth. The coach, or whirlicote such as it was, resembled a traditional long wagon from the outside, if not more elaborate in its decoration than one would usually see. However, the interior was completely different than any cart I had ever seen before; the center compartment was screened from the drivers by small square panels of glass set in sturdy metal frames so that one could talk in private without his attendants overhearing us. The sides contained plush, green velvet seating on benches with raised backs that too were padded for comfort. The main seating was comprised of two banquettes of similar padded velvet, facing each other, with slightly reclined backs—and they were set on spring-like leather straps so that once seated you bounced gently over every rut and rock rather than endure the jarring common to every coach ride. This was a curious invention, and one that seemed so elementary, but what was more curious was the metal box frame; the seats were set upon it, not in it, and the axles of the wheels rode below it, not through it, as if the box frame was a coffin of sorts. I suspected that it might be the very same contraption described by the steward that the dutchmen had crafted. I was very curious about its purpose but did not press David on the point. There were more important things to discuss.

We rode along in comfortable silence for some time which gave me the opportunity to collect my thoughts. David seemed content to gaze out at the countryside through the flaps in the cloth that had been pulled open, allowing in the crisp winter air. I struggled to begin the conversation as my mind raced with images of the event in the chapel—the visitor, whom I assumed was Christ although he never said so, to the writhing bodies of the tortured souls who had appeared beneath the floor of the chapel. The morning had been an assault on my senses and truthfully, I was content to some degree to not relive it for the time being and just enjoy a quiet ride on the comfortable seat. David broke the calm.

"Your king has acted as expected. We could ask for no more, so thank you."

I was surprised to hear this since I considered the morning to be a complete failure.

"Surely you jest?" I asked in astonishment. "This morning was not a success."

"We did not expect success, Robert. We expected nothing more than the opportunity to address him, and the others…precisely as it occurred."

This was a confusing admission. How could he have known

that the others would have forced their way into the audience, since only Edward, and Elizabeth, and me, knew of the plan. I asked David to elaborate on the meaning of his statement. There was a long pause before he spoke to me again, and even then, it was not until he had bidden the coach to stop by banging on the glass divider with his gloved hand. Alighting from the coach he asked me to join him as we stretched our legs, walking alongside the coach as it crept along the London road.

"Edward is not a curious man, Robert. We have known this for a very long time. Whereas the adventurers of other realms have begun to set sail from the shores of Europe, he has committed himself to only retaining his crown at home, even when it is doomed. This we know to be true."

"The algorithm?" I asked.

"Yes and no," he responded, with a certainty that alarmed me. "We know most things that will happen from this day forward. We have seen it already because of you."

I was very confused, and if I had not seen so many wonders this day I might dismiss this comment out of hand, but I could not. I believed David, even if I did not understand how he could possibly see the future.

"Let me explain in the simplest way that I know how to," he continued, pausing to stop, and allowing the coach to continue on its slow progress without us, my own guards following closely behind on horseback, "none of what you saw today was real. It was all a pantomime of sorts."

"It is not possible, I saw with my own eyes Christ come down from heaven through a hole in the chapel roof, I saw cherubs in the clouds!" I exclaimed. "I saw the floor open up, I saw the pit of hell and those lost souls writhing in agony."

"You saw what we wanted you to see. A projection, like a

shadow puppet behind a linen sheet illuminated by a candle. It is an image cast by light and transformed to something spectacular by your own imagination."

"This can't be true," I challenged. "Everyone in the room saw the same thing, we all witnessed Christ admonish the cardinal and the king, we heard his words and saw the wounds in his hands and on his feet."

"You just think you did," he responded. "What you actually saw was an image and voice of a Christ from the future, and what we didn't show you, your own mind created."

David then began a long and incredible explanation of how he cast this image using the light from the sun—saying it was as if he had harnessed millions of candles to project a shadow onto a mirror that reflected a copy of man that we only recognized as Christ-like.

He told me he could not explain it to me in a more meaningful way, because it was impossible for me to truly understand. My immediate thought was that this was some sort of sorcery, but he just laughed and said that there is no such thing.

He explained that what we saw was but a hollow version of a man, of a cherub, and of tortured corpses. And that he, himself, was not really here standing beside me, but rather that he existed in the future and was projected before me using the same light from the sun; concentrated into such an intensity that he, and his attendants, manifested in the physical form of the men we saw. He referred to himself as being a Solid and the image we saw as Jesus, as a Hollow.

I was too confused to ask questions except to claim my disbelief, and so he decided to show me what he meant by removing his glove and holding out his hand to me. I took it gingerly, afraid of what might happen next, but I was relieved when he gave my hand a gentle squeeze in return.

"Now take my hand in both of yours. Can you feel the warmth and the density of my skin? Now squeeze hard and do not worry about hurting me. Can you feel that there is no give to my flesh?"

He was right, it had no give. His flesh was warm and dry, and smooth, but with feel of grit—it reminded me of the outer flesh of a sole or skate—not scaly and not fishlike, and yet not human either, but still animal in texture. He said that his flesh was made from a form of glass that was blown from a crystalline-like sand, and the heat I felt was the energy that kept him all together. He reminded me of the time, at his first audience, when our guards had rushed him, and his men and they were repelled by some unseen force. And just as I replied that I did recall that moment, I felt a shock run from his hand into mine. It was not painful, but it made me jump just the same.

He explained that the shock was like the spark given off when you walk across a woolen carpet on a cold winter's day, and you reach out to touch a metal object like a door latch or candlestick. He called this feeling *static electricity* and said that it was harmless in small doses but like lightening, it could kill with an increased intensity. He said I should think of this energy like the rays of the sun; it gives life to plants but when passed through a glass disk it can start a fire. He said that his body, in the form as I saw him, was made up something he called a form of 'matter', which was created by an intense and very concentrated form of this electricity.

It was a puzzling description, and although I could understand lightning and static electricity since they were two activities that I had experienced. I did not understand the word matter, and his further explanation that it is everything, including

227

me, was too difficult to comprehend without a deeper conversation, and we had other, more pressing things to discuss.

I asked him where he was, if, in fact, what I could see of him was just an image of his true self in some solid form here before me? He told me that his true mind and body were far away and many hundreds of years in the future. He was not precise in his answer, but that I should have faith that what I saw of him was his true self.

How could I debate something I could not understand? But, his assertion that I have faith in him was quite preposterous. Up to this morning I had faith in Christ, yet he has ripped this from me with the admission that what I wanted to believe was a second coming, was in fact a lantern show, a pantomime, no better than a court entertainment. I told him so and he grimaced and said that he understood my point but reassured me that the morning's theatrics should not diminish my true faith. He added that the falsity of the projection was not meant to dispute the reality of Christ. He assured me that to his knowledge Christ had been real, as far as *he* knew, and therefore my faith could be too, if I so choose.

I disagreed and told him so. I was terribly shaken by what he was telling me, but I was willing to allow him to continue his explanation of what had transpired—hoping that he would soon get to *why* he has gone to such lengths to impress such a simple message on Edward, a man who had no interest in hearing it. David explained that the *why* of his mission was inextricably linked to the *how*. Like his explanation of matter and energy from the sun, they were not the same, but they were inseparable. Once again, I did not understand what he was talking about, so he suggested that he could illustrate what he meant with a stick he grabbed from the brush on the edge of the woods.

Using his foot to smooth out the dry, barren, dirt on the side of the road he created a drawing surface on which he drew a single straight, horizontal, line, having me imagine that this was a farmer's field. He then drew another line straight up from the field and asked me to imaging that this other straight line was the whip of young tree growing perpendicular to ground, and without any branches on its trunk—like a young poplar. He said that the whip was representative of time growing straight, but not perfectly straight, saying that time bends and curves ever so slightly due to unseen forces—just like a tree does. He said time moves, or grows, continuously in this way, like the trunk of a tree, until such time as a branch sprouts and grows.

He then asked that I consider that at this very moment, that his place in time is located at the top of the tree trunk and that my place in time was somewhere in the middle, but closer to the bottom. I could follow this logic clearly, so he went on.

"Imagine," he said, "that I wanted to visit you lower down on the trunk, well, we had found a way to harness the infinite power of the sun to create an illumination, one that is hearing and seeing, and send a life-like image of a me right to this very time, to your place on this trunk."

I understood what he was saying since the analogy was quite elementary, but I was struck by the thought that if he was altering time. Everything on the trunk that followed from this moment would then be changed in some way, and therefore it would also impact him in the future.

He said that this was precisely the point of the correction.

Although it was not as simple as I had made it sound. He explained that by inserting himself at a past place in time along the trunk it caused a branch to grow; meaning, another straight line of time would grow from the trunk, and upon it a new reality

229

while the original trunk continued to grow until it simply ceased or was cut down somehow.

He said that we were now on one of these new branches in time.

I was stunned by this revelation. If, in fact, David was telling the truth, it meant that that there were multiples of each of us living on different branches of time? David answered that, to his knowledge, that it wasn't the case, because according to the algorithm branches died from war, disease, and natural disasters including cataclysmic forces from the heavens. Basically, people die naturally and their time on earth dies with them. But, he agreed that it was theoretically possible that he and I both existed in two places in time: on the main trunk and now on this shared branch. Although, he thought it possible that the main trunk had ceased to grow or maybe even had died, saying that he would have no way of knowing.

I asked him how many branches were on this tree and he said he did not know that either since he was but one person among many working with the algorithm. He was aware of others doing the same thing as him, and by his estimate they numbered in the hundreds.

We returned to the coach, leaving the drawing in the dirt, and rode along in virtual silence for several hours with just the occasional question from me on the parts of the story that I found particularly confounding. Such as, how long have they been doing this? And what part of our common history has been altered? He said he did not know what has been altered by others before him, but for his part it began with the arrival of the ship and his first audience in the Tower.

He believed that the branch we are on is not directly attached to the main trunk—he knew that much—because his people had been in England before him, hence the fabrication of the ship and other tools they needed to make it happen. So, by his estimate we were on a branch of a branch, and as for how long they had been doing this manipulation of time, he said that in some form or another it had been, to his understanding, for several hundred years.

He qualified this buy saying that the tools they used to make this projection work were continuously changing and getting better. He said that the projection of Jesus we saw was really a very old example of what they were capable of since the Jesus we saw was what he called a Hollow, and not a Solid like himself.

The thought of the manipulations that David and his people were capable of horrified me. I told him that if they were able to create a Jesus out of nothing was it not possible that they had done so from the very beginning and created the story of Jesus to begin with, and he assured me that they had not. He said that we all had a common history and that they had never gone that far back in time, that they couldn't, and that they had no need to; or rather, they believed that the changes they needed to make in our future could be made without having to alter the basic faiths established long before my present time.

Whether I believed this or not was not important to either him, or in fact, to me. He could be lying or telling the truth, it would not alter that which I could not control. But there was one very perplexing question, and that was why he would need to go to such great lengths to create such a grand and fabulous mirage for Edward when all they had to do was kill him and insert someone in his place who would be more compliant. Why not do the same with Isabella, Phillip, the Pope, the Emperor? Why go to such an effort for someone who is as thick headed and noncompliant as Edward?

David's answer surprised me. Why was I so certain that Edward was the target of the correction, why did I assume that it was the king that the algorithm was targeting? I could only offer that as the most important person in England, that I just assumed it was so, and he admitted that he did not know who the actual target was, but that he had a feeling that it wasn't Edward. That he believed Edward was justifiably doomed regardless. There were others in the chapel this morning, and perhaps someone else was actually more important than Edward. I asked if it was me, and he just laughed saying he thought not. He claimed to not know himself, but if he was to make a wager on anyone it would be the young princess, Beth. I found this thought to be unlikely, she was but a child and a female, no less.

He also explained the true power of the correction was in its subtlety. He said that they were not prone to big things, that they didn't harm anyone directly anymore, or preemptively strike out anyone even to prevent a calamity. Rather, they had learnt to use subtle nudges to alter the judgement of men and women and to guide them towards a different outcome in the normal business of their time.

If they weren't prone to big things, then why create the hoax of the giant ship?

David said that it was a mistake on their part since they had only intended the projection to hide the *router* (his word and with a meaning unknown to me) and a much smaller ship would have done the trick. He said that when the ball was fired at the ship it was just pure luck that it hit the only actual solid part of it, the rest was a Hollow, a mirage of sorts. The ship was actually no bigger than the cart we were sitting in (which I guess is also what he calls a router), and he said that not only could they not have predicted that to happen, but that they also thought it was quite comical.

I told him that I though their actions were highly presumptuous of their own importance, and that they were toying with people's minds and souls. They were playing God, figuratively and literally.

He disagreed and spoke of an archer shooting at a target. He said that a good archer gauges the wind and notices its direction and strength and adjusts his aim using this knowledge to guide the arrow to its target. I said that he and his people must be very talented archers and he responded that I missed the point entirely.

"We are not the archers. We are the wind."

The sun had long set by the time we passed north of London, our lanterns lit for safety and my men well-armed, and so we were without fear on the well-traveled roads. We were fast approaching Hackney, and David beckoned me to come closer to the coach as I had long returned to my own horse to avoid further discussion. He asked me to allow him to beg for one final indulgence. I agreed and brought my horse to the coach. He leaned out as closely as possible and asked that I put down on to vellum all that I had seen and heard since the first audience. He asked that I be as truthful as I could be and not embellish nor withhold anything from the story. He said that it was essential that I give no care or worry to heresy or treason because the work, which needed to be in my hand and not that of a scribe, would be locked away for centuries to come.

He could sense my reluctance to agree to this indulgence, because if it ever came to light I would certainly lose my head. He assured me that I would not if I followed his instructions precisely and warned me that it was essential that I put quill to vellum without haste. I asked why this was so important to him and he just laughed and said that only a fool asks questions of the wind.

York Place

There had been no need to accompany David to the coast. Upon arrival at Temporal Hall, we each retired to our own chambers and of course he was nowhere to be found when I awoke in the morning. I checked his bedchamber and found his clothes placed neatly on the bed and found no other sign of him. The steward's wife caught me examining the floor. When I questioned her on David's whereabouts, she assured me that he and his attendants had left sometime before dawn. She asked me why I was so interested in the floor, and when I attempted to brush her off, she asked if I was looking for some sand because I would find none. She had swept the room out earlier that morning like she always did. Why the master and his people always tracked sand into the manor she didn't know, but she didn't like it one bit.

I found her husband in the yard and queried whether he had tended to our horses, and I was pleased that they had been fed and watered and were well rested. I enquired about the whereabouts of the coach, since his master had evidently departed, and he assured me that it, and David's own horses, were in the stable and that his master must have left on foot, as he usually did.

I returned to the Tower immediately, taking David's coach and horses as I certain that they were no longer needed. With David's final instructions ringing in my ears, and a firm commitment to honor this final indulgence; the horses would enter the king's stable and the whirlicote would be dismantled and the dutchmen's handiwork thoroughly inspected. If for no other reason but to complete the correction that I had so unwittingly enabled from the moment the cardinal brought David to court. I would, as instructed, commit in writing the entire story of the embassy that came from across the sea and with them the visitation of Jesus Christ from the future.

I would use the vellum sheets that I had taken from the scribe and place them as instructed in the child-sized ossuary David said was hidden in a groom's chamber at York Place—now being remodeled into a new palace by our very own king. He had given me a precise description of the location of the chamber and said that a mason had recently placed a neatly trimmed stone with a deeply incised mark of Pax—the kiss of peace—upon its face. He said that time was short, and that it was imperative that I complete this task within a fortnight as the stone would then be mortared and the vellum sheets sealed away for the centuries to come.

I would do as instructed, except, I would arrange for a leather binding and maybe even have a rosewood box to be crafted for it, since I could not bear the thought of the vellum laying loose in the ossuary like the bones of a child to be forgotten to time.

Chapter Twelve

The Chronicle

The transcription of the manuscript to a legible form of modern English was completed after a weeklong feigned illness (as far as the lab was concerned) and a tremendous amount of time AOLing medieval English words. Wondering all the while how I could have done this just a few years ago when all we had was Google! Nonetheless, I was able to use recognizable patterns in the sentence structure of Robert's writing to string together the dialogue and the descriptive paragraphs with some ease. I was frequently forced to look something up, which would result in a rabbit's warren of scholarly journals, political dissertations, architectural surveys, art compendiums, linguistic diatribes, textile analyses, animal husbandry practices, and image search results of all manner from porn to poetry. At the completion of the transaction I was left asking myself: why do so many people spend so much fucking time on medieval studies!

I lamented that even though the internet may be a vast resource of nonsense and contradictions, it did allow me to see directly into the medieval world at the same time I was reading about it. Admittedly, before I began the translation, I thought that so much of the past must have been lost to time, and so I was pleasantly surprised by how many remnants there are of medieval buildings preserved in situ or encapsulated within other buildings. I was amazed by the hundreds of illuminated manuscripts preserved in libraries around the world; scanned and catalogued, with their colorful illustrations of people in courtly dress, all accessible to me via open access portals. Even the preserved mapping from the fifteenth century gave me a glimpse of a medieval geography which surprised me by how very similar to our present-day it is with the same towns and villages still inhabited, and with the same place names no less. I felt as if my mind's eye was remarkably clear and while I read, researched, and transcribed I truly felt as if I had witnessed all that Robert had written.

By the time I had finished the transcription I noted that words such as whirlicote were no longer alien to me, and neither were the attitudes and moral workings of the medieval mind. I was quick to recognize that I must have unknowingly held some deep prejudices towards the peoples of the past, perhaps out of ignorance, or simply because I had no meaningful connection to them in my regular life. I had never previously considered how closely long-dead people thought like me or even considered whether they held the same fears and desires. To me they were just characters in moldy books and plays; entertainment in a version of the English language I barely understood. But at the completion of the transcription I genuinely felt connected to these people, I felt compelled to try and figure out, if I could, what happened to them. How did their lives progress after that morning in St. George's Chapel?

I already knew that Edward died soon after the chronicle was written because I had not waited to the end of the transcription to look that up. His death remains a mystery till today of whether he was poisoned or died of natural causes. But like with his own ascension from claimant to king, he left behind a trail of calamity and death that included the murder of his two young sons by his own brother Richard while they were held captive in the Tower, just as David had predicted. Richard, in turn, met his own end, as all highschoolers know from having read their Shakespeare, at the Battle of Bosworth and was succeeded by Henry Tudor the father of the infamous Henry VIII. I could now picture clearly how much tragedy and bloodshed must have occurred while the crown was conveyed from one head to another, exactly as David accused Edward of enabling, and still without any adherence to the warnings that he had been given.

The dukes, who read as hapless buffoons, all went on to some success. They rode the waves of war and courtly intrigue with their families' strengths ebbing and waning with whatever political intrigue befell them. The cardinal, interestingly, fled England upon Edward's death and retired to Rome, or rather a villa outside Rome, and lived many more years and reportedly dying with more amassed wealth than the Pope himself. I could find no contribution to charity or ecclesiastical scholarship ever attributed to him, but this did not surprise me.

Robert proved very difficult to trace through time. Although recognized by his father, his illegitimate birth meant that there was little record of him while he was alive and even less after Edward's death. The last mention of him in any written form was the record of a funeral mass said for him in 1485. There was little detail in the register except the date of the mass and the mention of a ship having floundered in a storm while crossing the channel. I earnestly hoped that it wasn't true, since I had become deeply invested in him as a person, and I really felt like I knew him as a friend.

He had mentioned that he had intended to plan his own exile, and in my heart, I hoped he had made it across the channel and remained hidden and hopefully happy until the end of his life.

But I don't think I will ever know the truth of his life or death.

Of all the characters in the manuscript the one with the most surprising legacy was the young princess—Beth. I had not pegged her to be of any significance to history, but I was terribly wrong, as was Robert in his dismissal of the importance of his niece at the event in the chapel. Not only was she the daughter of a king, but she would be sister of a king, the niece of a king, and eventually married a king to become queen consort in her own right. She gave birth to Henry VIII who in turn fathered Elizabeth I. This unassuming character who warranted only a small mention in Robert's telling, a perpetual teenager in my mind, would end up being the grandmother of the woman who propelled England towards the renaissance, and actual enlightenment. From her womb sprung the masters of the sea and the founders of an immense empire that once stretched across the entire globe. Yet she is all but invisible today.

Granted, none of this was achieved without bloodshed, war, famine, slavery, and environmental degradation. But of all the characters in Robert's writings she proved to be the most influential and I was quick to suppose that perhaps the entire correction was aimed at her, and that she was actually David's target the entire time. I could not shake the thought that without Beth, there would be no empire, no colonies, no universal form of parliamentary government, no form of modern banking, and probably no me. Had the mirage of Christ appeared for her alone, I wondered?

At the completion of the transcription, I was left with my own version of the manuscript that I deemed a *chronicle* rather than simply a story, since what I had translated was meant to be a record of fact rather than a tale of sorts. It sequentially laid out, in a narrative form, a series of detailed and related historical events and it contained a first-person account of an actual piece of history that had been unknown up to this point in time. I was proud of my work and printed an old-school copy for myself and for some insurance I saved a couple of copies on two thumb drives, filing one away in my wall safe and mailing the other to my sister with strict instructions to hold it for me. I didn't have to tell her why or what it contained; she would do as I asked. The original vellum manuscript was locked away, secure in my safe, but I was more than willing to give it to David when he reappeared, since I had photographed each page for my own records and had no need of it anymore.

I had my suspicions of what David wanted me to take away from the chronicle, but I had a lot of questions that needed answering if I was going to get anything really, truly, meaningful from the exercise. I was quite troubled that in all my AOLing I could not find any record of David and no mention anywhere of the visit of the embassy in any writings from the period. There is no mention that I can find in any journals, scans of court records and circulars, or even an anecdotal reference in the pamphlets of the time. I suspected, there was no mention of the second coming of Christ, even in theatrical form. That bastard Edward had successfully muffled the whole event and died the worse for it.

The only reference of any interest that I could find was related to Istoia, which is not recorded as a place name anywhere, but it shares the original name of a bank headquartered in Athens. Like so many other financial institutions, Istoia Bank SE, was established just over a century ago to take advantage of the lax regulatory environment in Greece that propelled Athens to the banking capital it is today. The buttoned-up fastidiousness of the Greeks, and the centuries of their overly diligent work-ethic made Athens the perfect place to hide money. Yet, I was surprised to learn that Istoia Bank SE was now known simply as IST: the largest venture capital firm in the world and the very same group that funded my own startup before we were sucked into the OSS. This could not be a coincidence. David would need to provide some explanation of his relationship to IST!

I needed to tell David that he had deeply impacted my faith, and that his weak assurance that Christ had been an actual person did little to nothing to soothe my fear that he, or someone else of his time, has been interfering in our religious history. If he could project such a massive charade on Edward and his courtiers, he could easily have manipulated so much more over the past two thousand years. I could not help but wonder how many other events in our history they altered, how much of what we believe to be fact, whether it be faith-based or political, was actually true or just some altered form of a reality.

The casual and reckless way in which he projected a Hollow of a Christ-like figure into that very superstitious time made me doubt his sincerity towards the correction in which I was participating. Medieval peoples believed, however naively, in the literal reading of the bible, as surely as they believed in witchcraft and sorcery and miasmic diseases. They sought miracles from the toe-bones of dead saints, and they slaughtered Jews and Muslims as a means to please God, believing that a crusade or pogrom gave them some form of holy dispensation. The people of that time were not only susceptible to subterfuge, but they were also victims of their own superstitious beliefs, and thus ripe for David and his manipulations.

It has taken us many centuries since then for man to overcome such superstitions and to develop the current level of tolerance for each other that we now enjoy, which is a fragile peace at best. In the hundred or so years since the last big war we have managed to carve out a co-existence of faiths and a level of political stability that has staved off any significant armed conflict. However, we still have not been able to separate the politics from faith where our adversaries are concerned. The USA, like the UK and our fellow Commonwealth brethren, consider ourselves JCI or prophet-based, and even though we are highly protective of all the other belief systems we struggle to maintain a peace with our primary adversaries: Canada, France, and Australia. This Gallic Axis offers little tolerance for anyone, or any country that is not fundamentalist Christian and deeply, intolerably, conservative.

This intolerance is often given over to aggression and if it were not for Russia and China, our allies in a very loose sense, we might be in a constant state of conflict since they help form a neutral buffer between our JCI ideologies and the fundamentalists. It's not that we are culturally or socially aligned in a meaningful way with either nation since they both remain mired, after all this time, in their non-faith based political systems—adhering to a strict form of collective capitalism born from a now defunct communal system that replaced all faith-based religions with the worship of wealth! We consider them faithless, but their political and economic structures knit with our own, and so we support their right to godlessness in the same way we support all other ally's belief systems.

I wanted David to know that my faith has been shaken, as I know Robert's had been as well. The other similarities between Robert and myself was not lost on me. His story was very much my story. The fact that David had imposed himself on both of us, and in a similar forthright manner, with little regard to whether we wanted to participate in a correction was pretty fucked up. David told the both of us that we had the ability to choose to participate along with him, but I clearly recognized my own naivete in Robert. Neither of us had been given a choice. The moment David projected into our lives we were thrust upon one of those allegorical branches that he liked to describe so much. We cannot/could not choose otherwise because he had the power to impose himself upon us at any time. In doing so he stripped me of any sense of freewill or self-determination. He could anticipate what I might do next. He could adjust his reactions to me using the machinations of the algorithm, altering his actions and his reactions with a prior knowledge of how it would impact me.

Reading about his interactions with Robert confirmed this for me. He had led Robert to believe that he was making his own decisions. He believe that he made the choice to meet David in that field near the cemetery and that he chose to arrange a second audience with Edward; when all along he was being manipulated into giving the algorithm what it wanted.

I was anxious to confront David with these questions—arguments really—but I was helpless in contacting him. Robert had been able to deliver a message to the manor at Hackney, but I had no such method. I was at the mercy of the algorithm, again.

Chapter Thirteen

The Correction

David's reappearance at the farmer's market was as unceremonious and as unoriginal as his projection onto the pavement outside Whitehall. Suddenly, he was just there. He chose to return to the scene of our first meeting, just as I had done—equally unceremoniously and unoriginally. I had been on the lookout for him for several weeks, suspicious that he might manifest at any moment and in any place, and yet I was still surprised to feel my pulse quicken when I caught a glimpse of him moving through the crowd and towards me. My anticipation had been more than a little bit feverish, which had caused me significant anxiety. I had been spending way too much time lately developing anger filled scenarios, each as confrontational as the next, of what I would say if I saw him again. I knew it was playing with my head, but I continued to craft these scenarios anyway, believing I would get some satisfaction if I was mentally armed for our next meeting. I certainly had a lot of questions, but most of all I wanted to hear from him why I was chosen and how could it be that my reading of the chronicle was enough to perform a meaningful correction?

But there was no confrontation to be had. David approached me, hand outstretched in greeting, a broad smile on his face. I smiled back and shook his hand. He motioned towards the tree at the edge of the parking lot and the bench that we had sat on at our first meeting. We walked together in silence and only began talking after we had sat down in the shade of the oak tree. I was immediately reminded of him and Robert doing the same thing on the edge of the field near the Roman cemetery.

"Did you find the manuscript interesting?" He asked, breaking the silence.

"I did. I also found it difficult to read, its calligraphic writing was challenging to decipher, and the prose, having been composed in middle-English, was almost like reading a foreign language," I answered, babbling nervously.

"Hence, your transcription."

It was not a question. Our familiar style of communication resuming.

"Yes, but of course you know all about that. It took me a good week and a lot of time on the web piecing it together. I learned a lot, that's for sure. My medieval vocabulary has increased immensely, but not that I think I will get much more use out of word whirlicote."

"The Jesus Chronicle, that's what you called it?"

"Yes," I laughed in response, "You like the name? Every book needs a title," I thought.

"I suppose I do, but it's more important that you found some meaning in the chronicle. Enough to give it a name at least," he added—a statement again, not a question.

I had not considered the psychology behind selecting a title for the transcription. It wasn't as if I was the original author, and I honestly could not remember why I thought it even needed a title. Perhaps David was right, maybe I had found enough value in it, possibly subconsciously, to give it a name.

"I think you may be correct. I certainly got invested in the story, maybe too deeply. I think I connected with the characters, especially Robert. There are a lot of parallels between him and I, but you know that already, don't you?"

David was quiet for a moment before responding.

"Yes, you two are very much alike. You both have engaging minds and share a similarly critical intellect. You seem to have the same curious personality type."

"I tried to find a historical record of him, all of them for that matter. I could trace almost everyone, except him. The only record of Robert, after Edward's death, was a funeral mass said for him and a reference to a ship's sinking. Did he drown, do you know what happened after his brother's death?"

"I don't," he responded in his typical matter-of-fact way.

"Aren't you curious about what became of him? I mean, he may have lived centuries ago, but you interacted with him for several months not that long ago, and your dealings with him read to me almost like a friendship."

David just shook his head, no. His eyes showing no discernable empathy.

"You manipulated his relationship with his brother, you challenged his faith, and you abandoned him to the repercussions of your changes to the course of history. Seems kind of callous of you not to have followed up to see how he fared!"

"Everyone dies, Paul. And he died a very long time ago."

It was a callous response, and he could tell that I found it unsatisfactory. He went on anyway, dismissing my comment out of hand.

"I know you're now wondering whether I hastened his death. Perhaps. But did I extend his life? It's just as likely that he lived longer for knowing me than he would have otherwise. But the algorithm doesn't grant me the luxury of tracking him or any other person through time."

'What about me? Are you are tracking me through time?"

"No," he answered. "And I thought you had a better understanding of what is happening here," David responded with more than a hint of frustration in his voice.

"We are in a correction; I am not stalking you. I know you *now* in your present time and I have read of you long after you are gone. You exist for but a brief moment in my long life. When the correction is complete, I will probably never think of you again...except maybe in passing. I will move on to my next projection and then another one, and another until it's time for me to stop and I can retire to some place warm and sunny...and with gravity."

His attempt at humor was not comforting, yet his dispassionate approach to his work was admirable. We wanted our pilots to exhibit the same sort of attitude, but their basic humanity kept getting in the way. David did not suffer from this trait.

"So, what next?" I asked. "I've read the chronicle. I have learned quite a bit about medieval life and Edward IV's court. And I now know that you and your colleagues manipulate past events. You are like the wind, right, isn't that how you think of yourselves?"

"You like that analogy?" he asked with a genuine laugh this time.

"I'd say you like your analogies. Trees, branches...wind."

"Ah, yes. We've got to use what's relatable to the time. I happen to think it is an apt analogy."

I had to agree with him, but I didn't want to say so.

"And Christ? You thought that projecting a Hollow of the son of God, complete with cherubim and a scene straight out of a Hieronymus Bosch hellscape was relatable to the time?"

"Yes, perfectly relatable. Whom else would they believe but their lord and saviour?"

"But it was such an elaborate projection. Music, clouds, the opening of the floor to reveal the torments of hell. You went to such an effort only to have Edward to cover it up. There is no record of the event, and everyone seemed to have gotten on with their lives afterward, unmoved by it all. Except for me of course, all you managed to do all those hundreds of years ago was to undermine *my* faith, today. The others seemed to just move on from it. Why the second embassy at all? What was its purpose?"

Only when I heard my own words aloud did they fully register with me. The elaborate projection was done for my benefit. I am what needs to be corrected. But it couldn't be so, I thought to myself. David had said that the correction was meant to prevent a terrible calamity of some sort—mass death and the like. Surely, I could have nothing to do with something like that? I had devoted my professional life to helping people, not harming them.

I asked him if this was the case and he said that it was a possibility, but also that it was highly egotistical of me to think that events in 1481 were altered just for me. He went on to explain that when the algorithm was first applied it was very simplistic and had a very narrow focus. With every computation it learned from itself, and if their first projections were meant to impact one person, or one event, the algorithm learned over time to predict the follow-on impacts so precisely that it could combine corrections to produce perambulations of corrective events that were so complex, that the human mind could not keep up. Like a complex web that only the algorithm could navigate.

The second embassy was a theatrical spectacle and somewhat ridiculous, he admitted that, but one that was suitable to the time. What it was meant to achieve is computationally impossible for our minds to predict. If he considered the history that followed the event from the reformation to colonization, to Anglo-world dominance and the peaceful world order of my own time, then maybe the theatrical had a significant purpose. Or more precisely, a thousand purposes. The algorithm needed to get from that point in time to where I am today, so the second embassy had to have a purpose for one or more people in the chapel that day.

It wasn't that he didn't care why it happened. He just accepted that the performance was deemed necessary by the algorithm and so it was orchestrated with David as its conductor.

So much for the wind analogy, I thought. How could David claim to be simply *nudging* an act in time when the same correction was skipping centuries and targeting multiple people at the same time? This was more than a nudge, it was a full-on shove!

He continued, what he admitted, was an uninformed answer to my question. Reminding me again that he was not the brains behind the correction, he was just the pilot. He was given instructions and his own actions were being corrected in real-time by the algorithm. He explained that even as we sat talking in the shade of the oak tree the algorithm was analyzing all the nuances of our conversation, including my facial expressions, my pulse rate, the placement of my hands, my posture, my eye movements...everything about me was being run through thousands of analytical equations to predict what I might say or do next.

I asked him more if I was the subject of the correction. Was it me? Did I need correcting? He said that by their calculations I should have figured out the answer to this question much earlier than I had. I think that was his attempt at a joke.

"Perhaps I have," I responded, "I have been deeply troubled for weeks now and I had anticipated our meeting again as a confrontation rather than a conversation because of this. I think subconsciously I have always known that it is me, and why wouldn't I be? You, David, are a product of my very own technology, you wouldn't be here if it wasn't for me."

He nodded in agreement.

"But am I the danger or am I *in* danger?" I asked.

"Both," he answered abruptly, and continued, "you know that there are few coincidences in life, correct?" he asked, but didn't wait for a response from me.

"Statistically, it is one hundred percent accurate to say that all that will happen can happen, and all that didn't happen could also have happened. So, now you are a witness to what *has* happened on our shared branch of time, and now you have been given the gift of determining what might not *yet* happen."

A complex scenario, but clearly the truth. He wanted me to determine what didn't happen in his history and what isn't going to happen in my future.

"Remember, none of this is coincidental," he continued, "this is your technology, and it is all predictable, so even you with your inferior twenty-first century brain, you must now know that you have an infinity of futures before you. You get to choose from all or none of them."

It sounded like a lot of bullshit to me, and I told him so, but he knew I believed every word he had said. I added that if I was going to make the right choice, I needed him to answer some more questions for me, and he agreed to provide them.

"Who else, besides me, was the target of the correction?"

He didn't know for certain, but he suspected, as he told

Robert, that it was the young princess they called Beth. She was an origin point of sorts for most of our shared history that followed, and her place in the chapel could not have been coincidental.

When I pressed him further on this possibility, based on what I now knew of Beth's life long after the episode in the chapel, he said that I just had to look at the historical treatment of women to find some truth there. He pointed out to me that my own faith has a very long history of beatifying women as either virgins or whores, at least until they are married. Then they become martyrs to their husband's infidelities and their children's needs; they then pass into obscurity while men write history. Just like the young princess.

"Beth is the most likely candidate," he said, "given what we know about her and yet she remains invisible, erased to time, except to the algorithm. Who better for the algorithm to nudge than Beth?"

I then asked if Robert was also a target, since like me he was critical to the correction, and David said that he believed that he wasn't. He said Robert was like the archer in the wind analogy. He wasn't the target or the arrow, he was just the useful muscle. This struck me as odd since Robert and I were so much alike, and so I had to press him further on this point.

"If Robert wasn't the target of the correction, how come I am, especially when our roles are so similar?"

He then corrected me and said that he never told me that I was the target. I had only assumed so, and he reminded me that he had responded benignly when I questioned him before, stating that he was surprised that I cared so much about my role in the correction. Why can't I just accept it for what it is he asked.

"But you did this to impact *my* faith, to show me that you

251

can manipulate anything or anyone, including the prophets. Did you not go to this effort to illustrate to me how easily our belief systems can be fucked with?"

He laughed at what he said was my very narrow view of events. He also called me egotistical, adding that it was both naïve and selfish of me to think that they would use so much precious time and energy to target my Christian beliefs alone; me, one person amongst billions.

He went on to say that religious faith as the defining nature of any political system was one of the greatest failures of mankind. When I asked him to explain this further, he was quite blunt reminding me that every war or armed conflict from ancient times to present day was justified by some religious belief. That no matter who fought whom both sides believed themselves to have a god on their side. This belief is the justification for all manner of horrors from atomic bombs dropping on cities to the massacres of woman and children in remote jungles. He said it didn't matter for whom, or when, but that in the last three thousand years or more the righteousness of the victor was always legitimized by the belief that they had a special covenant with an Abrahamic god. Usually, the very same god that the losers also claim as their own. Faith and nationalism are a recipe for calamity, according to David.

"So, no it isn't just *your* faith we are fucking with," he added candidly, "it's everyone's."

"Why? What could you hope to gain by doing that?" I asked.

"Your enlightenment, and everyone else's of course," he said without a hint of sarcasm in what was obviously his fucked-up idea of the truth. He went on to explain that if Robert was the archer in his analogy, then I should think of myself as the bow, the most important part really, because without the tensile strength of the bow the arrow would just be a stick thrown by a man.

Furthermore, the technology I had created could be a weapon if it was used for the wrong purposes. He reminded me that I already knew this to be the case, and that my team and I had been hiding our data from our bosses for years, and for this very reason. He said that I knew that with every advancement we made from Hollow to Solid that OSS and MI8 might want to militarize it and that we had chosen, so far anyway, to prevent this from happening.

He warned me of what I already knew. That if my work continued as planned it would eventually be turned over in its entirety to some government agency since I had long ago relinquished the rights to the technology—and my soul—to the OSS with the knowledge that whatever my team produced would eventually be weaponized. I could choose to think otherwise, but he said I knew in my heart that I needed to continue my work in secret.

He was right. Any altruistic thoughts I ever had about projecting had been long buried.

He said that I would soon be at the moment in the development of Solid projection technology where a decision would have to be made; continue to hide the data and shelve the work to keep it from my bosses or go back to IST for more funding and continue its development in secret…or inform the OSS and allow our solid projection tech to be weaponized.

"Why can't we continue to work through the data and then try and convince the government to see the benefits—I mean, other than the creation of an artificial army. That's what you are saying, correct? Why does my only alternative have to be *you* continuing to manipulate history or the government's creation of a ghost army of death?"

He answered that there were so many other alternatives, but for me these two were the most probable choices, although he accused me of oversimplifying the challenge.

I continued to press him.

"Why don't you just take my tech and in a couple of years manipulate the government yourselves to whatever purpose that suits you? Why should I have to go underground?" I asked, once again seeking what I thought was the simplest and most direct route to a solution.

"Do you really think your government, or any other government for that matter, is capable of being manipulated to stop them from killing one another? And as long as any monotheistic religion is at the core of any political structure there is no hope for any of us. You must accept this as fact."

It was a shocking statement, and one that cut to the very heart of the correction. It was now evident to me that David had been attempting for years to separate church and state, but he couldn't, not yet. He and his people had been inserting themselves at various points in time, as far back as their tech would allow them, with the express intent to eliminate mankind's reliance on religion. I could not even guess how many corrections, or nudges as he called them, had been performed over the centuries—all with the intent to fuck with people's belief in religion and faith in their government institutions.

"You want to remove religion from government? Get rid of the *In God We Trust*," I asked, guessing that I had finally figured out the correction. "And you think making me question my own Christian beliefs will achieve this goal?"

"Close," he answered, "but not quite. We need you to make the right choice that will help us eliminate government entirely.

It's a bigger nudge than we usually try, but now you know that this correction is bigger than whether you believe a man was nailed to a cross or some old guy talked to a burning bush on a mountain top. You are free to believe whatever you want, we just need you to continue what you are doing, free from the eyes of the OSS and we will do the rest."

"Surely people need structure and governance of some kind?" I asked, not clearly understanding the connection he was making between me and the elimination of all form of government.

He was obviously prepared for this question. He was quick to answer in a way that I could tell he had rehearsed. He explained that all life forms are programmed to survive, from the smallest virus to the billions of bacteria that live on our bodies—they are all designed to survive via replication. It was the same for higher order species, like mammals; they eat, sleep, and procreate. Ancient humans did the procreating and the hunting so well they had enough time on their hands to construct a belief in an afterlife where they could fuck and eat for all eternity unimpeded by fear of death—the one human certainty.

Humans got so good at surviving that they were able to craft hierarchical structures of worship and governance that evolved to subjugate them and dictate their most basic activities. They created laws that if followed correctly would lead to great reward in an afterlife—it's a near perfect scam he said, at least for those at the top.

It's funny, I thought to myself, we don't remember our own our birth but we spend our whole life avoiding, and at the same time preparing for, our eventual death. This faith-based reward of an afterlife still makes death palatable.

He went to on to describe that after tens of thousands of years these laws became entwined in earthly rewards too, not just in the afterlife, and the control of these rewards become the basis for power. We call it government in whatever form, from its tribal origins to the legislative bodies which we freely elect, and yet, David said that the resulting effects upon humanity have always proven to be the same; without fail, governments of all kinds have always used faith to justify their most destructive actions.

He had accused me of being far too simplistic in my understanding of the correction, but he was the one who reduced thousands of years of human life into a two-minute tirade on the origins of religion and governance.

I countered with all the amazing things that mankind has accomplished, from the eradication of most of those viruses he mentioned, to eliminating hunger in most of the world…to putting him on the moon. I added that none of this was possible without some form of government to organize and to give form and structure to our lives.

"You mean none of this has been possible without us?" He countered, gesturing to the both of us.

I had suspected, since the moment of our first contact, that he and I both worked for the OSS. But I had forgotten that he once mentioned in passing that in his time that there was no more government, or no government in a way that I could relate to my current experience. I was now realizing that he and I were too far removed from each other in time to be truly working for the same result. It was illogical to think so. It was like I was the ancient Mesopotamian guy who invented the wheel, and he was like Karl Benz inventing the automobile. One begot the other, but the Mesopotamian guy could never have imagined the combustion engine.

"What agency do you represent? Who do you work for?" I

finally asked the question that I should have led with weeks ago.

"IST, of course," he answered bluntly. "Remember, there are no coincidences."

I was stunned by his answer and by my own naivete. I had been so busy trying to figure out whether I was one of the targets of the correction that I failed to see that there was a much larger, and much more complex, manipulation occurring around me. It was like David was playing chess and I was playing checkers. More importantly though, it was now evident to me that Robert had been useful only up to a point and then he disappeared from history. Therefore I was also only useful to the algorithm as long as I played David's game, then I too would disappear from history.

IST was the venture capital arm of a Greek bank that had funded my start up. I asked him if it was the very same company.

"That's my understanding, although the term venture capitalist is not how we would describe ourselves now. We've changed a lot over the past couple of hundred years."

He went on to explain that they began as a traditional bank until money, or the construct of money as currency and as the means to conduct business, stopped being the norm. The entity I now know as Istoia Bank SE (trading as IST) evolved into a different entity with the advent of decentralized financing for basic corporate transactions. He said he couldn't give me the whole history. But basically, by the time cryptocurrency trickled down to the masses corporations had largely moved on to other non-fungible tokens because the very rich and powerful no longer needed currency. Debt had become as valuable as cash had once been, and so money was eventually rendered useless and quaint, the stuff of hobbyists—similar he explained to how people collected postage stamps in the nineteenth and twentieth centuries.

According to David, IST invested heavily in the tech boom of the early 2000s, quietly amassing control over the financing for most of the leading-edge information-based companies. In doing so they had taken significant ownership stakes in the actual hard tech, and not just the passive profits. They saw the value in owning, and not just funding. When the world was celebrating the new class of titans of the silicon age, with their super-yachts and toy rockets, IST was quietly amassing ownership of everything behind the scenes. IST became a shadow bank of sorts, and ended up owning the titans, and they didn't even notice their own irrelevancy until it was too late.

When I pointed out that IST had to be just another company with shareholders, no different really than the structure of every other public company, but he was quick to correct me. IST had never gone fully public, and the original Athenian-family of shareholders had long been bought out by a small clandestine cadre. This group successfully hid behind the corporate veils that had become so normal in everyday transactions that people rarely, if ever, questioned who, or what, IST had become. The entity had ceased to be an investment bank and had no one to report to. This included the governments of the countries whose debt they owned.

I now understood the reason why David said that they needed to eliminate all governments. However, I pointed out that governments are complex entities that operate at so many levels of society, from informal systems that govern our daily lives through to the complexities of centralized agencies and elected bodies that provide oversight. I told him that I didn't understand how anyone could simply eliminate all the basic structures that maintain the functions of a civilized society and not expect anarchy. I made the point that governments made and enforced laws that ensured order. Surely, this was still necessary in 2228.

He went on to explain that I was the one who originated the solution to this problem. It is my writings on the transactional requirements of projected technology, along with my experiments on the solid-caste state of projections, that eventually leads to the elimination of the monotheistic religions that he claimed are at the very core of nationalism.

For him to suggest that my work, or more accurately Sarah's research which I adapted to inform my own, would somehow lead to a form of faithless governance was incredible, and extremely distressing, to say the least.

He said that over time they had managed to eliminate wars that stem from nationalism by replacing organized religion and all fundamentalist belief systems with a more natural form of transactional reward. He said his people were certainly free today to keep faith within their own consciousness, but everyone came to agree that there was no collective determinant of order and structure to be found in stories from the past. The need to relive the past or make things great again was bad for everyone. Surely, I could see that, he asked.

"What is *your* transaction then, if not obeyance and the support of a civil society in exchange for personal wealth and safety?" I asked, not believing what I was hearing.

"Comfort, security, good health, education, peace…happiness," he answered. "Just as I told Edward at the second embassy. We just don't promise eternal salvation."

"And IST, what does it get in return?"

"Information. That's where the true wealth has always been," he answered smugly.

"But religion brings hope, it gives people peace of mind, and meaning to their lives. Information can't do that."

Religion is just another form of information he countered, seemingly not caring that religion has simply been replaced by a corporation.

"Words. Religion is just the sharing of words," he said.

"Everyone is still free to dream about an afterlife," he continued, "but the more pragmatic amongst us enjoy the rewards of a long life on earth, or on the moon for that matter, but a life without fear of disease, hunger, or strife."

"And you got this all from me?" I asked.

"No, you know that's not possible. Of course, you are important in the evolution of the technology that makes this all possible, but you're just one person in time."

"But I originated the idea that makes *you* possible, here with me. It comes from my intellect, my research, my thoughts."

"True, which is why you are important to this correction. We are working on together. If you choose to continue your present course of research the algorithm predicts that your technology will evolve to the point that it can be weaponized, and this will lead to untold deaths from wars that will continue in perpetuity. If you choose another course there is a different future, also according to the algorithm."

"But you already know what I choose. You are here with me now with all the knowledge gained from the next two hundred years. I mean, you've said that you've read all my journals, which must include this conversation."

"That's not how it works," he answered. "I don't know what happens to me tomorrow. All I know is what the algorithm says is possible, and my responsibility is to affect the probability of what is possible for my tomorrow and the tomorrow of many others. Personally, I care more about my future than yours because yours is baked into the algorithm already. Mine is not, it has many more possibilities than yours."

This was an abstract thought, but quite logical.

"Your future is my past. Do you understand?"

I did understand, and I was scared. I needed to use his tree branch analogy to keep it clear in my own mind, but I got it now.

He and I were on the same branch of time, but at different points along the branch.

He was on the part that continued to grow long after my time on the branch had expired.

If I did as he asked, then I was the assurance of the entirety of the past that he knew—the past that leads to his current place on the branch.

It was entirely possible that I might head off onto another branch, and he needed to prevent this. There might even be another entity out there that might entice me to do so, or maybe it had happened already. How would I know?

How many corrections have lead David to me, and my place in time? It was obvious that he now needed to guide me to his future.

I now knew for certain that my role in David's correction was the same as Robert's was in mine. Robert assured my past and I assure David's. If I didn't do exactly as he asked, his past would still occur in some form, but his future—or *a* future—according to the algorithm, would be in jeopardy.

I asked if I was really that important to algorithm and David responded that I was important to *him*, specifically. He explained that that's how IST works. He and I found ourselves by chance on the same branch of time. He said that he tried not to think too deeply about all the implications of what this meant for the billions of people he was responsible for, but that he had faith that the algorithm was choosing the correct probabilities, and acting to correct those that were possibly disastrous. To drive the point home, he reminded me again about the story of the Austrian baby they had killed. I got it now.

It wasn't lost on me that he was asking me to replace my faith in Christ with faith in a mathematical computation managed by a corporation, and I told him so. He said that what he was asking was no different than what he knew of Christianity, or any of the other Abrahamic faiths. It was just a question of *if this, then what*? If you abide by the teachings of Christ, Mohammed, or Moses then you receive a reward. It was the same as his faith in the algorithm.

"But," I asked, "why such an elaborate projection, over such a long period of time? Why did you go so far back in time just to have me find a manuscript hidden in a wall so many centuries later?"

He pondered this for a moment, before admitting that this had puzzled him as well. He explained that he thought that it came down to accepting, albeit blindly, that there are no coincidences. I could not reconcile the reason IST directed Robert to write a story of an event that they had fabricated and then sealed in a wall just so that I would find hundreds of years later. It all sounded so improbable, and yet it was all perfectly possible. The algorithm directed it and IST made it happen.

"But, why the chronicle at all," I asked, "why the need for it to be written down and sealed away, just for me to find it? You could have just projected to me at any time and told me all this without having to go to so much effort."

"For the same reason you have written it down all over again," he answered. "In case someone else, or another version of you, needs to find it on some other branch, or perhaps, for this version of you to find it some other time on this very same branch with the help of another pilot. I can't say for certain that this is the case, but I know that the chronicle, whether by your hand or Roberts', assures a future for me and a lot of other people."

I had many more questions, but David reminded me again that he was just a pilot and that he didn't know how it all worked. Although, he did say that he believed there were a lot of branches out there and we had found ourselves together on just one of them. How many there are he didn't know, and if he was being honest with himself, he told me that he thought the algorithm functioned mostly to preserve itself now. Like all organisms, its priority is its need to survive, hence the many branches.

This was an intriguing thought, and as we both pondered it quietly a sudden breeze caught the leaves of the oak above, causing us to look up at the same time.

"The challenge," he said, "for both of us, and for the algorithm for that matter, is that the wind blows from so many different directions."

He asked me again if I understood. I assured him that I did.

End.